Drowning in Lies

Ann Eichenmuller

Deltaville, Virginia

Thank you for purchasing an authorized edition of *Drowning in Lies*.

High Tide's mission is to find, encourage, promote, and publish the work of authors. We are a small, woman-owned enterprise that is dedicated to the author over 50.

When you buy an authorized copy, you help us to bring their work to you.

High Tide Publications, Inc.
Deltaville, Virginia 23043
www.HighTidePublications.com

Printed in the United States of America
ISBN: 978-1-945990-38-0

Edited by: Cindy L. Freeman
Book Design: Firebellied Frog Graphic Design

Publisher's Note: This is a work of fiction. Names, characters, businesses, places, events and incidents are either the products of the author's imagination or used in a fictitious manner. Any resemblance to actual persons, living or dead, or actual events is purely coincidental.

For Eric,
my love, my Muse
who has given me the gift
of time

Prologue

He slumps against the concrete pylon, his face shadowed by a dirty baseball cap pulled low over his brow. One of a thousand men in faded camouflage who haunt the waterfront of this city, he is all but invisible to those who pass. Later, no one will remember his hair color, how tall he was, whether he was young or old. They will describe him as homeless, as if that is the sum of his identity. That one word will be his disguise.

It is just past rush hour on a Monday in January, but the traffic never ceases, an endless stream of cars headed for the high-rise condominiums that crowd out the sky. Their residents descend on West Palm Beach each winter, their appetites for more and bigger reshaping the landscape—driving indigenous species into ever smaller, poorer neighborhoods, or westward, to stretches of filled swampland. It angers him, and yet it feeds him as well.

Their money has the power to both bless and curse.

The man turns his eyes to Lake Worth. A cargo ship is entering the channel, its lights reflected on the surface of the water, reminding him he is running behind. It is the girl's fault. He slides up the ragged sleeve of his jacket and darts a furtive glance at his watch. Six o'clock. It should have been finished by now.

The waiting makes the skin on his back tighten and itch.

Across the parking lot he hears the sound of a door opening. He raises his head slightly, just enough to catch a glimpse of her…long legs, short skirt, dark hair in a ponytail. She does not look around, but strides purposefully in a straight line to the dented silver Mazda. He stares down at the ground, listening as she starts the engine, gauging the distance as she pulls onto Blue Heron Boulevard and heads west, away from the waterfront. Thirty seconds, a minute, a minute-thirty, he counts to himself. The sound of her motor is lost in traffic, but still he does not move. He cannot take a chance she will return.

Another minute passes before the man edges away from the concrete pylon. The ragged stretch of grass along the parking lot is deserted, his movement swallowed by the falling darkness. He slips across to the front door and lounges against the wall, his head down, rolling the key between his gloved fingers. He looks across toward the parking lot. A couple passes, hand in hand, heading toward the bridge, but they barely glance at him.

It doesn't matter who is watching. He knows they will turn their eyes away.

His hand trembles as he holds the key up to the lock. Out on the main road a car horn blares, and he jumps. The key clatters and bounces on concrete before the man stomps on it with his boot. He bends and retrieves it, then fits it into the hole. A few seconds later, the man is inside, heart racing, leaning against the glass door.

The rush is always the same.

He pulls out a small flashlight and unfolds a piece of paper. The blueprint directs him to the cafeteria kitchen, where the man lays his backpack down on the counter and removes a can of spray paint. Sliding back into the hallway, he retraces his steps toward the front of the building, takes out the can, and sprays words on the wall. Returning to the kitchen, the man pulls a pipe cutter, three candles, and a pack of matches from the backpack. Scanning the room, he sees what he is looking for—milk crates, just tall enough to buy him the necessary time. The man works quickly, setting a candle on top of each crate and lighting them. Then he moves to the back of the large stainless gas oven, carefully slicing a thin line in the pipe and bending it till it leaves a gaping hole. Propane flows out in invisible waves, sinking and rolling along the linoleum floor.

He has time—the candles are a foot off the ground—but the flames are already flickering and growing brighter. The man stuffs the pipe cutter and matches in his bag and heads for the door. He is perhaps six feet away when it swings open.

The woman is in her early forties, short and heavyset but still pretty. She wears a dark skirt and white blouse, and something about her reminds him of the girl in the Mazda. She stares at him in surprise.

"¿Qué hace?"

He stands, frozen, as she pushes her cart of cleaning supplies toward him.

"You can't be here!" he cries out, though the words seem to stick in his throat.

Then panic takes him, and he rushes forward, but she shoves the cart in his abdomen, and suddenly he is falling backward. His arms flail out, clutching at a shelf beside him, sending dishes crashing to the floor. In the second before his head hits the tile, the man watches as the cart runs into the milk crate, and the candle rocks and turns on its side, its flame dancing and spreading on an invisible wave.

He does not have time to scream as the air around him explodes.

Chapter 1

Living on a sailboat changes you.

Your days are not divided into hours but into a hundred degrees of light and darkness—the soft glow of the horizon before moonrise, the low shadows of noon in winter, the wash of pink that lingers in the west long after the sky grows dark. Space is measured by water under the hull, and most of your forward motion is sideways, sails carefully balanced, knowing you must tack away to draw closer to where you want to be. Your world—everything you own, everything that matters most to you—is encapsulated around you, carried by the wind and tides, so that you are both always and never at home. There is freedom in that.

But it is not real life.

Sixty-five feet above us, a steady stream of traffic rattled concrete and steel as it crossed the Blue Heron Bridge. Commuters, rushing home from their jobs, picking up their children, stopping for takeout. They formed an endless line of blank faces staring through windshields, numb from the myriad chores of daily living. Below them, the narrow channel of Lake Worth's harbor was crowded with charter boats coming in from the ocean, their decks packed with tourists drunk on sun and beer. I clenched the wheel as *Andromeda* rocked in their wake, cursing under my breath at their disregard of the posted 6 mph speed limit. But then, time was money to them.

That's real life.

Josh was on the radio with the marina, a quarter mile ahead on the right. A fat bead of sweat dripped down his sunburned forehead and into his eye. It was January 13th, five o'clock in the evening, and the thermometer read eighty-nine degrees. It was a stark contrast from the morning we left Norfolk in late November. The air was cold and heavy then, wet fog blanketing the waterway. We huddled in the cockpit, shivering, and dreamed of Florida, of bare skin and translucent turquoise seas.

As the saying goes, be careful what you wish for.

It had been scorching for days, forcing us to slather lotion on our red skin and squeeze into what little shade there was on deck. And although the water was crystal clear, we'd spotted an alligator in a canal just to the north, and within the past hour a half-dozen Portuguese man-of-war slid past our hull. When I imagined sailing in Florida, I hadn't realized jumping overboard to cool off would be a life-threatening experience.

"B-2, third slip in on the right side of the dock," Josh repeated into the handheld microphone. "Thanks, but we don't need any help. We're about five minutes out."

We began a familiar dance. He slid behind the wheel as I dove into the cockpit storage compartment, grabbing four sets of lines and a boat hook. We had mastered a division of labor since I left my own boat in Morehead City to crew aboard *Andromeda*. It wasn't without the occasional disagreement, but for two very different people, we worked well together.

It helped that we were in love.

Josh maneuvered the boat toward the slip while I stood on the bow, prepared to lasso the first post. A huge tuna boat was berthed close to one side, a large trawler on the other, so he slowed the engine as he turned, letting the outgoing tide push us in gently. I secured the lines quickly, keeping us off the dock, as Josh killed the engine.

"Bravo!"

The captain of the trawler to our starboard stood on the pier, clapping.

"I must congratulate you," he shouted to me. "So often sailboats cannot seem to get in here without bumping every post."

There is a certain light-hearted feud between those who prefer sails and those who prefer power. Despite having seen disastrous docking attempts from members of both camps, I overlooked the back-handed nature of the compliment and thanked him as I stepped off the boat.

"How long are you here for?" he asked.

"Four or five days. After that we're going offshore."

"Ah! To the islands!" He raised his beer in a mock toast. "Well then, let me know if there is anything I can do for you while you are here. I'm Carlos. My wife and I live aboard. We did the Abacos before Christmas, and we're here now until the end of March. We have a rental car if you need a ride somewhere."

Josh came up to the bow and threw the end of our shore power line to me. He introduced both of us, labelling me as his fiancée, while I plugged in our electric. I didn't correct him, though the term was not completely accurate. I wore the ring he had given me in December when, with his signature optimism, he chose to interpret my maybe as more of a yes. In fairness, I didn't discourage him. The status of our engagement was something we had avoided discussing for more than five hundred miles of Intracoastal Waterway, and I wasn't going to bring it up in front of a perfect stranger.

"We do need some provisions," Josh said to Carlos. "Is there a grocery store nearby?"

"Yes, right over at the base of the bridge there's a Publix. Maybe three, four blocks away. I could take you," our neighbor offered.

An air-conditioned ride sounded wonderful. I grimaced when Josh said we'd been on the boat for three days straight and could use the walk. While I secured bumpers on either side of *Andromeda*, he and Carlos chatted for a few more minutes about the locations of local restaurants (over the bridge), beach access (also over the bridge) and where not to go (any farther west than a few blocks).

"Some rough neighborhoods there. We've been at this marina eight years in a row, and we see the city council is trying to clean things up, but with the drugs and the gangs, it's a hard thing to fix," our neighbor explained. "There is a nice mall on PGA Boulevard, maybe eight miles up the interstate. You let me know if you want to go there. We'd be glad to take you."

Josh thanked him, and while he was exchanging final pleasantries, I went below to wash the salt and sweat from my face. He came down as I was closing the hatches and starting the air conditioner.

"Good idea. We might need it when we get back," he said, stripping his soaked t-shirt off his tanned, muscled back. He must have felt my gaze because he turned and grinned. He was a big man with a difficult past, but he had a lopsided, boyish smile that melted my heart. Literally. I felt positively gooey, like warm caramel.

"Enjoying the show?" he teased.

"Absolutely."

He pulled me to him and kissed me. "It's a two-way street."

I hoped so, but that was one of the concerns that kept me from taking the vow to become Mrs. Culliver. I was thirty-six, nearly seven years older than Josh. When I looked in the mirror, I saw the beginnings of crow's feet around my eyes, and last week I found a strand of gray in my streaked blonde hair. I was attractive in a confident, tomboyish sort of way, and I could still pass for late twenties—but who knew how long that would last? Would Josh want me in the same way when I was forty? And then there was the question of children. Biological clocks kept ticking, whether you were ready to make a decision or not.

Those were the kinds of thoughts that ruined even the best kisses.

Josh must have sensed my mind was wandering. He released me, and when he spoke his voice had a forced lightness.

"Food first, right? And we need to pick up beer and wine—we're out. You grab the backpacks while I wash up. We'll check in at the office and then head to the store."

The winter sun was low in the sky when we left the marina. It was still warm, but a breeze had shifted in from the north, drying out the humid ocean air. We took the narrow alley toward the bridge, walking hand in hand. There were new condominiums on the east side facing the water, and peeking between their bright stucco walls, we saw the green of Peanut Island in the middle of the lagoon, and beyond it the stacked red and black containers of a cargo ship entering the inlet. The west side of the alley was less picturesque, lined with old metal buildings, some rusted and empty, others housing dilapidated boats, heating and air conditioning businesses, and diesel engine repair shops. In the distance we could see a block of single level duplexes crowded together, all in varying states of disrepair. I guessed this was the area Carlos had warned us about: abject poverty living within eyesight of wealth, separated by a thin dividing line of crumbling industrial warehouses.

It took only a few minutes to reach the commercial block that fronted Blue Heron Boulevard. A giant red and white dive flag fluttered over a new concrete strip mall, its windows displaying scuba gear, surfboards, and high-end fishing equipment. Across the road, at the base of the bridge, was a gated yacht club, its docks filled with gleaming white boats two and three stories tall, and beside it the green sign of the Publix. The grocery store itself was so well-disguised behind palm trees and a tile and stucco façade that it could easily have been mistaken for a five-star hotel.

Everything along the waterfront was new and shiny with one exception—a long, low brick schoolhouse of the sort built in the 1950s, stretched out across three hundred feet of prime waterfront. Its parking lot was empty, but according to the sign on the small patch of grass out front, it was the home of the Jerome P. Garrison Community Center. Though it had fresh paint on the windowsills and a new roof, it looked painfully out of place amid the more modern construction. A man I judged to be homeless, wearing too many clothes for the heat, lounged in the shadows by the door.

Josh motioned to the bridge. "Let's climb up and take a look."

We strolled across the community center's entrance toward the fenced pedestrian walkway that lined the eastbound side of the bridge. The highway was crowded with traffic, and close behind us I heard the rough knocking of an old engine as a car pulled into the parking lot. Though the traffic drowned out any further conversation, I knew what Josh was thinking. He wanted to see the next leg of our cruise, beyond the breakwater, into the Atlantic.

We climbed to the top and looked toward the inlet, where a thin strip of white sand was visible along the shoreline, disappearing into a wall of rock and the foamy crests of waves. Josh squeezed my hand, bending down to brush his lips against mine. I buried my fingers in the thick curls at the back of his neck, pulled him to me, and closed my eyes.

Suddenly there was a bright flash, and the concrete and steel beneath us shook. My eyes flew open, and then I was falling as a ball of flame exploded in the air. Someone near me screamed, and Josh's body covered me as the blast knocked us both to the ground.

Chapter 2

Josh grabbed my arm and pulled me up. We stared down at the community center we had passed just moments before. One wall and most of the roof were gone, the windows blown outward, flames shooting into the sky. But that was not the true horror. The car that had just pulled into the parking lot was buried in shattered wood, brick, and glass, and through the splintered, burning pieces we could see a woman's body pinned against the half-opened door.

"Call 911," Josh shouted, though his voice seemed small and far away. I fumbled in my backpack for the phone as he ran down the walkway toward the parking lot.

I made the call, my ears still ringing from the explosion. I could barely make out the dispatcher's questions, but I kept repeating my location and describing what had happened until he promised help was on the way. I started down the bridge just as Josh reached the car and began digging through the burning debris. By the time I reached the parking lot, he had dragged the woman free of the wreckage. Josh dropped to the ground, holding her against him, just as the car's gas tank erupted in fire.

The woman was screaming, blood pouring from a deep cut in her forehead, but she tore herself from his grasp and ran straight toward the yawning hole where the community center's door once stood. Josh ran in front of her, blocking her path as she beat at his chest with her fists. I came behind and put my arms around her, holding her tightly.

"My mother! I've got to get my mother!" she sobbed, and then she crumpled, her weight pulling us both to the pavement.

Josh's eyes met mine.

"Stay with her," he said, and he ran into the burning doorway.

Time slowed. I felt the heat of the fire on my face and tasted the acrid smoke that filled my lungs. I cradled the woman's head in my lap, pressing my palm against her wound, but my eyes—and hers—were pinned to the black hole that had swallowed all traces of Josh. A psalm from childhood ran through my head --The Lord is my shepherd, I shall not want—but that line kept repeating because I couldn't remember the words. Then even my thoughts were drowned in the harsh music of sirens.

There were shouting voices, and a man in uniform knelt beside me. I pointed toward the building, and as I did, there was a loud crack like thunder, and the remainder of the roof collapsed.

A cloud of dust and smoke rose from the doorway. Through it, the shape of a man appeared, carrying something over his shoulder. The woman pushed away my hand and struggled up, running toward him. I rose, frozen for an instant. I knew it had to be Josh, but he was unrecognizable--black with soot, shirt torn, one arm hanging limply at his side. He placed his burden down gently and the woman dropped beside it as paramedics rushed in. Josh took a few steps and pitched forward. A fireman caught him before he hit the asphalt.

What happened next is still unclear to me. In my memory, it comes back as flashes of red light and jagged images that don't quite fit together, like random photographs shot without focus. *The woman screaming... a police officer pulling her away... a faceless body on a stretcher...the back of an ambulance. Holding Josh's hand.*

"Mrs. Culliver?"

I started. A middle-aged woman in scrubs stood in front of me.

"I'm sorry?"

"Are you Mrs. Culliver? You came in with Joshua?"

"Yes...no. I came in with him, but my name is Sandi Beck. We're not—we're engaged."

She glanced around the ER waiting room, empty except for an elderly man slumped in the corner, and took the chair next to me.

"Miss Beck, I'm Helena. I'm one of the nurses who treated Joshua when he was brought in. He is out of trauma and being moved to the ICU. Doctor Hassan will come talk to you in a few minutes, but I wanted you to know your fiancé did just fine. As soon as Joshua is settled, I'll be out to get you and take you up to him."

I thanked her. As she rose to leave, a slight, dark-haired man entered the room, also in scrubs.

"Here he is now. Doctor Hassan, this is Sandi Beck, Joshua's fiancée."

He shook my hand. He was my age, perhaps a few years older, soft-spoken with a kind smile.

"Nice to meet you, Sandi. It was quite a heroic thing your boyfriend did," he said.

"The woman he brought out....?"

He shook his head. "No. I'm sorry to say she didn't make it. Her injuries were just too severe. But her daughter, the young lady Joshua pulled from the car, is doing very well. We'll keep her overnight for observation, but she should be released in the morning. I'm afraid Joshua's situation is a little more complicated."

A lump of fear hardened in the pit of my stomach.

"Joshua suffered a mild concussion. There was minimal fluid on the CAT scan, so we are hopeful he will have no long-term effects from his brain injury, but he will likely experience headaches and dizziness for up to six weeks. His shoulder was dislocated, but that has been reduced, meaning it has been put back in place. He also has a complex right humerus fracture, which is the bone between the shoulder and the elbow," he said, pointing to his own arm. "We have him in a temporary splint until the orthopedic surgeon can take a look in the morning. It is likely Joshua will need surgery; if so, we'll probably want to schedule that as soon as his overall condition improves. Joshua also sustained a number of deep lacerations on the back of his head, arms, and left hand which required stitches, but we aren't worried about those."

Dr. Hassan leaned forward. "Right now our main concern is the combination of burns and smoke inhalation. Joshua sustained extensive deep second degree burns to thirteen percent of his body, primarily the right hand and upper back. These contained a significant amount of debris. While the wounds have been debrided, it is common in these situations for bacteria to get into the bloodstream and cause infection. Added to the smoke particles in his lungs, this can create a serious challenge to the immune system. Joshua is being moved to the ICU in serious but stable condition. He is on oxygen and he's being monitored by a respiratory therapist. He's also receiving fluids, antibiotics, and pain medication through his IV, and right now he is resting as comfortably as he can under the circumstances."

I nodded numbly to show I understood. Dr. Hassan's eyes were sympathetic.

"I gathered you don't live locally. Joshua wasn't conscious long enough to fully explain your situation, so I'm not sure what arrangements you need to make, but I'd plan for his hospitalization to last a week at least, possibly longer based on how he responds to treatment."

I knew I should say something, but my mind was sluggish, still processing what he had told me.

"Okay," I managed.

The doctor smiled. "I know that's a lot of information at one time. The good news is that I believe he will heal without grafts, and with occupational therapy, he should regain full range of motion in the right hand. Your boyfriend is a strong, healthy young man. I see no reason why he won't make a complete recovery. It will just take some time. Do you have any questions?"

I did, but I was overwhelmed by a dizzying relief at his prognosis. All I could do was shake my head.

"All right then. Helena will be back for you in about fifteen minutes. Can I have them get you anything? Water, a soda?"

I was suddenly aware of my raw throat. "Water. Thank you."

He rose, patted my shoulder, and the security guard buzzed him back through the ER doors. A few minutes later a young woman came in to pick up the old man in the corner. As she helped him to his feet, she stared at me, eyes wide, then looked quickly away. For the first time, I realized I had not washed my face or used the bathroom since the explosion. I asked the guard for directions to the ladies' room, making him promise that he would tell anyone looking for me that I would be right back.

It was after nine and the corridor was empty. The whole night felt like one of those dreams where you start off in a pleasant, familiar place and suddenly you find yourself trapped on what could be the set of a horror movie. A look in the restroom mirror supported that scenario. The front of the gray t-shirt I wore was stained with a mixture of Josh's blood and that of the woman I had held. My hair, face, neck, and arms were streaked with smoke and ash. I washed up as well as I could with paper towels and hand soap, but underneath the grime my skin looked pale and drawn.

As I was leaving the restroom, the phone in my back pocket vibrated. I checked it and saw the number was Wayne Kremm's. I positioned myself where I could keep an eye on the ER door and answered it.

"Jesus, San, that was a hell of an explosion. Are you okay? How's your boyfriend?"

Wayne was a *Washington Post* reporter in D.C. While I knew he had an impressive network of sources, short of clairvoyance I didn't see how he could know what had happened to us.

"I'm fine. Josh is being transferred to the ICU. He's in stable condition. How—"

"Art Peerson called me. It was all over the news."

Arthur Peerson and his wife Alice were former clients of mine who had a winter place in Florida. Arthur was also a Virginia lawyer—or at least he had been, prior to his retirement. He represented Wayne in all three of his divorces, which was a testament to his loyalty because they were losing battles from the start. Wayne was a great guy, as long as you weren't married to him.

I hadn't even considered the news. I pictured Josh's parents seeing their son's collapse on national television. While I had called my mother and father from the hospital, Josh's family had totally slipped my mind. I only had his father's work number on my cell, and to be honest, my communication with his family was rocky from the start.

"Do you know what news? Did they report our names?"

"Just the local Palm Beach stations, and they weren't giving names. Art sent me the video—he was positive he recognized you."

I had a vague memory of bystanders holding up cell phones. Wayne went on.

"So far the report says two fatalities and one survivor from the blast, and one unnamed hero taken to Palm Beach Trauma Center. I assumed the hero was your boyfriend."

"Yes." I told him the story of the explosion, Josh freeing the woman, and then running in to look for her mother. "As far as I know, she was the only one inside."

"They're saying a second body was recovered. Look, Arthur and Alice are on their way to the hospital now. Before you argue, he insisted. He knows you're on the boat. You'll need a ride home."

I didn't argue—not even a little. The events of the evening had put a crack in my façade of fierce independence. Just hearing Wayne's voice was enough to choke me up.

"Okay. Thanks. Tell them I'm in the emergency waiting room." The ER door slid open and I saw Helena look around and then wave to me. "I've got to go. They're letting me up to see Josh. Have Arthur text me when they get here."

I ended the call without saying goodbye.

Helena met me in the hallway and led me to an elevator. We went to the third floor, another empty waiting room. I waited while Helena spoke to a nurse behind a glass window. A few minutes later, we were ushered through a heavy door to the end of a long, dimly lit corridor. We passed darkened rooms where patients lay sleeping in nests of tubes and sensors, the thick sound of ventilators pushing breath in and out while monitors blinked overhead. I followed them through a second doorway labeled Burn Unit and stopped at the sixth room.

"Ten minutes, that's it. You can come back after eight a.m. tomorrow," directed the ICU nurse in a tone that brooked no discussion. “This card has the number for the nurse’s station. I’m Adrienne, and I’ll be on duty until seven a.m., when Francis will take my place. You can call at any time for an update. And don’t expect him to hear you—he’s heavily sedated right now.”

I moved toward the bed. Josh was on oxygen, hooked to two IVs, with machines monitoring his heart rate, blood pressure, and oxygen saturation level. The broken arm was splinted and elevated, the right hand heavily bandaged. We had been together just a few months, and in that time I had seen his emotional vulnerability, but never any hint of physical frailty. I felt a rush of fear—for him and for me. I had barely survived Ryan’s death. I was stronger now, but not enough. I could not bear another loss.

I pulled the chair next to the left side of the bed and took his hand in mine, stroking his fingers, whispering the words I needed to believe. “I love you. You’re going to be fine. Everything’s going to be okay.”

Then I laid my head against his chest and closed my eyes, losing myself in the beating of his heart.

Chapter 3

You never realize how much you miss a Virginia accent until you go a few months without hearing one. It is a soft drawl, genteel, like sweet tea. When I heard Arthur's voice, my eyes filled with tears.

"Oh, darlin', come over heah and let me hug you," he said, opening his arms wide. He was a big man with a shock of wavy white hair and a physique that closely resembled a teddy bear. I melted in his embrace.

"You po' thing," his wife said, patting my back. She was tiny, perhaps five feet tall, thin with long gray hair wound in a braid around her head. "We'll take you to get your things, and you can come stay with us. You don't want to be all alone on that boat right now."

I protested that I'd be fine, but my wet cheeks and red eyes suggested otherwise. They were adamant, and I let it drop, surprised at how relieved I felt. I used to prefer being alone. I spent three years living solo on my sailboat after my husband died, going months without exchanging two words with another person. But the job and the time with Josh had changed me. Now I wanted—needed—human touch.

On the drive back to the marina, Arthur and Alice kept up a steady stream of chatter while I laid my head back and closed my eyes.

"I can't believe it's been two yeahs," she said. "I was weahin' my necklace last week, and I told Arthah how grateful I was you got it back."

That was how I had met the Peersons. They were living in Alexandria at the time and spent weekends at their second home on Carters Creek, not far from where my boat was docked. Two summers ago, while they were there, Alice suffered a stroke. When she was released from the hospital, Arthur thought she would recover faster in their vacation house, so he brought in help from a local caregiving agency. Sometime in the weeks that followed, Alice's diamond and ruby necklace, a thirtieth anniversary gift from her husband, disappeared. Alice—whose memory was still spotty—thought she had lost it, but Arthur knew better. The culprit had to be one of the girls from the agency, but he was torn; Alice had grown fond of the two nursing assistants who stayed with her. Despite his reputation as a pit bull in the courtroom, Arthur was kindhearted. He didn't want to ruin either girl's life by bringing in the police, but he knew enough about human nature to realize that if he never mentioned the theft, there would be more pieces missing, and if he did, both would deny it and probably quit. Either way, the necklace would be lost. He mentioned his dilemma to Wayne, who recommended me.

That's what I do—or at least, what I did before setting sail last November. I solved problems. My job title was personal advocacy consultant, but the job itself was more complicated. Private investigator, negotiator, counselor, and friend, I helped my clients by finding the lever that would push the guilty into following their better natures. If I was successful, there was never a police report or a newspaper story, and everyone got to live happily ever after.

In the Peersons' case, it didn't take long to find that one of the caregivers was living paycheck-to-paycheck with her mother, who was dying of stage four liver cancer. A new experimental treatment was offered at a clinic in Boston, and the daughter had promised she would come up with the cash. She was a good person in a bad situation, which is how most crimes begin. Arthur, being Arthur, rounded up donations to cover the treatment, and amidst tears and apologies, the necklace was returned to him. As for Alice, Arthur told her I had tracked it down after he accidentally packaged it up with donations for the church bazaar. It was a plausible story, and if she thought it odd that Arthur was cleaning out closets, she never said so aloud.

We reached the marina, and they waited while I went on board and threw together a bag with some clothes and my laptop. The boat beside us was closed up, and there was no sign of Carlos. On the way out, we passed what was left of the community center, surrounded by crime scene tape, a fire truck and several police cars still on site. News crews were filming from the sidewalk across the street. I craned my neck to look back as we crossed the bridge.

"What do you think caused it?" I asked.

Arthur shrugged. "Hard to say for sure. Given the explosion, probably propane. This area along Lake Worth nevah got natural gas, but a lot of people hereabouts still use propane tanks for heatin' hot water and stoves. The community center used to be an elementary school back in the day. It had an ol' commercial kitchen, so that would be my guess."

"Have they identified the woman who was killed?"

He shook his head. "Not officially, no. But Alice is on the board. The woman your boyfriend pulled from the car was the director of the center, Vianca Baptiste. Her mother owned the maid service that had the contract for the center. We think she must have been in there cleanin' when it happened."

Alice added quickly, "Mind you, Mariana—that was Vianca's mother—did it at cost, just what she had to pay her employees. She didn't even charge for supplies, God bless her."

"What about the second victim? Was that someone who worked for her?" I asked.

"That we don't know. We haven't been able to get through to Vianca yet. We are just prayin' she's all right."

"The doctor said they were keeping her overnight, but they expected to release her in the morning," I reassured them.

We pulled into the underground parking garage of a high-rise oceanfront condominium. A uniformed doorman opened the entrance to a wide, marble-tiled lobby, comfortably outfitted with potted palms and overstuffed deep sofas. We rode the attended elevator to the tenth floor, where the Peersons made their winter home. A chorus of yapping began when Arthur went to unlock the door.

"That's just Maxi. Don't pay him any mind," Alice said. "He's all bark and no bite."

"Well, what do you think?" Arthur asked, swinging open the door as a small white ball of fluff bolted toward me.

Maxi's tail wagged in full circles as he jumped up and down, his nails leaving scratches on my legs. Alice scooped up the puppy, scolding him, and carried him back to their bedroom while Arthur led me inside.

My experience with condos was limited to my parents' two-bedroom Myrtle Beach retirement home and vacation rentals Ryan and I had done in the Outer Banks. This was more of a penthouse, at least three thousand square feet, with floor-to-ceiling windows and a wide balcony overlooking the Atlantic.

"It's beautiful."

"We like it. Hot as hell in the summer, though—humidity's worse than Virginia, if you can imagine it. That's why we head back to the Northern Neck every April. And Alice likes to see her azaleas and rhododendron bloom."

He showed me to the guest room—one of three, each with a bath as big as *Andromeda*'s entire cabin. Maxi, liberated from Alice's attention, rushed in and jumped on the bed, sniffing my bag while his mistress bustled to the kitchen to heat up some leftovers.

"You mean to tell me you haven't had a bite to eat since lunchtime? Bless your heart. You go shower, and I'll have dinner for you faster than a hot knife through buttah."

As I went to close the door, Arthur pressed an overfull glass of Chardonnay in my hand.

"You look like you could use a drink."

I sipped it, felt the cool liquid slip down my throat.

"Thank you."

Arthur put his arm around my shoulder and squeezed. "It'll be all right, darlin'. Everything looks bettah in the mornin'."

He was right. After a meal of shrimp and grits and a second glass of wine, I fell into a heavy, dreamless sleep. I didn't wake until after eight, feeling rested and optimistic until the images of the previous night flooded back. Then I was struck with remorse that I had not been at the hospital for the start of visiting hours. I called the ICU at once, and Francis told me Josh was stable and still under sedation. I dressed quickly and found Arthur and Alice having coffee on the balcony. I told them Josh's condition and asked if one of them could drop me at the hospital. Arthur got up and handed me a set of keys.

"I can do you one bettah. These are for the Mustang. And don't even think about sayin' no. We have three cars here and nevah use more than one at a time. There's a door key to the condo on the ring. Just promise to give us a call and let us know how your boyfriend's doin'."

My eyes teared up unexpectedly, and I blinked. Alice rose and gave me a hug.

"You just tell us what you need, sweetheart. We'll be heah all day."

I hurried to the downstairs parking garage and found the Mustang. It was far nicer than any car I had ever owned. Unfortunately, West Palm Beach's city streets were significantly more crowded than the sleepy little Virginia town I recently called home. The last thing I wanted was to repay the Peersons' kindness by denting a bumper. I drove slowly enough to draw glares and the occasional expletive, but at least I made it to the hospital without incident.

I joined a long line of visitors at the reception desk, where everyone entering the hospital had to present a driver's license and be photographed for a personalized, disposable identification badge. When I finally got to the attendant, she took a hard look at my name, shook her head, and pushed my license back across the desk.

"There's a policeman waiting for you over there. You'll need to take care of that first," she said, with a frown that suggested I had no business visiting anyone. She stood and waved to what had to be a plainclothes officer sitting in the main waiting room, then pointed to me.

"She's right here, Detective!"

Everyone behind me took a step backward.

Face burning, I left the line as the officer rose and walked toward me. He was Hispanic, somewhere between thirty-five and forty, about my height.

"*Buenas días*, Miss Beck. Detective Tony Ramirez. I recovered this at the scene this morning and came to return it to your friend. I understand he's still sedated in the ICU."

He held up Josh's backpack. In the chaos of last night, I had forgotten all about it. Josh must have pulled it off when he went to rescue Vianca Baptiste from her car.

"There was no wallet or I.D. in the bag, but I took the liberty of checking the phone. It was unlocked. Other than that, the backpack was empty. Hopefully nothing was stolen."

I explained that Josh kept his wallet in his pocket, and the pack was empty because we were on our way from the marina to pick up groceries.

"Ah. That makes sense, then," he said. He glanced around the waiting room, then leaned closer and lowered his voice. "Miss Beck, I was wondering if you could talk with me for a few minutes. I understand you're probably anxious to see your friend, but I'd really appreciate it. I'm investigating the explosion at the Garrison Community Center, and I was hoping you might have seen or heard something that could help me."

I checked my impatience. If Josh was still sedated, a few more minutes wouldn't make any difference. I knew from my experience that the sooner you interview witnesses, the better. Memories are notoriously unreliable to begin with, and they don't improve with time.

"Of course."

"Do you mind if we step outside? There's a place we can sit around the corner."

I followed him to a small courtyard sandwiched between hospital wings where a lone man in scrubs was eating from a styrofoam container. Ramirez sat down at the table nearest us, and I slid in across from him. He pulled out a small spiral notepad and pencil.

"If you don't mind, I'll just jot down some things while we talk. How long have you and Mr. Culliver been in West Palm Beach?"

"We just got in last night."

"It says in the EMT's report that you are from Virginia, and Mr. Culliver is from Maryland."

"That's correct."

"You are a little young to be snowbirds," he commented, looking up from his notebook. "Neither of you are currently employed?"

I swallowed my annoyance. He was just doing his job.

"Not exactly. Josh recently left the Army, and I have my own business. This is a sort of extended vacation. Sailing to the islands is something Josh has always wanted to do."

Ramirez nodded. "I can see why. I have to say I'm jealous. It must be nice to have a situation where you can take that much time off," he said pleasantly.

"It's the first vacation either of us has taken in years," I said, defensiveness creeping into my voice.

"Of course. Now, you said you were headed for the grocery store. Were you in the parking lot or crossing the street when you saw the explosion?"

"Neither. We were on the bridge." I went on to tell the story of going to the top to look out over the inlet, how we had planned to head to the Bahamas within the week. He smiled sympathetically.

"So things have not turned out like you expected. I'm sorry. When you passed by the parking lot, or on the way up the bridge, did you see anyone else in the vicinity of the community center?"

I described the homeless man lounging in the doorway, but I knew it was not much to go on. I had been some distance away, and he had been standing in the shadows. The best I could do was guess at medium height and build. As for clothing, I had the impression of military camouflage, but I couldn't be sure. Ramirez sighed.

"Don't feel bad. That's the same description I've gotten from every other witness. I don't know if you noticed the park. It's under the bridge—you would have seen it when you came through on your boat. It's popular with the homeless population because it has public restrooms and lots of shade. It closes at sunset, and then they scatter to parking lots and alleys nearby. Probably a dead end," he said, but I noticed he still wrote it down. "Now tell me what happened after that."

I replayed the sound of an engine pulling into the parking lot behind us, the blast a few minutes later, and Josh running to free the woman from the car. When I got to Vianca's plea for her mother, he stopped me.

"So just her mother, Mariana Baptiste. She never mentioned another person inside?"

"No. The media reported a second body was recovered. Is that true?"

Ramirez kept his expression carefully blank. "I'm not at liberty to say at this time. Please go on, Miss Beck."

I described Josh rushing into the burning building, the roof collapse, and his exit with Vianca's mother.

"Was he conscious at all after that? Did he say anything?"

"I don't think so. He was wearing an oxygen mask, and it was so chaotic…I can't say for sure. But I never saw his eyes open," I replied, shuddering as I pictured his face, white beneath the soot and blood.

Ramirez put down his notebook.

"I'm sorry. I know it's hard to talk about. We can leave it there for today. Will you be staying on your boat at the marina while your boyfriend is hospitalized?"

I told him about Arthur and Alice. He knew the building and jotted down their names and address. "If you should think of anything else, please call me." He scribbled something on the back of a business card, then handed it to me. The front listed an office in District Two of the Florida Bureau of Fire, Arson, and Explosives Investigations. On the flip side he had written a room number and name of a Palm Beach hotel.

"You're an arson investigator?" I asked in surprise. "Then you think the explosion was intentional?"

"We have made no determination as to cause. My office received a request last night for assistance from the Palm Beach County police department. I drove up from Miami this morning. I'll be staying in town until the investigation is complete."

"So this is just routine?"

He looked at me and pressed his lips together as if weighing his options.

"No. We are not usually called in unless the local PD believes there is compelling evidence suggesting arson."

I digested this.

"But if someone caused that explosion on purpose, that means—"

Tony Ramirez fixed his eyes on mine and finished my sentence.

"It means Mariana Baptiste was murdered."

Chapter 4

I rode the elevator to the third floor, barely aware of the people around me. Ramirez had refused to say more, and he looked like he wished he had said a good bit less. If there was a second body recovered from the building, wasn't it likely to be that of the culprit? Was it the man I had seen?

The ICU waiting room was crowded with a mix of adults and children being ushered through the security door two at a time to visit elderly patients. As I signed in, a stunning ebony-haired girl in her early twenties rose from one of the chairs and came toward me. If not for the bandage on her forehead, I would never have recognized her as the bleeding, ragged woman Josh pulled from the debris. Despite the dark circles under her eyes, Vianca Baptiste was achingly beautiful.

"I was hoping I'd see you before I left. They said your boyfriend couldn't have any non-family visitors yet. I wanted to thank you both for what you did last night."

"I'm glad you're all right," I said, taking in the bloodshot eyes and quivering lip. "I'm so sorry about your mother."

She blinked and a tear threatened to spill over. She wiped it away before it could fall.

"Thank you. Your boyfriend, Joshua—is he going to be okay? Alice Peerson called this morning. I understand you're staying with her. She said he was going to be fine, but Alice always says everything is going to be fine...."

I smiled at that. Like most southern women, Alice believed there was no point in dwelling on the negative. She still referred to her stroke as "that little trouble I had."

"They expect him to make a full recovery."

"Thank God," Vianca said, emotion overwhelming her. "I felt so guilty, knowing it was because of me—"

Her eyes filled again. I took her elbow and steered her gently to a nearby chair, then sat down beside her.

"No. Josh would have gone in regardless if he knew there was a person inside. Don't blame yourself."

"That's what the detective said, but I can't help it. I just don't understand how this could have happened. Our inspections were up to date. We'd just had the gas oven serviced a month ago, and it was fine. I keep asking myself, what did I miss, but...."

Then Ramirez had not told her his suspicion. I wondered why.

"I'm sure it wasn't your fault, Vianca."

She continued as if I hadn't spoken.

"I know it's wrong, but I blame Angelina. She's the girl who was supposed to clean the center yesterday. If she had shown up for work when she was supposed to, my mother wouldn't have come in, and she'd still be alive." Vianca shook her head. "That's horrible, isn't it, to wish another person had died instead? But I can't help it."

"It's not horrible, it's normal," I assured her. "You don't really wish she was dead. You just want your mother back."

"Mamá was...she was everything to me. She worked so hard to put me through school, and she was so proud of me, so supportive. It just doesn't seem real that she could be gone."

I knew that feeling. I grabbed a Kleenex from the table beside me and gave it to her. She wiped her nose, then stared at the crumpled tissue in her hand.

"Vianca?"

She squared her shoulders and looked directly into my eyes.

"Alice Peerson told me something else. She said you are like a private investigator. You look into things for people. She thought you might be willing to help find out what really happened."

"Detective Ramirez—" I began.

She shook her head. "No. I know how this must sound to you, but I don't trust him. I don't trust anybody connected to law enforcement here. Most of them don't care about people like me. Please—"

She was interrupted by the sound of the window at the desk sliding open. The receptionist called my name. I stood up, but Vianca put her hand on my arm.

"I'm sorry," she said. "I know I shouldn't impose on you. I understand you need to see your boyfriend. But please, just think about it. I can pay you." She rummaged in her purse and handed me a brochure for the community center that listed her cell phone number and email address. "Either way, will you call and let me know how your boyfriend's doing? And if he's awake, tell him how much I appreciate what he did."

"Of course."

The receptionist called my name again.

"Vianca, I have to—"

"I know. Thank you."

I left her sitting there and went back through the security door to Josh's room. As I took his hand, his eyelids fluttered and opened.

"San?" he whispered.

"I'm right here."

"The...girl?"

"Her name is Vianca Baptiste, and she's fine. I just saw her in the waiting room. She said to tell you thank you."

"The other...." He gave me an anguished look. "Dead?"

"Yes. The doctor said there was nothing they could do."

He closed his eyes.

I waited beside him for nearly an hour, but he did not reawaken. Francis, a young man in his twenties, came in to check Josh's vitals and told me he was still receiving a heavy dose of pain medication.

"We had to change the bandages on the burn wounds again this morning. It's a painful process. He will probably sleep most of the day. I can call you when he wakes up, unless you really want to stay. But like I said, he won't be awake again for a while. There's no point in sitting here all morning."

I hated the thought of Josh waking without me there, but Francis was right. I thanked him and gave him my cell number. Once in the elevator, I looked again at the backpack Ramirez had brought me. I would have to be the one to call the Cullivers.

I waited till I was in the car before turning on Josh's phone. My stomach dropped. There were ten missed calls, eight from Joanne Culliver, one from Josh's father, and another from his sister, all with voicemails. I checked the transcript of the first message. Even in writing, I could hear his mother's sharp voice, anger bordering on hysteria.

Oh my God, Josh, are you all right? What were you thinking, going into that building? Are you hurt? Answer the phone, Josh. You need to pick up the phone if you're there. Call me, Josh. Call me back.

I didn't bother to look at the rest. I was sure they were more of the same. I briefly considered sending a text, but I knew that would only make the situation worse. I touched the call-back button.

Joanne Culliver picked up on the first ring.

"Thank God, Josh. I'm—"

"It's not Josh, Mrs. Culliver. It's Sandi."

There was dead air, followed by a flat "Oh."

"Josh is in stable condition. He's in the ICU at Saint Mary's Palm Beach. He's still sedated, but--"

She cut me off before I could finish my sentence. "We talked to the nurse an hour ago. Andrew and I are on our way down there now. We're at BWI. Our plane boards in five minutes."

"Do you want me to pick you up at the airport?" I asked, thinking about the Mustang's cramped rear seat.

"We reserved a rental car. We land at two-thirty, and we're coming right to the hospital. The nurse told us they only allow two visitors at a time…if you're planning to be there."

It was on the tip of my tongue to ask her where else I would be, but there was a loud PA announcement in the background and then she was gone. No goodbye. I looked down at the phone, resisting the desire to smash it on the asphalt and run the wheels over it once or twice. The situation was difficult enough without the addition of Joanne Culliver.

It was only ten-thirty. If I got back to the hospital by two, at least I could plant myself by Josh's side before they arrived. Until then, I had some questions I'd like answered, like why Tony Ramirez did not tell Vianca Baptiste her mother was probably murdered. The girl was already tortured with grief over her loss; knowing it wasn't due to her own negligence would have given her some solace. Not telling her seemed a deliberate decision—why? Was Vianca right—was there a reason she could not trust law enforcement? Or did Detective Ramirez believe Vianca knew more than she was saying?

I would bet my life Vianca had nothing to do with the fire. I had seen her face when she called out for her mother. She would have run into the flames to save her. Plus Vianca asked me to find out who was responsible. Most criminals don't try to hire someone to investigate their own crimes. All Vianca Baptiste wanted was to know the truth—and so did I.

Now that the initial shock was over, I felt a growing anger. Someone had killed a woman, and in doing so they had also jeopardized Josh's life. Now our future plans were in limbo, and I was stuck in West Palm until—if—he recovered. Even if it did nothing to hasten Josh's healing, finding whoever was responsible for the explosion would give me a sense of purpose while I waited, and it might help allay Vianca's feeling of responsibility.

Detective Ramirez had refused to give specifics, saying only that he was "looking into every possibility." If he believed it was arson, the fundamental question was whether the target was the facility itself or the person inside. Detective Ramirez had wider resources available to find that answer than I did, but he also had a liability—he was a police officer. Even the innocent avoid talking to law enforcement, and based on Vianca's distrust of police, I doubted the local community would be any more forthcoming. I might have better luck.

I didn't have my laptop with me, but according to my iPhone's all-knowing Siri, the main branch of the Palm Beach County library was not far away. Before I approached Ramirez or Vianca again, I wanted to have information and some idea of who might benefit from either the fire or Mariana's death.

***

"I'm sorry, but those are the rules."

The gray-haired librarian behind the desk pursed her lips. She had already explained to me that I needed a library card to use a computer, and she was understandably hesitant to issue one to a person living on a boat with no fixed address.

"But I gave you the marina address. I'll be there for at least a few weeks, maybe longer. My boyfriend's in the hospital here."

She made a compassionate clucking noise, but her face didn't change. "I'm sorry to hear that; unfortunately, there is no waiver for your circumstance."

I sighed. "Then maybe you could help me. I'm trying to find information about the community center. My boyfriend was injured in the explosion—"

A teenage boy organizing books on a cart behind the counter looked up. "Was he the dude who saved Vianca?"

My answer catapulted me to instant fame. The community center sponsored several youth programs at the library, and Vianca was a local heroine there. Apparently her rescue, starring a now-identified Joshua Culliver, was being played as a trailer for every upcoming twelve o'clock news broadcast in the city. The entire staff extended their thanks and well wishes, along with a temporary library card good for thirty days and a promise of help if there was anything else I needed.

I settled in at a computer as far from the check-out desk as possible and started with a Google search for the community center that turned up dozens of hits. The brainchild of Palm Beach philanthropist Jerry Garrison, owner of a commercial HVAC company, it had gotten lots of press when it opened. The story went that he bought the defunct school building from the county for next to nothing a decade ago, when the area near the bridge was considered undesirable. He began the lengthy process of finding additional donors and created a foundation to serve needy families. It had taken seven years to get the building upgraded and the center staffed. Meanwhile, property values underwent a drastic change as the city worked with developers to bring upscale shopping and housing to the area.

Greed stepped in.

While many applauded Garrison's efforts to help the diverse, struggling community, those profiting from the gentrification of the waterfront were vocally opposed to the Garrison Community Center. They banded together to form the Lake Worth Improvement Society, a citizens' action committee to force the center's closure, claiming it would lead to increased crime in the area and substantially lower property values. Newspaper editorials accused the largely white group of racism—a charge they vehemently denied. The LWIS went on to petition the city and the county, both of which refused their request to shut down the center.

Meanwhile, Garrison was battling stage four cancer. He lost his fight a few weeks later, and the terms of his will infuriated the LWIS. The foundation charged with operating the community center was treated in the will as a single entity and given a lifetime estate on the property. As long as it was actively used in accordance with the terms of its community mission, the property could not be sold or repurposed. In other words, the center could be there forever.

The LWIS filed a lawsuit, arguing that the lifetime estate was invalid because owner-of-right status was meant for individuals, not charitable organizations with an infinite lifespan. But before the case could be heard in court, a video surfaced of one member taking part in a white supremacist rally. That turned public opinion against them, and a counter movement began to boycott any business owned by the group's members. A few days later, the lawsuit was dropped.

If the arsonist's target was the facility, the LWIS could be behind it.

I turned to Mariana Baptiste. An immigrant from Guatemala, she had almost no digital footprint—one marriage record from 1992 to Joseph Baptiste, a Haitian-American United States citizen, and nothing else: no court records, no speeding tickets, not even a personal Facebook profile. Her company, St. Agnes Maid Services, LLC (SAMS), was rated at five stars on

Yelp. A business directory listed SAMS as employing twenty to thirty people with an estimated revenue between $500,000 and $750,000—a respectable profit, but hardly enough to make its owner a target. Mariana was looking more and more like an unintended victim in the wrong place at the wrong time.

While there was little information about Vianca's mother, Vianca herself was the subject of numerous online articles. She attended local schools, winning a variety of academic and athletic awards, along with a scholarship to the University of Florida. Despite her father's death in her senior year, she graduated at the top of her class with a degree in public administration and went on to get her master's. She was hired as the center director right out of grad school, and her innovative programs to combat violence between rival Haitian-American, Hispanic, and African-American gangs won accolades at state and national levels. She'd even been interviewed by Oprah. By all accounts, Vianca Baptiste could go anywhere she chose—but she continued working in the old brick building for a mere $46,000 a year.

It was in the posts after the news articles about the center that I saw the ugly side of Vianca's notoriety.

Another illegal crybaby. Send her back where she came from.

Socialists like her are destroying our country.

Just like the rest of the liberal elite. To hell with hard-working Americans. This black bitch is giving our tax dollars to a bunch of crack babies.

Her center is full of drug dealers and gang bangers. The police should burn the damn building down.

I was taken aback by the venom in the comments. Somehow Vianca, a quintessential American success story, had become a reviled symbol of anti-Americanism to a small but vocal population. Had one of them carried it a step too far and acted on that hatred?

Perhaps I had been asking the wrong question. Maybe the arson wasn't an either/or, it was both. Burning down the center and killing Mariana Baptiste accomplished the same goal—destroying Vianca Baptiste.

Chapter 5

Josh was propped up on his pillows, eyes open when I got back to the hospital. When I entered, Francis, the nurse I had spoken to earlier, was adjusting his IV drip.

"I was about to call you. He just got up about ten minutes ago."

"Hey, babe," Josh muttered, his voice hoarse.

"How are you?" I asked, reaching for his hand.

"Better… than I… look," he said, managing a faint grin.

"His temperature is slightly elevated. Blood pressure is normal. Oxygen saturation is still a little low, so we'll keep him on that for now," Francis said. "Also, he should be hungry. He didn't wake up for lunch. Do you think you're up to swallowing some soft food?"

Josh nodded.

"I'll have them send something up," Francis said. "Enjoy your visit."

I leaned over and kissed Josh's forehead. "How do you really feel?"

"Drugged up. Not bad." He had trouble saying more than a few words before running out of breath.

He closed his eyes, drifting off. Francis returned with what looked like baby food, juice, and Jell-O.

"He fell back asleep."

"That's okay. I'll leave it here for a while in case he wants it when he wakes up. He'll be in and out all day. Doctor Hassan and the orthopedic surgeon, Doctor Kristofferson, made their rounds earlier. Your boyfriend will need surgery for the fracture. They've scheduled him for tomorrow at eight a.m., assuming he doesn't spike a fever or have any complications prior to."

Fifteen minutes passed before Josh opened his eyes. I watched him get his bearings.

"Hey," I said, pulling closer. "There's some food here. Are you hungry?"

He reached for my hand. "Our trip…sorry, San."

"Don't worry about it. We'll figure something out," I said, raising his fingers to my lips.

"My girl," he whispered. He motioned to a business card lying on the bedside table. "Detective was here. I was asleep. Wants to talk to me."

It was the same one Ramirez had given me.

"I met him this morning. He's an arson investigator."

Josh nodded. "Thought so. There was another body… on the floor." He looked over at the tray.

"Do you want to try it?"

He nodded.

I adjusted the tray table over his lap and raised the head of the bed. He lifted his bandaged right hand, then laid it down.

"Forgot," he said, trying to smile.

He positioned the spoon in his left hand and was able to get the pureed food to his mouth.

"What's it taste like?"

"Chicken." It was a weak joke—he said it whenever we were in a restaurant and he ordered something unusual. I laughed anyway.

When he finished the puree, he started on the Jell-O and juice. He did it slowly, with small swallows, but some of the color returned to his face and his voice seemed stronger.

"Best Jell-O… I've ever had."

I cleared away the dishes and tray. He patted the bed and I perched beside him. I chose my words carefully.

"Did the nurse talk to you about your injuries?"

His green eyes grew wary. "No. Why?"

I summarized what Dr. Hassan told me the night before and the information about tomorrow's surgery.

"And…the hand?"

I mentally kicked myself. I should have started with that. Between the bandage and the swelling, it was the size of a baseball glove. No wonder he was worried. "They believe it will heal without grafts. You may need occupational therapy, but you should regain full function."

He let the meager air out of his lungs in a shaky sigh.

"I was…afraid you'd have…to sail the boat alone."

"Well, it's not like I can't. In fact, I might be a better sailor than you," I teased.

"Those are…fighting words," he said, but he was smiling.

"Josh, you said you saw a second body. Can you describe it?"

"Always…the investigator." He closed his eyes and frowned, thinking. "Hard to see…. Male, I think. Medium build."

"Where was he?"

"In the kitchen…in front of the woman," he coughed, then took a minute to catch his breath. I started to protest that he'd talked enough, but he raised his good hand to stop me. "You said… you saw… her daughter."

"I did. Vianca Baptiste. Her mother was Mariana." I described the center's director and her request that I look into the fire. "I wonder if the body was the homeless man we passed in the doorway."

Josh shrugged. "Couldn't see…through the smoke. The body…was on its back. Had to have been down…before the blast."

"What about Mariana Baptiste?"

"It blew her…against the wall…across from the kitchen."

I tried to picture the scene. "So maybe he thought the center was empty. He would have seen Vianca leave. There were no other cars in the parking lot. He could have been setting up explosives when she walked in on him."

"Not terrorism…too few casualties. Confident. Went in…while it was still light. Pro. Maybe ex-military."

He spoke with knowledge borne of experience, and I was reminded again of how little I truly understood him. There were two halves to Josh—the sniper who had taken human life with cold efficiency, and the warm, gentle lover whose ring I wore. On the surface at least, he had successfully flipped the switch and rejoined civilian life. But sometimes, when he did not know I was watching, I imagined a hollowness behind his eyes. I did not know if it was because of the things he had seen, or the things he had missed.

"What did…Ramirez say?"

"Nothing. Just that he thought it was intentional. But there are obviously things he wasn't telling me." I shared everything I had learned at the library. Josh frowned.

"If Vianca was…a target, she could…still be a target."

"Possibly. Or maybe killing her mother was intended to hurt her, drive her off. How much danger she is in could depend on whether they try to rebuild the community center."

I glanced over at the clock on the wall. Five after three.

"Josh, I almost forgot. Your parents are coming," I said, taking his phone from my purse. "You left your backpack in the parking lot and Ramirez gave it to me. When I checked the phone, your family had been trying to call you. I guess they heard what happened."

He groaned.

"I called your mother back this morning. Your parents were boarding a plane for Palm Beach."

He looked at the call log on his phone and grimaced. "Man…I never even…thought about them. Someone in the Bureau…must have called… my dad. I bet Mom is…fit to be tied."

"She sounded that way."

"When will they…be here?"

"Right about now." Suddenly facing Joanne Culliver didn't sound so appealing. "You're only allowed two visitors at once. Maybe I should let them have some time with you alone when they get here. I need to check in with the Peersons, and I can come back later tonight."

He gave me a feeble grin. "Throwing me…under the bus, huh?"

"They are your parents."

"I'll…remember this. Kiss."

I leaned down and kissed his lips.

"I'll be back. Call me when the coast is clear. Love you."

"Love you."

The waiting room was empty, though one of the two elevators was on its way up. I got in the other hurriedly and pushed the button. As the door closed, I thought I heard Joanne Culliver's voice.

That reunion could wait for another day.

Chapter 6

I picked up a bottle of wine to thank the Peersons for their hospitality and headed toward Singer Island. As I drew near the Blue Heron Bridge, I saw two Bureau of Fire, Arson, and Explosives Investigations vans in the community center parking lot, along with a navy Chevy Silverado and a small sedan. Forensic techs in hazmat suits, masks, and gloves were combing through the wreckage, while Tony Ramirez and Vianca Baptiste sat on the Silverado's open tailgate, heads bowed in quiet conversation.

Neither looked up when I pulled in, and I was able to get within a few feet before Ramirez finally saw me.

"Miss Beck," he said, surprised. "Were you looking for me?"

Simultaneously, Vianca asked, "Is Josh all right?"

"He's fine, thanks," I replied, choosing to answer her question first. "His family is coming in to see him. I'm going back later tonight."

Ramirez was still looking at me quizzically.

"I was on my way to Singer Island and saw you. I thought I'd let you know Josh is awake in case you wanted to talk to him."

It was a lame excuse, and Ramirez knew it.

"Thanks. The hospital called me a few hours ago. I'll go by there later this afternoon."

His tone was dismissive. When I didn't move, his eyebrows rose slightly.

"Was there something else, Miss Beck?"

I glanced over at the agents who were carefully bagging what looked like fragments of a burned hat. "I just wondered if you had identified the second victim. Josh said it was a male. I thought it might have been the homeless man we saw."

His jaw tightened, though his expression remained pleasant. "I'm not at liberty---"

"Second victim?" Vianca's eyes were wide. "There was no one but my mother in the center when I left."

"Oh," I said, avoiding Tony Ramirez's eyes. "I thought you knew. It was on the news."

Vianca looked at Ramirez accusingly.

"You didn't tell me that."

"I was just about to ask Miss Baptiste about the second individual," he snapped, directing his words toward me. "Miss Beck, I'd appreciate it if you'd wait in your car while I finish up here. Then I'd like to speak with you."

Chastened, I returned to the Mustang. Five minutes passed, then ten. The conversation looked heated, and Vianca stood up once as if to leave and then sat back down. At some point Ramirez must have gotten something of interest, because his notebook was open and he wrote nonstop while she was speaking. Meanwhile the sun flitted in and out of the clouds and the car got progressively hotter. I finally put down the top, causing Vianca to pause and drawing a steely stare from Ramirez. Another fifteen minutes passed. Finally he rose and shook Vianca's hand. She glanced over at me, and I thought she might come to the car, but Ramirez steered her to the sedan and waited until she drove away. Then he slid into the passenger seat beside me.

"I'm sorry, Detective. I really thought she knew."

He ignored the apology and stared me full in the face. "What's your story, Miss Beck?"

"What do you mean?"

"The couple you're staying with, the Peersons. I don't suppose you knew Alice Peerson had a connection to the community center?"

I hesitated. "Yes. I mean, I didn't before the fire. I just found out last night."

"She is in fact on the Garrison Foundation Board of Directors," he prompted.

"Yes."

"That might have been a relevant fact to bring up this morning, don't you think?"

"No. I mean, yes, but I didn't even think of it," I stumbled. I really hadn't thought of it, but I could see his point.

"I stopped by to talk with her about the center, and naturally your name came up. By the way, the Peersons both think very highly of you," he said, flipping through his notebook. "Here we are. According to Arthur Peerson, you're 'a gifted private detective.' Is that true, Miss Beck?" he asked, and I saw a glint of humor in his eyes.

"Not exactly."

"But you do investigate crimes, is that correct?"

"Sometimes."

"And did Vianca Baptiste ask you to investigate the fire at the center?"

I couldn't come up with a nuanced response. "Yes."

"And what was your answer?"

"Maybe."

His mouth turned up in a half-smile. "Miss Beck, this conversation is going to take a lot longer if you keep giving me one-word answers. I'm just trying to figure out whether you're going to be a help or a liability here."

I am used to having an adversarial relationship with law enforcement. They typically don't appreciate amateurs inserting themselves into investigations, and I can't say I blame them. They operate within a strict framework of procedures, and I have more of an instinctual, fly-by-the-seat-of-my-pants philosophy. I admit it can get a little messy.

But I got a different vibe from Tony Ramirez. For a detective, he was amazingly likeable. I smiled back.

"Definitely a help."

"You know, this is where I usually explain that the investigation is a police matter, and you should let us handle it...but I'm not going to do that. It's clear Vianca Baptiste doesn't trust local law enforcement, and right now she has no reason to trust me. Neither does the Garrison Foundation Board. But for whatever reason, they seem to trust you." He gave me an assessing look. "My father was a cop—a good one—and he always told me it's a foolish man who doesn't accept any help he can get. So I am inclined to take your offer of assistance."

"Sounds like a smart guy."

He gave a rueful laugh. "You have no idea. Smarter than I will ever be. He passed away last year—heart attack. But not a day goes by that I don't think about him."

"I'm sorry."

"Thanks. Just wanted you to understand where I'm coming from. Anything I tell you, I didn't tell you. You have no official capacity here, and if I get called on the carpet for something you say or do, I'll lay all the blame back on you. Got it?"

"Doesn't sound like a very good deal for me, Detective Ramirez," I pointed out.

"Only one you'll get. And call me Tony," he said, putting out his hand. I shook it.

"Okay, Tony."

Ramirez sat back. "Glad we got that settled. I also understand your boyfriend's father is Andrew Culliver."

I felt the sting of betrayal. Was that what this was all about? Had he talked with Culliver about me?

"He is Josh's father, yes. Why? Do you know him?"

Ramirez eyed me thoughtfully. "I do not. I'm hoping you and Andrew Culliver have a good personal relationship."

"What does that have to do with anything?" It was more accusation than question.

"So, I take it the answer is no," he said.

"Let's just say I'm not his first choice for daughter-in-law."

"Really? I'm surprised," he said, and I wasn't sure if he was being serious or sarcastic. "The reason I asked is because Andrew Culliver was recently named the head of the FBI's hate crimes task force. Sooner or later, I'm going to have to bring him in. I'd rather do it quietly, without stirring up the press. It would be nice to have a connection."

I felt the heat in my face. "If that's the reason you're talking to me—"

He held up his hand, "Hold on a minute. You came to me. I'm just seeing how you can help."

I swallowed my pride. It was a reasonable request. While Andrew Culliver had no affection for me, I believed he had respect.

"I can try."

Tony smiled. "All right then. Let's move on. "

Ramirez got out his cell phone and handed it to me. The screen showed a blackened section of concrete wall. The crudely sprayed red letters were barely legible beneath the soot, but I could guess at the words: cruel and spewing hatred, they were directed at blacks and Hispanics.

"This is an interior wall near the front door. The graffiti was applied with high temperature spray paint. The perpetrator wanted it to survive the fire. There are some neo-Nazi gangs in the area, but the language is off. This is more sophisticated vernacular, not street talk. I'm assuming it was done by whoever created the explosion, but it's possible, even likely, he did not work alone."

"You think it was a white supremacist group or some kind of militia?" I asked.

"Or the arsonist wanted it to look that way. When this gets out, it's going to create a real shit storm, if you'll pardon my language. This community is already on edge."

Based on the contentious posts I had read about Vianca, I could envision the rising tensions and protests that would follow.

"How long before you call the FBI?"

"A day, maybe two, but that's it," he said, taking back the phone. "We don't have the resources in this area that they do. I'm hoping we get a positive I.D. on the body. As soon as it breaks that this was arson, there will be a lot of pressure to get it solved. The LWIS—that's the local citizen's action group-has already made a public statement saying they'll oppose any rebuilding attempt. And now it looks like the center was seriously underinsured, which makes you wonder. If they can't replace the building, the land reverts to the estate, and it's worth a fortune. Garrison's daughter has a seat on the board, and her husband handles the legal affairs for the foundation."

"You think the family was involved in this?"

Ramirez couldn't keep the frustration from his voice. "I don't know what to think. This has the look of an inside job. Vianca swears she locked the door when she left, and her mother would never have let a stranger in. So, Mariana Baptiste either knew the person who set off the explosion—which seems unlikely—or he had a key. If he did, we haven't found it yet. As far as I can tell, there were six people who had access to keys: Vianca, her assistant director Rufus Frey, who is in Cozumel on his honeymoon, Melissa Reid, Garrison's daughter, and the three other officers on the board."

I thought back to something Vianca had said.

"There was a girl who worked for Mariana Baptiste. Vianca said she was supposed to come in and clean yesterday afternoon but didn't show. Would she have had a key?"

"Angelina Torres," he said, checking over his notes. "No. She's supposed to come in at three, while Vianca's still there. The center's closed to the public on Monday afternoons. Vianca does the books, goes out to do a bank run and get supplies, then comes back at five to lock all the doors when Angelina is done. Yesterday, when the girl didn't show up, Vianca called her mother, and Mariana Baptiste got dropped off at the center at four p.m. to clean it in Angelina's place. Vianca was in the office doing paperwork until five-forty, when she left to get takeout for herself and her mother."

I frowned. "The explosion happened right around six. That means normally no one would have been there. And there were no cars except Vianca's. Whoever did this must have watched and waited till she left. They would have no reason to think Mariana Baptiste was inside."

"That's the assumption we're working on."

"Then the purpose of the explosion wasn't to kill anyone."

"It looks that way. But I'd sure like to talk to Angelina Torres and find out why she didn't come to work." Ramirez's phone rang. He answered it, listened for a minute, then ended the call and turned to me.

"It seems that might be more difficult than I thought."

"Why?"

"Angelina Torres's sister just called Palm Beach PD. She says Angelina is missing."

Chapter 7

"Missing" is a relative term. Not every missing teen is abducted or injured. Kids don't come home for myriad reasons—drunkenness, rebellion, selfishness, love—and in those cases they turn up, hours or days or months later, seemingly unaware of the chaos they created with their absence. But there are those few who are never found, their faces adorning bulletin boards and rest stop walls, computer aged as the years go by. I hoped the best for Angelina Torres, but that's all it was—hope.

"Are you all right, darlin'?"

Arthur had come up, a drink in hand, and was standing in front of me with a worried expression.

"Fine. Just tired," I said, taking the glass of wine he offered. In the five hours since I had talked to Ramirez, I had showered, eaten dinner at a drive-thru, visited Josh at five-thirty when his parents left, and then had come back to help a flustered Alice with a hastily-called emergency board meeting.

The foundation usually met in the center, but since that was an impossibility, Alice as president arranged for them to meet in the condominium complex's large first-floor library. The group always used a local caterer for post-meeting drinks and hors d'oeuvres, one of the few perks of their otherwise unpaid positions. But no caterer was available on three hours' notice, and Alice was in a state of panic when she called me at the hospital. She assured me nothing I could pick up from the Publix deli would do. Fortunately, last minute appetizers are one of my strengths; now the ten board members, as well as their lawyer, were enjoying the bacon-wrapped scallops, shrimp cocktail, and warm crab dip I'd thrown together in forty-five minutes from the contents of Alice's pantry.

Though everyone appeared to be chatting cordially, according to Arthur the meeting itself had not gone so smoothly. He was charged with videotaping the proceedings, which were posted to the group's Facebook page each month. He told me that five board members were in favor of getting a reconstruction loan and rebuilding the center as soon as possible, but the other five favored moving to an existing site elsewhere, insisting it would be less expensive than new construction. That would mean losing the life estate.

But that wasn't all. The Garrison Foundation was partially funded by a trust tied to the operation of the community center. If the center wasn't engaged in its mission for ninety consecutive days, the money was automatically redistributed to other charity organizations Garrison supported. If another site couldn't be found and placed in operation within that time period, how would the center survive without the trust fund?

Not surprisingly, four of the five members who favored moving the center owned businesses nearby and stood to benefit from increasing property values, a topic Alice broached without hesitation. The conversation became briefly heated, and in the end it came to a vote. One of the five members supporting relocation changed sides, so the final decision was to seek donations first and rebuild on the existing site as soon as possible; if that failed, they would turn their efforts to finding a new location. The lack of clear commitment to either option probably spelled the end of the community center, but it was the only compromise they could reach.

The contentious meeting behind them, the board members were now mingling with forced politeness over food and drinks. They were a mostly older crowd, seventies and eighties, but tanned and otherwise well-preserved. The majority oozed wealth—not the nouveau riche kind, but the old family money type, transplanted from Boston or New York or other northern cities. The only Florida natives—and the only couple who interested me—were Melissa and David Reid, the couple who also stood the most to gain if the center folded.

She was perhaps thirty, average-looking, with medium brown hair that was too long to be stylish and too short to be sexy, a pasty complexion, and large dark-framed glasses that magnified small gray eyes. She moved with a nervous energy, and her hands fluttered when she spoke. But her voice was melodic and sweet, and combined with a warm, genuine smile, it was enough to make her almost pretty. Melissa Reid did not look or act like an accomplice to arson.

Her husband was the opposite. Tall and dark, with a perfectly chiseled nose and broad shoulders, he was undeniably handsome, but he had a strident voice and his smile never reached his eyes. I could easily imagine him choosing dollars over ethics, though to be fair, I had not yet had a conversation with him. It seemed that was about to change, for David Reid and his wife were purposefully headed my way.

"Miss Beck, I'm Melissa Reid, and this is my husband David. We are so glad to have the chance to meet you. We are so grateful for what you and your fiancé did. It would have been devastating for the foundation to lose Vianca. We are greatly in your debt," Melissa effused.

"How is your boyfriend? We understand he will require additional time in the hospital and several surgeries," her husband probed.

"He's doing well," I replied.

He pulled out a card from his wallet. "Have him call me. Obviously, the foundation cannot accept responsibility or financial liability for his voluntary actions. We've contacted our property insurer, but I understand they are waiting for the outcome of the investigation. However, if you should need some limited temporary assistance with medical expenses, the foundation has asked me to offer it. Within reason, of course."

I took the card, but the distaste I felt must have shown on my face. Melissa put a hand on his arm.

"You'll have to excuse my husband. He thinks like a lawyer. He can't help it. I'm sure Sandi—it is Sandi, isn't it? I'm sure the last thing Sandi wants to do tonight is talk about money. Just know we are here to help, in any way you need."

David Reid's eyes narrowed, but he nodded with stiff civility.

"Of course. If you'll excuse me, I need a refill," he said.

Arthur jumped in and offered to pour him another bourbon, and the two men walked off. Melissa turned to me apologetically.

"He thinks everyone is out to sue us. It's an occupational hazard, I'm afraid, but sometimes I could just strangle him."

I couldn't suppress a smile.

"I know, not a very wifely thing to say in public," she said with a conspiratorial glint in her eye.

"I'm sure plenty of wives feel the same way."

"I know he means well, but to tell you the truth, David doesn't understand how much the center means to me. It was Daddy's legacy. Not that David doesn't support our work," she added hastily. "It's just that he's much more practical, and he doesn't see why we can't accomplish the same thing somewhere else."

I wondered what Tony Ramirez would think of that.

"Sandi, there's another reason I wanted to talk to you," Melissa said, moving closer. "Alice tells me you were a college professor."

The turn in conversation surprised me.

"I was. Junior college. But that was a few years ago."

She leaned her head toward me and lowered her voice. "I don't want David to hear. He hates it when I try to step in between him and his brother, but I'm worried about Julian's grades. He's a junior in high school. He had a paper due before the holidays that he didn't turn in, and his teacher called me. She said he was in danger of failing. I got her to agree to take it when he gets back this month. I didn't tell David. The problem is, I don't think Julian is putting much effort into it. I know it's rude of me to ask, but if you could just look over what he's done and give him some suggestions, it might motivate him to finish."

"Melissa, I'm sure you can find a tutor—" I started, but she shook her head.

"I've tried. But first it was Christmas and then New Years, and no one was available. He goes back to Saint Timothy's this weekend. Please. I'd be happy to pay you whatever you want."

The school name caught my attention. "Saint Timothy's Boarding School? In Urbanna, Virginia?"

"Yes. Do you know it? It's a fine school, though a little too far away. But it's where David went, and so that's where Julian has to go. They're from there, originally. David's parents lived in Falls Church when he grew up, and later they moved to Richmond. Julian was born when David was in law school—an oops baby, you know, late in life. But seven years ago their parents were killed, and David brought his brother down here with us to live. It's been hard on Julian. Being so far apart in age, they were never close, and David is so busy. Julian has had trouble adjusting…we all have. We'd just gotten married, and neither one of us was ready to have children. Not, of course, that we think of Julian as a son. But he was just nine years old, and he needed parenting, and I know I haven't always done the best job…."

Whatever David Reid might feel for his sibling, Melissa clearly bore the weight of the child's presence in their life. I could feel myself relenting.

"I'm not asking you to write it for him," she added, as if the thought suddenly occurred to her. "I'd never do that. I'd just like to get him some help, that's all."

"What will you tell David?"

"He'll probably never notice. He thinks Julian's working on a project for next semester, so I'll just say I asked you to proofread it. If that's all right."

I sighed inwardly.

"That's fine. When do you want me to meet with Julian?"

Melissa beamed. "Would tomorrow afternoon work? If you give me your number, I'll text you the address."

Josh's surgery was at eight in the morning, and while I planned to spend most of the day with him, his parents would be there as well. Having an appointment in the late afternoon would give me an out. We set a tentative time of four, though I explained the situation and said I would text her if I ran behind. I saw David look our way while we exchanged cell numbers, but he continued his conversation with Arthur and another man at the opposite end of the room.

"Then we'll see you tomorrow. And Sandi, don't be put off by Julian. He doesn't always communicate well. He can be–abrupt, and he has had issues with self-control. But he's getting better," she added quickly. "He's really very bright."

I reassured her that I had worked with a variety of students and that everything would be fine, but I found myself having second thoughts as she walked away. For a brief instant when she was talking about Julian, I thought I saw fear in Melissa Reid's eyes.

Chapter 8

I got to the hospital at six-thirty a.m. to meet Josh in pre-op. The antibiotics had done their job; Josh had not spiked a fever. His lungs sounded clearer, and though he was still on oxygen, he was able to speak more comfortably. I was both surprised and relieved to see that neither Culliver parent was there.

"I told them the surgery was at nine," he admitted. "I figured there would be less drama that way."

We were in a curtained cubicle, waiting for the anesthesiologist. The orthopedic surgeon had already been in to explain the procedure, called an open reduction and internal fixation, which included making an incision, lining up the broken bones, and pinning them in place. The arm would be splinted, and Josh would need to wear a sling to immobilize it while it healed.

"I talked to Doctor Hassan. He said your burns cleaned up nicely," Dr. Kristofferson, the orthopedic surgeon had said before he went to scrub up. "We would only keep you overnight for today's procedure, but I understand he expects you to be here for four or five more days while they monitor the healing of your back and hand."

That was good news, though I wondered how well Josh would be able to negotiate getting on and off *Andromeda* with his injuries. As if he read my thoughts, Dr. Kristofferson hinted at this as well.

"I understand from Joshua that the two of you live aboard a sailboat," he had added, directing his comments to me. "You might want to consider getting a hotel room for a couple of weeks, until the arm heals and you regain use of the hand. Any fall could cause serious damage, and then you'd both be sitting right back here."

Josh didn't say anything, but I saw from the stubborn set of his face that he wasn't willing to stay anywhere but on his boat.

"Thank you. I'll see what we can do," I had said, staying carefully noncommittal. It was a battle that could wait.

After that Dr. Kristofferson had gone.

Josh took my hand.

"I'll be fine, San. Really. "

"I know you will." I hugged him gingerly, working my way around the tubes and bandages.

"Hey, I meant to tell you. I had a visitor last night after you left. Detective Ramirez."

The investigator had asked for Josh's description of the second victim, since the fire had erased any identifiable features before the body could be recovered. That was the extent of his questions regarding the explosion, but he had evinced a strong interest in me.

"You must have made quite an impression," Josh teased. "He wanted to know all about the scientist you found in North Carolina."

I had never once mentioned that incident, and for good reason. Having a dead man's hand hit you in the face while diving was not an experience I was eager to relive, and I had been sworn to secrecy by no less than the CIA. Ramirez probably read the news reports, which barely grazed the surface of the real story.

"I hope you didn't say anything."

"Not me. My lips were sealed," Josh assured me. "I did refer him to the appropriate agency. That got his attention."

I sighed. "Great. Thanks."

He grinned. "I wouldn't worry. He's too smart to expect any answers from the CIA."

The anesthesiologist came in then and went over her checklist, followed by an orderly and an OR nurse who prepared to wheel Josh away. The nursing assistant took my cell number and ushered me to the closest waiting room.

"Joshua is scheduled for ninety minutes in the OR, and then it will be another thirty minutes or so in post-op before he goes back to his room. I'll come get you, and if you're not here, I'll send a text."

I checked my watch, then headed for the cafeteria to grab a bite to eat. I was in the middle of the hallway when I heard footsteps behind me.

"Sandi?"

I turned. It was Vianca Baptiste.

The passage of a day had brought color to her face and lightened the dark circles beneath her eyes. She wore her long hair pulled back in a single braid and was dressed professionally in a pair of navy pants and a white blouse. I saw she had a visitor's temporary badge.

"The front desk sent me to the OR, but they said Josh was already in surgery."

"They just took him in. I was getting some breakfast. You're welcome to join me."

I picked up a bagel and some fruit, along with a Diet Coke. Vianca, who could afford a few extra pounds, filled her plate with bacon, eggs, and waffles. The cafeteria was uncrowded, just a few staff members on break, so we had a corner table to ourselves.

"I hope you don't mind. I wanted to see how Josh was doing, but I also… well…." she hesitated, looking around uncomfortably.

"Go on."

"I wanted to know if you'd thought about what I said…about helping me. I know Detective Ramirez isn't telling me everything, and David Reid, our lawyer, keeps calling and badgering me about what's going on."

I bet he was. Before I could answer, Vianca pulled out her checkbook.

"I really can pay you, Sandi. My mother saved up money in case I wanted to go back to school for my doctorate. I'm not asking you to do it for free."

I shook my head. "It's not the money. You need to understand, Vianca, that I have no authority here. I don't even have a network of sources I can go to for information. I'm willing to look into what happened, but I'll need your help. And if Detective Ramirez is right and the fire was deliberate, that could put both of us in danger."

She paled, but her face was set.

"I don't care. I want to know the truth."

Famous last words. I sighed.

"I assume Ramirez told you about the second body."

She nodded. "The detective seems to think he was the man who started the fire. He wanted to know who would want to burn down the center. I told him probably half the people in this city. But Sandi, I don't think any of them would actually do it. I mean, people get upset and say things, but they don't act on them."

"Sometimes they do," I disagreed. "Have you talked to Detective Ramirez since I saw you yesterday?"

"No. Why?"

"After you left, he found out Angelina Torres is missing."

Her eyes grew round. "Missing? What do you mean?"

I explained about the report filed by her sister.

"Is that all?" she asked, her mouth curling in a sour smile.

"You don't seem surprised."

She shrugged. "Look, Angelina was one of my mother's projects. You know how some people bring home stray kittens? Mamá brought home troubled girls. She saw Angelina coming out of this club while she was out on a job. Mamá said she was crying, and she looked so lost that she felt sorry for her. Anyway, my mother gave her a Coke and sat her down in the van, and that's how Mamá learned that Angelina's parents threw her out for doing drugs. Angelina was applying for a job at the club, but the owner told her if she wanted to work there, she'd have to, you know…" she paused, embarrassed, before continuing, "…do something for him."

"That's terrible."

"It happens more than you think. Anyway, that was all Mamá needed to hear. She took Angelina in, cleaned her up, and gave her a job. Then she went to Angelina's sister and convinced her to move Angelina into her house."

"Your mother sounds like a good person," I said.

Vianca looked down at her food. "She was. Mamá is the one who taught me to put others first. I know this will sound selfish, but it made me mad sometimes, the way she let those girls take advantage of her. All her employees were like Angelina in one way or the other—throwaways, victims. I understood they needed her help…but sometimes I felt like they mattered more to her than me."

She pulled at the silver chain around her neck, holding up the charm.

"A Saint Agnes medal. She's the patron saint of young girls. That's where Mamá got the name for her business. All her girls wear one of these. She said it would remind them of who they were."

I could hear the guilt in her voice. "Did you and your mother argue about Angelina Monday?"

Vianca nodded miserably. "Yes. Angelina's been late for a few jobs. She's supposed to take the bus to Keesha Taylor's every morning—that's Mamá's team manager—and go out in her van, and twice she didn't show up and Keesha had to go get her. But Angelina only works the afternoon on Mondays, so she takes the bus from her first job to the center and I drive her home. When she didn't show up, I called Mamá. She tried calling Angelina, but it went right to voicemail."

"So your mom came to the center to do her work."

"Yes, but not right away. She was out with a crew. In between clients, she had them drop her off and go on to the last job of the day without her. I told her then Angelina should be fired, but my mother did what she always does—she made excuses for her. I lost my temper, told Mamá she needed to stop trying to be everybody's mother and start to be their boss." She looked away, lip trembling. "That was the last thing I said before I left to get us dinner...."

Last words carry a heavy price when there is no time to ask forgiveness for them. When my husband Ryan died, I was grateful that the last words I spoke to him were "I love you." I waited till Vianca composed herself and turned her gaze back to her plate before I spoke.

"Did Angelina ever give a reason for being late on those other jobs?"

"I guess you could call it a reason. She told my mother that she had a new boyfriend," Vianca said with a roll of her eyes. "When he snapped his fingers, Angelina went running. She seemed to think he was her ticket out, said she wasn't going to have to spend the rest of her life cleaning other people's toilets."

"Did she tell your mother his name?"

"No. It was a big secret. But she had new clothes—designer labels, really expensive. Mamá figured it was probably some older married man. She tried to talk some sense into Angelina, but that girl told Mamá to mind her own business."

Gullible and looking for an easy way out—Angelina Torres would have been easy to manipulate. Could she have somehow gotten a key for the arsonist? Could she have been warned about the explosion, and that's why she didn't show up for work?

Vianca was watching me intently. "Why are you so interested in Angelina? Does Detective Ramirez think she had something to do with the fire?"

I wasn't sure how to answer her. I had seen a photo of the graffiti, possible evidence of white supremacist involvement. It was unlikely such a group would recruit a Hispanic girl, but Ramirez acknowledged that Angelina's disappearance on the same day the center was destroyed was an interesting coincidence. I couldn't shake the feeling it was something more.

"I don't know," I answered. "But I'm sure he'd like to talk with her. What will happen to your mother's business now?"

"I met with Keesha last night. She was like a sister to Mamá, and whenever we went away, she handled everything. She's going to try and get a loan to buy out the business. I told her she can set the price, as long as she keeps on all the girls. It's what my mother would have wanted. "

Vianca put her checkbook on the table. "You understand now why this is important to me. I want to pay you. I want to make it official. What do you usually take as your, what do they call it—retainer?"

I could see she wasn't going to give up. "Why don't we start with two hundred dollars. If I don't find anything after I've logged that much time, then we'll leave it to the police."

Vianca opened her mouth to argue with my last sentence, but instead she bit her lip and wrote the check. I put it in my purse, and we ate for a few minutes in silence. Or I ate—Vianca pushed her food around the plate, but very little found its way to her mouth. She finally gave up and laid her napkin across the top.

"Not hungry?"

"I thought I was. But whenever I try to eat, nothing tastes right. I just feel...paralyzed, like in a dream. None of this seems real."

"It will get better."

She attempted at a wan smile. "I hope so. But right now everything is up in the air. I don't know how long I'll have a job. I don't know what's going to happen with the center. The insurance adjuster is supposed to come today, but the building was only valued at $130,000. There's no way we can rebuild for that."

"I thought last night the board members voted to form a committee to solicit donations."

"They did, but the way the lifetime estate is written, if the property isn't in active use as a community center, it reverts back to the heirs of Mr. Garrison's estate. According to David Reid, we'd have to have funding and begin construction within ninety days or lose the land. I talked to a local contractor who was a client of my mother's. He estimated new construction would cost over a million dollars. There's no way we can raise that in the next ninety days, and the board is opposed to a loan."

"Couldn't Melissa Reid still choose to renew the lifetime estate or provide a new one?"

Vianca sighed. "I asked that. I mean, the terms of the will were written to keep the building from sitting there empty or have the foundation profit if the center didn't make it. But David Reid never really gave me an answer."

No wonder the girl couldn't eat.

I turned the conversation to the library staff I'd met yesterday, describing how supportive they were of the work Vianca was doing. Her face lit up with the praise, and she launched into a summary of the many programs the Garrison Center had instituted. The transformation was startling—

Vianca became animated and excited, and the passion she had for helping people suffused her voice. With a handful of part-time staff and an army of volunteers from churches and civic groups, the center provided after-school meals and tutoring for local students four days a week, along with weekend programs for families, all geared toward breaking the cycle of violence that existed between different ethnic and cultural groups within the community.

"People see black or Hispanic or Asian, but it's much more complicated than that," she explained. "Immigrants come from China or Vietnam or South Korea, we think they're all one. Immigrants come from Guatemala or Ecuador or Colombia, and we see them as all one. Back home, there were tensions between those countries, between their people. Here, they're just expected to blend together."

She was right--I had never thought of it that way.

"The same is true of blacks," she went on. "Haitian immigrants, Jamaican Immigrants, Cuban immigrants—they all have very different cultures than African-Americans born in the United States. You can't just throw them all together and expect them to get along. And kids who have grown up on the streets of Central America and Haiti and even Miami have all been traumatized by violence to varying degrees. So everyone is looking for their own group, a place they feel can offer protection and belonging, and that is often a gang. As a multi-racial child of two cultures, I felt like I had a voice they might trust. All of us at the center were trying to help them to see each other as individuals and give them something better."

She went on to explain that the center also provided advocacy counseling for immigrants, and job training and interviewing skills classes for adults. They regularly served more than two hundred families.

"We're the only place like this. And we were starting to see real results. I just hate to think what will happen if we close…." she said, her voice trailing off.

I tried to think of something comforting to say, but all of the words seemed false. In the end I reached for her arm and squeezed it gently.

Vianca's phone beeped. The insurance adjuster wanted to meet her in the center parking lot in ten minutes.

"I hope Josh's surgery goes well. Tell him I came by to see how he was doing," Vianca said. "And Sandi, thank you. I appreciate your help." Then she emptied her plate in the trash can and strode quickly out the door.

I tried to finish my bagel, but my own appetite was gone. I put the apple in my sweater pocket and went back to the waiting room, stopping short at the doorway.

The Cullivers had arrived.

Of the two, Joanne Culliver was the one I most wished to avoid. A short, stocky woman in her fifties, she had close-clipped brunette hair, a brusque manner, and absolutely no regard for anyone's opinions but her own. Her husband Andrew was a few years older, with more gray in his dark hair than the last time we met. A quiet man, he had minimal warmth, no discernible sense of humor, and was as unlike Josh as a father and son could be.

The one thing the couple had in common was that neither of them could understand what Josh saw in me.

The last time we were together was in November, at Josh's aunt's funeral. I spent Thanksgiving with them, and while Andrew Culliver treated me with cool politeness, Joanne Culliver got drunk enough to tell me why I could never marry her son. It ranked as one of the most awkward and unpleasant experiences in my life, and given that I've had women point guns at me on two separate occasions, that is saying a lot.

Mr. Culliver saw me first, bowing his head and speaking to his wife in a low voice. She looked up, and her expression soured, though she did rise to greet me.

"Sandi. The nurse says Josh's surgery was at eight, not nine."

The tone was accusatory, as if I had made the error.

"Hi Joanne, Andrew," I said, forcing a smile. "I'm glad you're here. I think they changed the time late last night."

"But you got here before he went in?"

I opened my mouth to answer, but her husband stepped between us and took my hand.

"Hello, Sandi. It's nice to see you. I'm sorry it's under these circumstances."

Josh's father was at least putting on the pretense of civility. I hugged him lightly, imagining Mrs. Culliver's eyes drilling holes in the back of his neck.

"Me, too. He should be out soon. How is your hotel?"

Joanne Culliver slid around him and spent several minutes complaining about their accommodations, which were too expensive and too far from the hospital to be convenient.

"But what could we expect under the circumstances? After all, the only way we knew what had happened at all is that some communications analyst Andrew never even met had the decency to call and tell us our son had been nearly blown to pieces!"

This latter was clearly aimed at me, but I pretended not to notice, while Mr. Culliver had the decency to look slightly pained. I was relieved when the nursing assistant popped her head around the corner.

"Miss Beck? Josh is awake and in recovery. You can come on back."

Mrs. Culliver started to move with me, but the girl held up her hand. "Just Miss Beck right now. We'll be taking him up to his room in about ten minutes, and you can see him there."

I wanted to hug her.

Josh was fine, just a little groggy, and according to Dr. Kristofferson, everything about the surgery had gone as planned. The nursing assistant, with a flash of insight, rolled Josh out of a back corridor to the elevator. With a wink she mentioned she had a few additional stops to make after dropping him off, so it would be another ten or fifteen minutes before she could let Josh's relatives know where to find him.

"You saw my parents?" he asked after she left.

"Mmm hmm."

"That good, huh?" His green eyes twinkled in spite of the anesthesia. "Don't let them bother you. I think you're amazing."

"They gave you drugs. You think everything is amazing," I joked, but hearing him say it still boosted my mood.

The rest of the morning did not go badly. Perhaps Andrew Culliver had urged his wife to be more pleasant, or perhaps she was wily enough to know that frontal attacks wouldn't work in front of Josh. For whatever reason, she was almost friendly, and I barely saw her wince when she noticed my diamond ring. There was an uncomfortable silence before Andrew's father offered a subdued "Congratulations."

"You haven't set a date yet, have you?" Mrs. Culliver asked.

"Nothing definite," Josh answered, and I saw her shoulders relax.

It was the last they spoke of it.

I made a valiant effort to take part in the conversation, but Joanne Culliver spent most of her time talking about relatives and friends I didn't know, so I was effectively silenced. By three p.m., the Cullivers showed no sign of leaving, and I started sneaking quick glances at my watch. Andrew Culliver said little, appearing preoccupied and stepping out frequently to take work-related calls. Each time Josh's eyes followed him as he left.

I knew from the stories of Josh's childhood that Andrew Culliver had always been distant and aloof. It was Josh's Uncle Alan, not his father, who became the central figure in Josh's life. Few men can divide themselves equally between driving forces. While Josh and his sister knew their father loved them, they always understood that his first loyalty was to the Bureau. It is what made him so good at what he did, but the price was his relationship with his children. Even as a grown man, I could see Josh was hurt by his father's preoccupation with work.

On the last of his calls, Mr. Culliver motioned to me from the doorway and made a subtle gesture for me to join him. I excused myself and followed him to a secluded section of the hallway, out of Joanne's earshot.

"I just got off the phone with a Tony Ramirez. He's an arson investigator with the state of Florida. He says you've met."

Ramirez had warned he might try to use me as a liaison between his investigation and the FBI's. I wished I had dissuaded him of that notion. Andrew Culliver colored within the lines, and while he might work with Ramirez, he would never allow a civilian to play any role in an investigation, future daughter-in-law or not.

"It wasn't a social visit. He interviewed me about the fire."

Andrew Culliver raised his eyebrows slightly. "It sounds like a good deal more than that. He tells me you are working for the girl whose mother was killed. He also said you had agreed to provide ongoing information."

I am a terrible liar unless at least part of what I am saying is factual. I couldn't think of a single lie fulfilling that requirement, so I told him the truth.

"I am looking into the fire for Vianca Baptiste. But I'm also staying with a friend who happens to be on the board of the community center. Detective Ramirez thought I might hear something pertinent to the investigation."

"I see," he said, his tone suggesting the opposite. "Why don't you fill me in on everything you've found and everything you've heard."

I gave up trying to play the innocent and recounted both my conversations with Tony as well as the photo he had shown me on his cell phone. Culliver's expression darkened at that, though I couldn't say whether it was because of the actual graffiti or the fact that I'd seen it.

"And this girl? Angelina Torres?"

I shared my conversation with Vianca, emphasizing that I hadn't yet passed any of that information on to Ramirez. As a play for Andrew Culliver's trust, it was mildly successful. At least he didn't tell me to leave the investigation to the professionals.

"And I assume you have an opinion as to who might be behind this?"

The question was laced with sarcasm, but I decided to answer it anyway.

"There's the graffiti. That suggests a white supremacist group, and there are racial tensions and gang activity in the community. But there's also the fact that the Reids, a number of real estate developers, and local property owners would all benefit from the center's closing. The Reids could sell or develop the land, and either way it would make a fortune and drive up property values for everyone else. That seems the most likely to me," I said.

Culliver nodded. "A reasonable assumption. In the interest of being thorough, tell me about the unlikely suspects."

"Well…." I paused, considering. "Let's say it's not about the center, it's about the people. There's Mariana Baptiste's assistant, Keesha Taylor. She's in a position to take over the cleaning business, and Vianca's going to let it go pretty cheaply. But it's not like it's worth a million dollars."

"No. But people have committed crimes for less," Andrew Culliver observed.

"Keesha has been close to Mariana for years. It doesn't feel right to me," I countered.

Andrew Culliver's eyes narrowed. "Let's stick to facts, shall we? Is there anyone else?"

"The girls who work for Saint Agnes Maid Service. According to Vianca, they come from rough backgrounds, and Mariana Baptiste's mission was to clean them up. Maybe one of them resented her, or maybe some boyfriend or drug dealer didn't like her influence in their lives. But Mariana wasn't supposed to be at the center that night, so if this was about her, then Angelina has to be connected."

"A succinct analysis," Andrew Culliver acceded. "So you take the Reids and the developers over personal motives and ideology."

"David Reid, yes," I clarified. "Based on her commitment to the center, I don't see Melissa Reid as involved. But I do think it comes down to money."

"I am inclined to agree with you. Thank you, Sandi."

It was by far the nicest thing either Culliver had ever said to me and I beamed, flushed with his praise. I could swear he even looked mildly proud.

I should have known that appearances can be deceiving.

Chapter 9

I left the hospital shortly after my conversation with Andrew Culliver and made it to the Reid mansion at exactly four p.m.

It was impressively Floridian, all pink stucco and red tile, its six adjoining structures stretched along at least five acres on the west side of South Ocean Boulevard. The compound was walled and gated, with uniformed rent-a-guards at the entrance. I followed a staff member driving a golf cart down the stone driveway, winding past two tennis courts and a lagoon-sized crystal blue pool before ending at a covered carport, where another staff member in a matching polo shirt opened the door and took my keys. A third staff member met me there and ushered me down a landscaped path to a patio overlooking a smaller pool and beyond it, Lake Worth.

"Mrs. Reid will be out in a few minutes," he said, beckoning for me to sit. "What can I get you to drink? Soda, tea, cocktail?"

After my day spent with the Cullivers, I could have used a real drink, but it didn't seem appropriate for a tutor to start off with alcohol. I asked for an unsweet tea, which was brought on a tray with sliced lemons and a silver bowl of ice.

"Sandi, thank you so much for coming," Melissa Reid said from the doorway. "Julian is inside, working on his computer. Follow me. Don't worry about the tea—I'll have Timothy get it."

We crossed through a game room and a home theater with reclining armchair seats, stopping in front of a closed door. Melissa knocked softly.

"Julian? Sandi is here."

There was no answer. Melissa turned the door handle, but nothing happened. She smiled to cover her embarrassment.

"You know how teenagers are. They like their privacy," she said to me.

She knocked more aggressively this time and raised her voice. "Julian? Please unlock the door."

There was a click. Melissa pushed the door open.

Her young brother-in-law's room was the size of our entire house growing up. It was roughly divided into three open areas, one a living area with a full kitchen, sectional sofa and wall-sized flatscreen, a second with a king-size platform bed and dressers, and a third with a pool table, air hockey table, bookshelves and a computer desk. It was clearly the home of a gamer; vintage pinball and arcade games were lined up along the walls, and the coffee table in front of the sofa was piled with virtual reality headsets and custom controllers. But there was plenty of adolescent boy about the room, too—discarded clothes lay in piles on the floor, empty soda cans littered the desk, and a half-dozen guitars and a full drum set were haphazardly arranged in the corner.

I wondered how a child could be expected to grow up normally amidst such dangerous opulence.

The boy who stood in front of us was skinny and pale, with a bird's nest of frizzy light brown hair. He was dressed in a wrinkled Black Sabbath t-shirt and shorts that hung on his bony frame. His features were thin and sharp, and he wore wire-rimmed glasses.

"Julian, this is Sandi. She's here to help with your paper."

He glanced at me without enthusiasm. "Hey."

I said hello. The boy sat down at his computer and began typing, and Melissa backed out the door.

"Let me know if you need anything," she said, though she didn't say where I could find her. Then she disappeared, leaving me with Julian and no sign of Timothy and iced tea.

I walked over to the desk and stood behind him.

"That's it?" I asked.

"Yeah."

"Why don't you tell me about it."

He turned in his chair, his expression blank. "It's a paper. I have to do it."

I was not one of those sweet, patient teachers. I dealt with enough narcissistic freshmen to know you don't build better writers by sugar-coated grades and smiles. I had high standards and a reputation for thinly veiled sarcasm, which meant not all my students liked me, but all of them learned something—whether they wanted to or not.

"You have to do it. I don't."

Julian squinted up at me. "What's that supposed to mean?"

"You're failing. You need to get a passing grade. I, on the other hand, can walk out the door and never think about you or your paper again. If you want my help, fine. If you don't, good luck."

He smirked a little. "You don't sound like much of a tutor."

"You don't sound like much of a student," I shot back.

"Yeah, so what? This paper's all bullshit anyway. Nobody cares about what happened to a bunch of Indians like a hundred years ago."

"Trail of Tears?" I guessed. "That's more like two hundred years ago, and the 'bunch' was 60,000 people."

He looked at me in disbelief. "You know about that? I thought you were an English teacher."

"I was. But those who don't remember history are destined to repeat it."

The words seemed to jar the boy. His eyes widened behind the glasses.

"My dad used to say that," he murmured. "He took me to the Smithsonian all the time when I was a kid." His lips turned upward in the slightest of smiles. "Sorry for being a douche. Yeah, this is my paper. It's supposed to be 2,500 words on the consequences of Native American resettlement, MLA style. I have to turn it in as soon as I get back to school."

He slid out from his chair and motioned for me to take his seat.

Melissa was right—Julian was bright, and he knew how to write. He also knew how to cut corners and spin five words into twenty-five without providing a single piece of information, and there were more than a few passages of flagrant plagiarism. I went over it with him page by page as I typed in comments, though he showed little interest in correcting the paper. He did seem glad to have a captive audience, and in between my corrections he complained at length about his boarding school, voicing his resentment over being forced to go away.

"But isn't it a family tradition?" I finally asked. "It's where your brother went."

He snorted. "That's just what he tells people. The real reason is he doesn't want me around. He's afraid I'll ruin his perfect life."

I stopped in the middle of typing a comment, disturbed by the rancor in his voice.

"I'm sure that's not true."

The boy jumped up from his perch on the edge of the desk. His dark eyes burned behind the glasses.

"You don't know anything about it. David had to take me—Dad made him my guardian. Everybody thinks he's this great guy, but it's all an act. I see the stuff he does. And he knows it."

That is the moment where I should have steered the conversation back to the term paper, but Julian was echoing my own negative impression of David Reid. I thought back to my conversation with Andrew Culliver. If Reid was involved in the destruction of the center, it was possible that this boy knew something about it.

"What does he do?" I asked.

"Girls, for one thing. He has them here when Melissa's gone. I caught him once—talk about gross." He made a face. "That's why he bought me the Strat, that electric guitar over there—it's a pre-CBS, like Jimmy Hendrix played. It was a bribe so I wouldn't talk. But Melissa knows. She's just too afraid to say anything."

"Why should she be afraid?"

"Cause his last girlfriend before he married Melissa got her teeth knocked out. At least, that's what I've heard."

Julian relished telling the story. I was sorry I had asked. Extramarital affairs were not part of my investigation into the fire, though they did speak to David Reid's morality. Even if untrue, what Julian said made me sad for Melissa Reid. This was not a happy home.

I finished the rest of my editing in silence while Julian turned to a discussion of his prowess as an online gamer. Before I left I tried going over my comments with him, but he became argumentative and resistant to every point, so that when I walked out the door an hour later I wasn't sure if he would make a single correction. I said as much to Melissa when I found her by the pool.

"You lasted longer with him than anyone I've ever brought in," Melissa assured me. "Even if he didn't act like it, he must have been listening to you."

I thought her optimism was misplaced, but I didn't voice my disagreement. Melissa Reid wanted to see the best in the boy—that was her nature. It explained why she had married David Reid, why she might look the other way at his indiscretions if what Julian told me was true.

"I have an extra suit if you want to get in the pool," she offered. "Julian says the water is a little cold, but I only put my feet in. I never did learn how to swim. I sink like a stone, but he loves it."

I declined politely. While the valet was getting my car, Melissa tried to hand me a check for three hundred dollars. I gave it back to her.

"You have to take something. I didn't expect you to give your time for free," she insisted.

"Donate it to the rebuilding of the center."

She pressed me to at least let her buy me lunch. We agreed to meet at Chez Jean-Pierre's the following Monday. As I got in the Mustang, Melissa Reid reached down and gave me a hug.

"I feel so much better about Julian. Thank you."

As soon as I was out on South Ocean Boulevard I called Tony Ramirez's cell. Though it was past six, I caught him at his borrowed desk at the downtown police station.

"Hey, San, thanks. Whatever you said to Andrew Culliver worked. He was almost human," he joked.

"I doubt that was me. I need to share a conversation I had this morning with Vianca Baptiste. But first, have you heard anything off about David Reid?"

His voice grew serious. "Like what?"

"A history of domestic abuse? Adultery?"

"No," he answered, and I could hear the sudden interest in his voice. "There have been rumors about some insurance claims in the past. Apparently seven or eight years ago, right after he married Melissa Garrison, he invested in a high-rise project down in Fort Lauderdale that was hemorrhaging money. The place burnt to the ground. The fire marshal ruled it as an electrical fire, but the insurance company's investigator concluded it was arson. The insurer tried to point fingers at Reid and his partner, but it didn't stick. The company dragged it out for two years before they paid the claim."

"Any similarity to the center fire?"

"None—except our department believed it was accidental, so if the insurance company was right, it was a flawless professional job."

"If no one had been in the center, it might have been a flawless professional job, too," I noted, thinking of what Josh had said.

"Good point. We should know more when we figure out the identity of the body," Ramirez said. "So why the questions about Reid's personal life? Did you hear something?"

I hesitated. The accusations of a disgruntled teenager were not credible evidence, and I did not want to damage Melissa Reid's husband's reputation unfairly. Still, they might be a window into who David was and what he was capable of doing. I shared what Julian had told me.

"Probably just pissed off at his brother," Tony observed. "But I'll ask around." There was a commotion on his end, followed by muffled conversation. A minute later he got back on. "Sandi, I've got to get over to the Palm Beach County medical examiner's office. I'll call you later."

I had originally planned to go straight back to the Peersons. It was the second day I had taken their car, and despite their assurances, I felt I was imposing. As much as I appreciated their kindness, it was time to make other plans. If Josh needed extensive occupational therapy, we could be in West Palm for another two or three months. I agreed with Dr. Kristofferson that a sailboat was not the best place to live following orthopedic surgery, so that meant finding other accommodations and renting a car. I had already arranged for an Enterprise drop off at the Peersons' building the next morning. The challenge was locating an apartment before Josh's release from the hospital. I decided to head to the boat to pick up some extra clothes and stop by the marina office. It was on the bottom floor of a three-story condominium complex, and I was hoping the manager would have a contact number for any empty units overlooking the docks. Based on the lack of cars when we arrived, I guessed several were unoccupied. If one was open as a short-term rental, Josh might be more willing to stay there with *Andromeda* in his sight.

The marina manager's name was Willy. He was a short, heavy man in his late forties with a balding head and skin like worn leather. His face broke into a smile of a thousand wrinkles when he saw me.

"How's your boyfriend doing? Carlos told me he's the one who's been on the news. He's got some guts to run into a burning building."

I briefly described Josh's condition and explained our situation. He shook his head.

"None of the Ocean Breeze Apartments can be sublet. It's in the covenants. Owners and their families only. But you know…" He paused and looked out of the window thoughtfully. "See the trawler on the end?"

I followed his gaze down C dock to a forty-something-foot Grand Banks. She looked older—perhaps mid-1980s—but in pristine condition.

"She's a little unusual because one of the owners had some health problems and had her refitted to be more handicapped accessible. She's still got steps, but they're wider and they all have railings, and the heads have railings for the toilets and showers. The couple who own it are from Michigan. They usually winter down here, but their daughter had a baby in December, so they called to say they weren't coming. We had already prepped it for them, so I can tell you it's clean as can be. They might be willing to rent it out to you for a couple of months. Do you want me to call them?"

It was a great idea—and one Josh might accept. Willy agreed to contact the owners while I went down and checked on *Andromeda*.

"Give me ten or fifteen minutes," he suggested. "Then you can stop on back."

It was dark as I headed down the dock. The lights were on in Carlos's boat, and I could see him and his wife eating dinner. I felt a longing for the quiet companionship Josh and I shared as we sailed, a feeling intensified by the fact that *Andromeda* was exactly as we'd left her just over forty-eight hours before. The ICW chartbook was open on the table, dirty glasses in the sink, Josh's sweaty shirt and damp towel still in a ball where he'd thrown them on the cabin floor—commonplace items bearing witness to our rush to get off the boat, and a reminder how thin the line is that separates our everyday lives from disaster.

Just fifteen minutes more, and we would be sailing to the island of Grand Bahama tomorrow, then on to the Abacos. Josh would probably have spent today on his surfboard, still stored on the rear quarter berth, and I would have been deep in a novel, lying on the beach. We would be blissfully ignorant of the lives affected by the explosion, aware only that some unfortunate accident had occurred. Just fifteen minutes, long enough to do the dishes, pick up the laundry....

Just fifteen minutes, and Vianca Baptiste might be dead.

I cleaned up the cabin and packed a few extra clothes for myself and a couple of books to take to Josh. As I locked up, I saw Willy heading down the dock toward me.

"They weren't too keen on the idea at first, but I told them what your boyfriend had done. The Johnsons—they're the owners—volunteered at the center food bank while they were here. When they heard about what happened, they were all for it. They said you could stay there as long as you needed. All they want is for you to cover the electricity and pay to have the cabin cleaned when you leave."

It was an extraordinarily generous offer, but one Josh would need to approve. I thanked Willy and promised him I'd run it by my boyfriend and let him know the next day. As I left the marina for the Peersons, my thoughts were on the future, and I didn't even glance at the center's debris-filled lot as I passed.

Chapter 10

"Where are you now?"

The voice was Tony Ramirez's. I wiped the sleep from my eyes and readjusted the phone.

"In bed. What time is it?"

There was the sound of a horn blaring, and the detective muttered what I took to be an expletive in Spanish. "Sorry, Sandi. Some idiot came across three lanes and cut me off. What did you say?"

By then my vision had cleared and I could see the numbers on my cell phone.

"You do know it's 7:03 in the morning, right?"

He groaned. "*Huy*, I'm sorry. I thought it was later. I wanted to meet you for breakfast."

I rolled out of bed. "That's okay, I should have been up already. I've got a rental car coming in half-an-hour, and I'm supposed to be at the hospital at nine. Where did you want to meet?"

"There's a coffee shop on Greenwood, about a mile before the hospital on the right. How about eight?"

Arthur and Alice were still in bed, but Maxi greeted me in the kitchen with a wet tongue and wagging tail. I left them a brief note, promising to call later. By the time I made it to the lobby, the Enterprise representative was in front of the building waiting. It took only a few minutes to do the walk-around and pick up the keys.

I pulled into the Cappuccino Connection on Greenwood with a few minutes to spare. Tony Ramirez waved from a table inside.

"Pick anything you want. My treat," he said, handing me a menu when I sat down.

I scanned it and chose a nova and cream cheese bagel, New York style, and a regular coffee. He took the menu with him to the counter and returned with two coffees.

"To what do I owe this breakfast?" I asked.

"You put in a good word with Culliver. He is letting us handle the arson investigation, and he agreed to keep the racial angle quiet until we have a lead. He's providing background and support," he explained. I noticed he did not meet my eyes when he spoke.

"What aren't you telling me?"

Tony sighed. "He also said he didn't want any cooperation between your investigation and ours. In other words, I'm not supposed to talk to you."

So much for Andrew Culliver's approval.

"Yet here I am," I pointed out.

"*Si*. Here you are." He looked up then, his eyes gleaming.

"You're going to disobey the order of the head of the FBI task force?"

"Not disobey, no. I am using my professional judgment in the handling of a valuable source."

He parroted the line like it came right out of a procedural manual. I laughed. "That might look good on paper, but I wouldn't want to be you when Culliver finds out."

"Goes with the territory," he said, waving his hand dismissively. "Now, why don't you prove what a valuable source you are and tell me what Vianca said."

"It's about Angelina Torres." I gave him the condensed version of Angelina's history and Mariana Baptiste's mission to help troubled girls, ending with the possible sale of SAMS to the company's team manager.

"Yeah, that confirms what Angelina's sister told Palm Beach PD, though she didn't have anything on the boyfriend. Chances are Angelina's shacked up with this guy somewhere. They put out a missing person's bulletin, so maybe they'll get a tip on her location, but I've got to tell you, they aren't taking her disappearance too seriously."

I understood why not, but still it bothered me.

"What about the body in the center? Did the coroner's office identify it?"

The boy at the counter called Tony's name and he picked up our food. He motioned for me to eat and managed to somehow swallow bites of his sausage and cheddar bagel between words. "I wish they had," Ramirez complained, pausing to drink his coffee. "Guy's literally a ghost. Not enough left for fingerprints. All the coroner can say is a white male, five foot ten, probably mid-forties, dark hair and eyes. One partial print, no match in military or law enforcement databases. No DNA match. No identifying marks left, if there ever were any. Fabric fragments under the body are military-style camouflage. No wallet. No cell phone. One interesting piece of evidence—he was wearing false facial hair. It was synthetic, melted right into his skin."

"Ugh," I said, putting down my bagel. "Thanks for that image. So how did he get there? Have you checked parking lots nearby for an abandoned vehicle?"

"Didn't have to. Palm Beach PD questioned the public transit bus driver on that route. He remembers the guy getting on in front of the VA home by Beeline. He remembers because he asked if he had a service card. Disabled vets ride for free. Guy mumbled no and paid cash." He stuffed the last bite of his breakfast in his mouth and drained his coffee before continuing.

"All Palm Trans buses have security cameras, so we were able to check the footage. Guy keeps his hat low the whole time, so all you can see is this unkept beard—which, as we know, is not much of a clue. He gets off at the Publix across from the center at four. Security cameras there and on the bridge show him walking up the bridge. A security camera picks him up at the park entrance, heading toward the beach under the bridge. We lose him there until five, when he comes back out, crosses back to the west end, and then hangs out by the bridge pylon and sea wall next to the center. He crosses the parking lot after Vianca leaves, but there are no cameras on the building itself, so we lose him again before he gets to the door."

I thought about all that security footage. With modern artificial intelligence and machine learning, computers could usually create a composite image with even limited views and match it to the millions of faces on social media and drivers' license databases.

"You're saying there were no facial recognition hits with all that camera time?" I asked.

"None," Ramirez said, stopping to wipe the grease from his face. "The angles are all bad. He must have scoped out camera locations ahead of time."

"So, what now?"

He shrugged. "We're questioning the guards at the VA hospital, and we've asked for their security camera footage and the footage of every business in the three surrounding blocks. But a lot of those places scrub the memory every couple of days, so that could be a bust. We're putting out a video of the dead guy on the news, and my team is combing through missing person reports to see if anyone is looking for a five-foot-ten white guy. Otherwise, I'm hoping for a lucky break."

It didn't sound too promising.

"I know," Tony agreed, reading my expression. "If I don't come up with something before that graffiti gets leaked, I am *frito*."

I raised my eyebrows. He laughed.

"Sorry. I'm fried—in trouble."

"What makes you think they'll be leaked?"

"Sandi, that is what I like about you. You seem so world wise, but at heart you are *muy ingenuo*—very innocent," he said, showing his white teeth in a wide smile. "Allow me to disillusion you. Photos like that, they always leak."

It was a prediction he would regret.

We parted shortly after, Ramirez to wheedle video footage without having to wait for subpoenas, and me to spend time with Josh. I stayed at the hospital most of the day, doing what supportive girlfriends are supposed to do, but I couldn't keep my mind off the arson investigation. Josh must have noticed I was preoccupied, but we never had a moment alone to discuss it. Josh's parents arrived at the same time I did, and only Joanne left at lunchtime to get carryout. Since Andrew Culliver clearly wouldn't approve of my continued contact with Tony Ramirez, I didn't bring it up.

I did tell Josh about the trawler. His doctors had been in earlier to discuss his recovery plan, explaining that between physical therapy for the arm and occupational therapy to keep the scar tissue from limiting the use of his hand, he might need to keep regular appointments for the next ten to twelve weeks. Josh was still stubbornly insistent he could stay on *Andromeda*, and he attempted to prove his independence while they were there by using the bathroom on his own. With one arm and hand useless, the pain from any shoulder movement, and continued balance issues from the concussion, he fell and had to push the call button for help. That single trip to the toilet made clear what I could not—there was no way Josh could go up and down the ladder on *Andromeda*. His parents agreed with me for once, though they tried to convince him to recuperate at their home in Maryland instead. Given the two options, Josh took the trawler, a decision that made Joanne Culliver's lips press into a thin tight line.

I waited until almost five, hoping his parents would leave, but his father sat in a chair reading the *Wall Street Journal* and his mother got up every five minutes to fuss with Josh's pillows or fill his water glass. I finally told them I was going, and I bent to kiss Josh goodbye. He squeezed my hand, and there was a twinkle in his eye.

"You're not going to stay and tuck me in?"

"No. I'm taking Alice and Arthur to dinner. It's the least I can do."

"Save me some seafood. Something soft," he added. "And call me when you get home."

I promised I would.

I stopped at Publix for some diet soda and chocolate—the Peersons were impossibly healthy eaters, and I needed a caffeine and sugar fix to stay awake through dinner. The store was on the west side of the divided highway, so I spent another ten minutes getting across the Blue Heron Parkway. It was just after sunset when the traffic light stopped me in front of the center. A makeshift memorial had sprung up just beyond the police tape, with flowers, candles, and balloons surrounding a poster of Mariana Baptiste. But that isn't what drew my attention. There was a truck in the parking lot, and from inside the charred remains of the center, a bright light flashed on and off. Just as traffic began to move, a man came out of the ruins carrying a camera and climbed over the crime scene tape. He was a big guy, overweight, wearing jeans, a denim shirt and baseball cap. He opened the door of the truck, and the streetlight reflected off the metal signage. *Kreski's Tree Service.*

Why would a tree trimmer be taking photographs at the site of an ongoing arson investigation?

I pulled in at once.

The man began to climb in the driver's seat, but he stopped when he heard my car. He got back out and shut the door as I started toward him.

When you have no idea what's going on, the best tactic is to pretend that you do. I pitched my voice an octave higher than usual and smiled brightly.

"Hi! I'm sorry I'm late. I was afraid you would be gone before I got here," I called out while we were still thirty feet apart.

He stopped and looked at me blankly. "You were supposed to meet me here?"

"Yes—well, I mean, he said you would be here, so I should stop and check in with you."

I was mentally scrambling to figure out who I was going to say "he" was if asked. Instead, the man nodded.

"Oh, okay. Yeah, I was a little late myself. I had a job. But you can tell Gorman I got the pictures."

"Great!" I said with enthusiasm. "He'll be glad to hear it."

The man walked toward me, and I saw his shirt bore the name Jimmy above the Kreski Tree Service logo. "Did he give you my money? He promised me half would be deposited today, half when the pictures went up, but I ain't got it yet. I just checked my account."

Gorman must have agreed to pay Jimmy to photograph the graffiti. Since the only people thus far who knew it existed were the arsonist, first responders, and Tony's team, it was a good bet Gorman started the fire, which meant he was the unidentified body on the slab in the morgue. Dead men can't pay debts.

"No, I'm sorry. He said to tell you the transfer won't go through till tomorrow. Something about a bank holiday."

His brow furrowed and his voice took on a suspicious tone. "Today ain't no holiday I know of."

I threw some attitude in my voice while I scrambled for a good excuse. "You didn't think he was using a U.S. account for this, did you? Don't you know how easily those can be traced?"

He blinked.

"I'm talking about his offshore account…on the island," I said, scouring my memory for the name of some Caribbean haven for tax evaders that might conceivably have a holiday, but I came up empty.

Despite the slight lapse in delivery, my answer seemed to placate Jimmy.

"All right then. You tell him I'll go ahead and send 'em in like we agreed. But if I don't see that deposit, I'm going to put in a note saying Trevor Gorman's the one who took them."

"I understand, Jimmy. I really do. If you want me to handle the pictures, I'd be glad to—"

His face reddened. "What is this, some kind of con? I ain't givin' the pictures to you. They're mine until I get paid, you got that? You want your own you kin' go into the mess yourself."

I put up my hands. "No, that's your job. I just thought maybe you were getting nervous."

The man snorted. "Nervous! Only thing makin' me nervous is standin' here jawin' with you, girl. Go on and git."

"All right. You, uh, have a good night, Jimmy."

I got back in the car and drove off without looking back. As soon as I got across the bridge, I pulled into a store parking lot and called Ramirez. It went straight to voicemail. I explained in as few words as possible what had happened and described both Jimmy and the truck. I considered calling the Palm Beach police but I didn't want to risk making things worse. While I couldn't say for sure to whom the photos were being sent, my guess was the media. All I could hope was that Ramirez would get the message in time to track down Jimmy and stop the leak. I made a mental note to try him again in an hour.

When I got to the Peersons' condo, they were on their balcony watching the moon rise over the ocean. I had insisted they pick the restaurant for dinner, and Arthur chose a bar and grill within walking distance. We could go as we were, he said, and since it offered pet-friendly outdoor seating, Maxi could join us on the excursion.

"And let's take the beach down instead of the sidewalk," Alice suggested. "Maxi loves to run on the beach. And besides, Sandi, you look a mite peaked. The sea air will do you good," she added, patting my cheek.

The private beach in front of their condo adjoined a public park, and as we walked, we passed a few fishermen casting into the surf. Arthur regaled us with a story of the biggest swordfish he'd ever caught, a tale Alice described as an out-and-out falsehood.

"That man is talkin' with his tongue out of his shoe. Don't believe a word he says."

I was still laughing when we started up the sandy dune access path that led from the beach to the community playground and parking lot. It passed through a narrow hollow that was overgrown on both sides with palmettos and a curtain of thick, tangled vines.

"If anyone asks you for money, just keep walking," Alice admonished.

"We had a problem with the homeless begging here at night," Arthur explained. "They were sleepin' up here in the bushes, and there were some needles and such lyin' around, so there must have been some drug use. Folks complained, and the police have been runnin' them out."

I glanced into the shadows on the right side of the path. A shaft of moonlight pierced through the tangled leaves and reflected off something pale and white. Maxi made a low growling sound in his throat and pulled at his leash.

"What in the dickens—" Arthur began as the little dog jerked the lead from his hand. Maxi disappeared into the undergrowth, then reappeared in the moonlight. He began digging furiously.

"I'll get him," I said, dropping to my knees.

"Be careful. Those palmetto fronds are sharp as knives," Alice warned.

I crawled through an opening in the vines, thorns pulling at my hair. The ground was littered with trash, and all around me there was a sickly sweet, damp smell mixed with the odor of urine. I could see Maxi ahead of me in a cloud of dirt and sand, paws working frantically. I reached out my hand to grasp his back leg, scratching my wrist on a piece of broken glass. He whined as I pulled him toward me, but he let me capture him under my chest.

“Shh. It’s all right,” I said soothingly. He began to whine again, nose pointed toward the hole he had dug. The pale object I had seen protruded from it.

“What is he carryin’ on about?” Alice called.

I rose up on one elbow. It was a white canvas sneaker, toe pointed upward.

“It’s just an old shoe,” I called out.

I wriggled backwards, dragging a reluctant Maxi with me. When I made it back to the path, I looked down to see my tan capris and white shirt were covered in grass stains, dirt, and one or two other wet substances I couldn’t identify.

“Oh, darlin’! Ah am so sorry!” Alice exclaimed. “Do you want to run on back and change?”

I’m not fastidious when it comes to my appearance, but I could smell a pungent and entirely unappetizing odor emanating from my shirt.

“I’ll just be ten minutes,” I promised. “You go on and order me a Chardonnay.”

I jogged along the beach and back to the building. Even though the doorman had seen me come and go several times, he stepped forward and asked which guest I was visiting, all the while staring pointedly at my clothing. I caught the stares of several other residents, and the only other person on the elevator, the stooped, gray-haired attendant, sniffed loudly in my direction.

Once in the condo, I threw the offending shirt and pants in the washer and did a quick wipe off with a wet washcloth. I changed, ran a comb through my hair, and was back on the beach a few minutes later.

Several couples strolled together in the moonlight, and ahead of me, on the path to the playground and parking lot, a gaggle of pre-teens were jostling against each other, tossing a football in the air, their voices loud and erupting in laughter. I could see there was no room to squeeze by, so I slowed to a walk. When they reached the sidewalk beside the unlit playground, the group headed toward the swings, ignoring the posted “Closed at dusk” sign. I jogged past, then slowed again as I approached a uniformed police officer on patrol who was looking intently over my shoulder. From his vantage point he could not see the adolescents, but he could definitely hear them.

“Good evening, miss. Did you pass a group of kids in the playground?”

As I opened my mouth to answer, a terrified scream split the night air.

Chapter 11

Arthur, Alice, and I sat on the deck of Benny's Seafood Bar and Grill, our faces stained red by the lights of the ambulance parked in front of us. Across the park we could see movement in the spotlights of police cars parked by the beach path, focused on the place where Maxi had been digging earlier. The pre-teens were lined up on picnic tables, no longer laughing, as a grim-faced policewoman wrote on a clipboard. One girl leaned over a trash can, a second policewoman rubbing her back and talking to her quietly.

The patrons on the deck watched this tableau with hushed voices. Thus far no one knew what had happened. The restaurant manager spent several minutes talking to the closest policewoman, but she refused to divulge any information. Try as we might, none of us could conjure up an appetite, too mesmerized by the scene unfolding before us.

Two uniformed emergency medical technicians emerged from the beach path, wheeling a gurney through the thick sand to the sidewalk that led to the parking lot. They stopped twenty feet from us to open the back doors of the ambulance as a breeze lifted the edge of the sheet, revealing a swollen mottled ankle and a female's narrow white canvas shoe.

Alice's eyes met mine and the color drained from her face.

"Dear God," she whispered, and fainted.

Arthur grabbed her just as she slumped forward. A woman at a nearby table rushed over, identifying herself as a nurse, and she and Arthur lowered Alice's body gently to the patio floor while another patron balled up his sweater to place under her head. As the nurse checked her pulse, Alice's eyes fluttered open.

"Oh my," she murmured as she realized where she was.

The nurse asked her several questions in a calm, soothing voice, then had Arthur lift Alice's head so she could drink a few sips of water.

"Sandi, would you go back and get the car? I think we need to get Alice home," he directed.

"But we haven't even touched our dinnah'," Alice protested weakly.

"Sandi will have the waiter box it up for us," he said, fishing his keys from his pocket and handing them to me.

I waved to our server, who went to fetch to-go boxes and the check while I ran down the street to the condominium parking garage and fetched the couple's SUV. By the time I got back to the restaurant's front parking lot, Arthur and the nurse were standing on either side of Alice, propping her up. They loaded her gently into the passenger seat while I moved to the back with Maxi, and Arthur drove us home. Once inside, Arthur took Alice's elbow and steered her behind a potted palm to the elevator, avoiding the crowd of residents in the first-floor lobby buzzing with news of a body found in the park.

Arthur's face was ashen in the elevator's fluorescent light, and beside him Alice seemed shrunken and frail. Their lives had been sheltered from ugliness; beyond the evening news, their only acquaintance with death was that of loved ones and friends passing away in clean white rooms, surrounded by family. They were shocked by the horror of a corpse lying a few feet from where they had stood. It was not my first dead body, but even I was shaken by how close I had been to touching the stiff limb, unaware of what I was seeing. In the close confines of the elevator, my stomach heaved at the smell of death that still clung to Maxi's fur.

When we reached the condo, I wanted nothing more than to disinfect in a hot shower, but Arthur asked if I would wash Maxi while he helped Alice get ready for bed. I understood without words that all evidence of the incident must be erased for his wife. Fortunately, Maxi had his own bathroom, complete with dog shampoo, brushes, and a doggie fur dryer, so I turned on the exhaust fan, filled his tub and proceeded to dump him in.

The little dog loved the water and submitted happily to scrubbing. As I was doing a second soaping, the phone in my back pocket vibrated. I grabbed a towel, leaving Maxi in the water with a toy, and fished my cell out of my pocket. It was Wayne Kremm.

"Hey. What's up?"

"Hi, San. Is everything okay down there? I've been trying to get Arthur for the last hour, but he isn't picking up."

"It depends on your definition of okay." I replayed the events of the evening. "He's helping Alice get settled for the night. This really upset her."

"Dead bodies do that to normal people, San."

I bristled. "What's that supposed to mean? You don't think they bother me, too?"

"Whoa, don't get all defensive on me," he broke in quickly. "I was just joking."

I bit back a retort. He was right—I was overreacting. "I'm sorry. It's been a rough couple of days."

"I gathered. Why don't you tell me about it."

I did—everything from my first encounter with Tony Ramirez to Josh's parents to the tutoring session at the Reids'. I ended with the body by the beach.

"Any info on what happened?"

"No. But they have a problem with drug addicts and homeless people sleeping in the park. The woman might have overdosed, or she might have died of natural causes. I didn't see a medical examiner on scene. They just took the body away."

"Well, you gotta' admit, your life is never boring."

"I could use a little boring," I said with grim humor. "Do you still need me to get Arthur?"

There was a pause.

"Wayne?"

"Yeah, I'm here. I'll catch him tomorrow." His voice sounded strange.

"Anything important?"

Wayne cleared his throat. "Yeah. I, uh…I need to talk to him about a prenup. I'm, uh, thinking about getting married."

Nothing he said could have surprised me more, though I don't know why. All three of Wayne's marriages were spur-of-the-moment, impulsive decisions. The last one was over right after Ryan died, and it hadn't lasted through the honeymoon.

"Who is she? Where did you meet her?"

"She's a marine biologist at the Virginia Institute of Marine Science. I met her doing a story."

"And?"

"And her name is Kylie Kennedy."

Wayne usually spilled all the details about his conquests. His reticence was out of character.

"That's it?"

"She volunteers for Greenpeace."

I couldn't help it—I laughed out loud. Wayne was one of those rare humans who has no true political leaning, and he is a vocal cynic about all fondly held beliefs of the far right and left. I have heard him refer to Greenpeace as "tree huggers" and "little girls who grew up wanting to play with Flipper."

"Did I laugh when you said what's-his-name gave you a ring?" he asked, sounding offended.

"His name, as you know, is Josh," I reminded him. "And yes, you did, right after you told me you didn't think Boy Scouts were my type."

"I still don't. But what do I know? Look, San, I'd like you up here for the wedding. I think we're going to do it at the vineyard in Irvington. We're, uh, thinking about Valentine's Day."

"This Valentine's Day? When did you meet this girl?"

There was a moment's pause. "December."

"Isn't this a little fast?"

"She's got a one-year research project in Alaska starting in April. So it's either now or next summer."

February 14th was more than three weeks away. Hopefully Josh would be able to travel, because I was curious to meet the woman who had lured Wayne into a fourth marriage.

"I wouldn't miss it."

Maxi, who had been fairly compliant to this point, decided he needed attention. He began jumping up and down in the tub, sending waves splashing over the sides and putting an end to further conversation. I promised to tell Arthur about Wayne's call as soon as I was done washing the dog.

I went through the motions of finishing Maxi's bath, but my mind was elsewhere. Wayne and I were close friends, and friendships between men and women can be tricky propositions. There was always an element of flirtation in our relationship, a script we acted out over and over, Wayne pretending to pursue while I pretended to reject. Yet, for both of us, there was an undercurrent of attraction. Not physical, at least not on my part, but I appreciated his mind and his sense of humor. I suppose, in a way, I loved him.

This marriage might change all that. The one constant in the nearly four years since Ryan's death was Wayne. I had called him at all hours of day and night. He had been my confidante and at times a partner in my investigations.

I would miss my friend.

I toweled off the little dog and took him in to Alice, who was lying in bed.

She looked small and frail beneath the sheet.

"How are you doing?"

She smiled wanly. "Weak as dishwatah, an' that's a fact."

I put Maxi in her arms, and he snuggled happily against her chest and licked her chin.

"Get some rest."

"You, too, darlin'."

I found Arthur in his bathroom, door open, washing his face. When I told him about Wayne's call, he shook his head.

"That boy doesn't know when to quit," he said. "Well, let's not be pessimistic. Maybe this one will take. I'll give him a quick ring since you just talked with him. And Sandi, you get yourself to bed. You look tuckered out."

As soon as he said it, I realized how exhausted I was. I took a long, hot shower, washing the smell from my body and hair, and threw on a big t-shirt and sweats. Then I turned on the T.V. and sat down on the bed to drink the cup of herbal tea Arthur had placed on the nightstand. The local news was on, and I watched to see if there was any more on the girl they had found. There was a breaking news alert, but it wasn't about the body.

The screen was filled with grainy photographs showing the graffiti on the center's smoke-stained wall.

I forgot to call Tony.

The reporter was explaining that the photographs were sent to the station from an anonymous source, but the pictures suggested the explosion was the work of local gangs. She went on to detail the complaints of some community leaders against the center and noted that the police department had not released any information about the photos and refused to comment. This was exactly what Ramirez hoped to avoid. By tomorrow morning, there would be accusations and finger-pointing between factions, and it would escalate from there. I pulled out my phone to see a text from Tony: Thanks. Got it.

It was sent fifteen minutes before. And I had never given him the name of Trevor Gorman.

Chapter 12

By six o'clock Friday evening, a protest was taking place at the center, decrying Mariana Baptiste's murder as a racially motivated act by radical white supremacists.

I watched it from Josh's hospital room, both of us lying on his bed, our eyes pinned to the television. I had tried to call Tony a dozen times, but they went straight to a voicemail box that was already full. The police were reporting that James (Jimmy) Kreski had been taken in for questioning. I was certain he'd given up Gorman's name by now, though no further information was released by investigators. However, it didn't take long for the media to do an investigation of their own. They uncovered Kreski's social media trail of bigoted posts and his involvement with PWA, Patriots for a White America. The group had participated in white nationalist rallies across the South and had even sent a volunteer vigilante force to Texas to "police the border" before being asked by the Border Patrol to return home. Though he had never been a physical part of any of the group's actions in the past, Kreski fit the profile of a homegrown terrorist. Socially isolated, with a string of dust-ups with the police for bar scuffles and disturbing the peace, reporters suggested he could have been radicalized by the online rhetoric and violence of others.

I knew better, and if Kreski had talked, so did Tony Ramirez. Kreski was there to make money, and PWA's biggest crime thus far had been marching and carrying tiki torches. It seemed more likely that the arsonist spray-painted graffiti and paid Kreski to photograph it to create the illusion that white supremacist gangs were involved. What better way to deflect suspicion from those who stood to profit from the fire, like David Reid and members of the Lake Worth Improvement Society?

But that's not how most people saw it.

Some demonstrators carried signs naming Kreski as part of a racist conspiracy; others had signs denouncing specific neo-Nazi gangs in the area.

They crowded in the center parking lot, chanting slogans and calling on police to protect the neighborhoods they were called to serve. Fortunately, the vast majority appeared peaceful, there to celebrate Mariana Baptiste's life and call for justice for her killer.

For an impromptu event, the protest was well-organized. A local bishop addressed the crowd first, leading them in prayer for the city. Then Vianca came forward, thanking the demonstrators for showing their love for her mother, urging them to unite in her memory to make their city a better place. She talked about how her own biracial identity had shaped her life and quoted poetry by both Maya Angelou and Langston Hughes. Watching her was like watching the morning sun hit the windows of a skyscraper—she was transformed, on fire, illuminated by the depth of her loss and her unshakeable belief in the potential of the youth around her.

"She is amazing," I murmured.

"She is…I hope she can hold on to it," Josh said.

His voice was dull. I looked at him in surprise.

"Aren't you the glass-half-full guy?"

He tried a smile, but it faded from his lips. "In my experience, people who believe in a cause most are the ones who become its martyrs."

"I hope that doesn't happen to her," I responded. "Maybe she should let the center go. There are other places she could have an impact without putting herself in danger."

He put his good arm around me. "That's not your call or mine. You've done what you can to help, but in the end, we all have to do what we believe is right for us."

The way he said it made me wonder if he was talking about Vianca, or me, or himself.

It was the first private conversation we'd had in two days. The Cullivers had gone back to their hotel, preparing to catch a redeye flight home. When the news of the graffiti broke and protests began, Andrew Culliver was called back to D.C. for an interagency meeting with the attorney general. Before they left the hospital, Joanne made a last-ditch push to get Josh to come back with them, arguing that Johns Hopkins in Baltimore had the best doctors and physical therapists in the world. I took the opportunity to bring up Wayne's wedding, and suggested instead that we could spend a few extra days with Josh's family when we flew up to Virginia. Josh welcomed the plan, as did his father, who had other, more pressing things on his mind than his son. Joanne Culliver had no choice but to agree, though I got the impression she was inwardly seething.

I banished all thoughts of the Cullivers and snuggled into Josh's chest, nestling my face in his neck. He turned his head to kiss my lips at the same moment that Cassie, his new nurse, walked in. She gave us both a stern stare. In the ICU, Francis had been lax with visitation hours, but we were on a regular floor now, and Cassie had more of a hardline military approach to rules. She was in her mid-forties and looked like she pushed iron and rode Harleys on her days off. Blushing, I pulled back and tried to sit up.

"I see I got here just in time. No visitors in patient's beds unless you want to be billed for them. Josh needs his wound cleaned, and visiting hours are over in twenty minutes, so you two lovebirds might want to say your goodbyes."

I took the hint. I got my purse and sweater and kissed Josh goodnight.

"Call me when you get back to the Peersons," he said. "The police might have closed some streets. I want to know you made it all right."

The police didn't just close a few streets—they closed the entire highway from Congress Avenue to the bridge. The detour took me to the north end of the island by John D. Macarthur Beach, with traffic barely moving. By nine o'clock I was finally nearing the south end, where the Peersons lived. There were more brake lights ahead and temporary road signs announcing the bridge and road closures. I slowed to a stop, peering into the darkness, puzzled by dark shapes moving in the distance. This section of the island was purely residential, with a few high-rises interspersed between expensive beach and lagoon-front homes. There were no streetlights, and a light fog was drifting in from the ocean, so I did not realize what was happening until I heard screams and the smashing of car windows.

I was driving into a riot.

The cars were packed closely together on the roadway. There was not enough room to turn around. I was trapped.

The wave of bodies was roiling and breaking upon hoods and doors, engulfing whole cars in its wake. In the glare of headlights, I saw a man pulled from his convertible and thrown to the ground. Panic rose in my throat as four figures in black hooded sweatshirts and masks swarmed around my car, pounding on the hood and windows with their fists. The noise of helicopter blades overhead drowned out the sound of splintering glass. A circle of white light centered on my car as a voice barked over a loudspeaker for the crowd to disperse. There was shouting and running as the sea of rioters turned and fled, the searchlight following them. The last of the hooded shapes pressed against my window, fist slamming into the glass. I slunk back in my seat, willing myself to be still. The mask had slipped, and for an instant I saw a face, chalk-white and bloodless, and blank eyes staring through my own reflection in wire-framed lenses. Then it was gone.

I watched, shaken, as police cars approached from behind me, sirens blaring, driving south in the northbound lane. One pulled to the shoulder near me and two officers jumped out and began knocking on car windows, asking if anyone inside had been injured. I pointed to the convertible in front of me, where a man lay crumpled on the pavement. Ambulances arrived, and neighbors in surrounding houses came out with offers of water. Two images stuck in my mind—a little girl, blood dripping from her forehead, sobbing in her mother's arm, and drones like fireflies, dancing overhead, filming the aftermath of the chaos.

Josh called as I waited in my car for the road to clear.

"Oh, babe, am I glad to hear your voice. I've been trying to get you for the last hour and the calls wouldn't go through. Are you all right?"

"I'm okay, but I can't say the same for the rental car. The hood and driver's side door are dented, the left front window is cracked, and the side mirror is gone."

"Geez, San. What happened?"

I described the riot as I had seen it. "It was crazy, Josh—I mean, there was no purpose. This wasn't a protest. They were just smashing things. How did this get so out of hand?"

"News came out about the girl whose body was found in the park by Riviera Beach. She was a Haitian-American U.S. citizen, a senior in high school, worked over at the golf course, no criminal history at all. The police initially assumed it was an overdose, but now it looks like it was homicide. Her parents are accusing authorities of jumping to conclusions based on her skin color."

I could see where that spark could ignite the powder keg of anger and frustration in the community following the burning of the center and the graffiti found there.

"There's something else, Sandi. The girl who was killed used to work part-time for Saint Agnes Maid Service."

I digested this for a moment. "Is someone suggesting there's a connection between her death and Mariana's?"

"Yeah. Some guy in the crowd took the microphone and said women of color were being targeted by neo-Nazis, and that's when all hell broke loose. The memorial was still streaming live, and it looked to me like a separate group of protesters showed up. They wore hoodies and masks, and they started breaking out windows in the fishing store and the dive shop. People came out of the woodwork—I mean, they poured in from the alleys behind the shops and started taking anything they could carry. It was crazy. Then the police boxed them in and they fled across the bridge."

"I wasn't sure what it was at first. It was so dark...." I shuddered, remembering the sound of fists against metal and glass.

"Oh babe, I'm so sorry you had to go through that," Josh said soothingly. "I was praying you made it back to the Peersons before then."

I hadn't even thought about the Peersons. Their condo was barely a mile down the road. "Do you know if their building is okay?"

"Yeah. The news is reporting some minor damage to cars in their complex, but armed security guards ran the rioters off before they could do too much harm. I don't think—"

A police officer stepped in front of my car, waving me forward with his flashlight.

"They're letting us go now," I interrupted. "I'll call you when I get inside."

I wove the Subaru through a battlefield of broken cars until I reached the entrance to the Peersons' condo. A security guard flashed his light in my face. I pulled my guest pass from the dash and he stepped aside. Residents stood in tight knots on the front walk and in the lobby, their nervous voices blending in a restrained chorus of fear. Alice and Arthur were seated in chairs near the elevator, their eyes scanning the crowd. When she saw me, Alice jumped up and ran to embrace me.

"Oh, my deah' girl, we have been worried sick about you! Where on earth have you been all this time? Your Joshua called and said you left the hospital before seven."

I told them about the detour and my encounter. Arthur put his arm around me, while Alice squeezed my hand and led me to the elevator. "My goodness, child. If you nevah so much as set foot in Florida again, I can't say as I'd blame you. But I sweah, honey, it's nevah' been like this."

"No, Sandi. Sometimes it's worse," Arthur joked, but given the past hours, I had trouble manufacturing a smile.

Maxi greeted me with his usual enthusiasm, Arthur handed me a bourbon, and Alice made me shrimp salad on French bread, all of which made me feel warm and fuzzy. The hard edges of the night softened and drowsiness crept in. Seeing me blink to stay awake, Alice insisted I shower and go to bed at once, and I gratefully complied. Maxi, who had a sixth sense for emotional need, planted himself next to my pillow and licked my hand. I closed my eyes and fell into a heavy sleep.

The dream, when it came, was a replay of the riot, only this time as I shrank against the seat the window splintered and cracked, and a hand pushed through the jagged fissure and grabbed my throat. I woke gasping for breath, but certain of what I had seen. The face in my dream was the same as the one I had seen tonight, pressed against the glass. When the mask slipped, it revealed pale skin and sharp, thin features. But it was the eyes that caught me—alight with madness behind wire-framed glasses.

Yes, it was a dream, but I was certain—Julian Reid had been one of the shapes in the darkness.

Chapter 13

My alarm went off at 7 a.m., winter sunlight already streaming through the condominium windows. Dreams and theories do not always survive the bright light of day, but I was still certain the face I saw last night in the riot belonged to Melissa Reid's young brother-in-law. The question was why he had been there.

Julian was troubled—I had seen that from the way he talked about David. He felt unwanted at home, so it would not be surprising if, like so many teens, he found acceptance and a sense of purpose in the streets. Josh had said the violence began when hooded, masked protesters showed up late in the demonstration. I was certain at least one of the four people surrounding my car was white. Was the riot part of a coordinated effort to stir up unrest and turn public opinion against the center?

Julian must have recognized me in the glare of the searchlight, yet he continued smashing his fist into my window. Would he have harmed me? Try as I might, I could conjure up no expression of guilt or remorse on his face. The eyes had been soulless, empty of humanity, gleaming with hatred.

I reminded myself he was little more than a child, one who had already suffered great loss. His actions could be a cry for help, but if Julian continued to take part in events like last night, neither his youth nor his family's money would protect him. I hated to involve myself further in the Reids' life, but there was no choice. I would have to tell Melissa. I contemplated calling her right then, but I had to meet Willy at seven-thirty. I was supposed to pick up keys to the trawler and begin moving our things aboard, and I barely had time to dress as it was.

At least that's the excuse I told myself. The truth was I hated confrontation, and I knew all too well that it is the messenger who gets the blame.

Willy was waiting for me by the trawler and once we stepped on board, all thoughts of Julian Reid were forgotten. *Tortoise* was a lovely, roomy boat that had only one drawback—its owners' preoccupation with turtles. Green was their color of choice, and the pilothouse captain's chair, settee, club chairs and bar stools were all upholstered in a bright lime-colored leather. Whimsical shelled creatures adorned pillows, valances, bedspreads, and glassware.

"They're real nice people, but I can't say I'm a fan of their decorating," Willy said, laughing at the expression on my face.

"It certainly is unique," I agreed.

"If you need anything or have any questions, I'll be up in the office. If you move something, just remember where it came from. Mrs. Johnson is a sweetheart, but she is particular. If there's anything you want out of the boat, I might be able to find a place for it in the back room."

After he left, I went through all of *Tortoise*'s closets and cabinets. The boat was well-stocked, with every appliance I could ever use, and some I'd never owned, including a Keurig. I stored the couple's personal items and linens in bags under the bed and then moved our clothes, bedding, and what little food we had over from *Andromeda*. At nine-thirty I called the rental company to report the damage to my car, and they agreed to send someone over with an exchange vehicle at one p.m. Next I ran to Publix and picked up groceries to stock the trawler's much larger fridge. By eleven I felt like I'd run a marathon, so I fired up the Keurig and treated myself to a caramel vanilla cream coffee on *Tortoise*'s shaded upper deck.

The day was seasonable, in the upper seventies with a southwesterly breeze. The lagoon was crowded with weekend boaters coming in and out of the inlet. Off in the distance, sunbathers and snorkelers were laying out blankets and coolers on the park's beach. It stretched under the bridge on the southeast side, providing a sheltered spot for swimming. Buoys marked the underwater dive and snorkel park, where a few red-and-white flags floated on the surface, warning of divers below. I closed my eyes and felt the cool air on my face.

It was the first time since the explosion that I had truly relaxed and let myself breathe.

"Hello! Anyone home?" a male voice called from the dock. I looked over the rail and saw Tony Ramirez, wearing sunglasses, shorts and a t-shirt and carrying a Panera bag.

"Hey. Come on up."

He climbed aboard and took the stairs to the upper deck. "I'm glad I caught you. The marina manager said you were here. Didn't you say you had a sailboat?"

"We do. That's *Andromeda* over there," I said pointing.

"So you're just having coffee on a stranger's deck?"

I laughed and explained our rental arrangement. "It should be easier for Josh to get around here."

"Makes sense." Tony lifted up the bag in his hand. "I took a chance and brought an early lunch. A thank you gift for the lead on Kreski. I'm sorry I didn't see it sooner. It would have saved a hell of a lot of trouble."

I gestured to the chair behind him. "I know. I tried to call you. I couldn't get through, and your voicemail was full."

"Yeah, I saw the missed calls. Everybody in the department was blowing up my phone." He put down the food and sat across from me. "You see what happened at the protest?"

"I didn't just see it—I was in it." I detailed my experience from the previous night, leaving out the identity of my attacker. Tony nodded.

"Yeah, eyewitnesses are blaming the escalation on a group of ten or twelve white teenagers. The police are trying to track them down, but surveillance video isn't showing much. So you know about the murdered girl. Her name is Nephtalie Aristide. Did you also hear she worked for Mariana Baptiste?"

I nodded.

"I can't see any way she ties to the fire, but she was one of the girls who cleaned the Reids' house for six months. According to the manager at Playa del Lago country club, David Reid is the one who got her the job waiting tables in the clubhouse there."

Tony paused and looked out over the water.

"Do you think he was involved with her?"

"I don't know. Wouldn't be the first guy to sleep with the help. I was thinking about what his little brother told you. But unless her murder has something to do with the explosion at the center, it's not part of my investigation. Still, you know, as a cop I have a responsibility to share what the kid said. Since you're the one who got the information from Julian Reid, I wanted to tell you first—in case there's any backlash."

I cringed. I should have kept my mouth shut.

"I know," Tony said, reading my face. "Look, I really don't think the girl's death has anything to do with Reid. Guys like David Reid don't kill their mistresses—they buy them off."

He was probably right. I didn't like David Reid, but that didn't make him a murderer.

"That riot really screwed things up," Tony added. "After the chaos of last night, the FBI is sending fifteen agents down. They'll be here late this afternoon. We're supposed to be conducting a joint investigation into the fire, but now that it has become such a shitshow, I'll probably lose all control. I just wanted to let you know going forward I might not be able to share what's going on."

"Thanks for the heads up," I said in a tone that was anything but appreciative.

"That's not the only reason I came. Kreski gave us the name Trevor Gorman, but I'm guessing you already knew it. He said he talked to some girl who worked for Gorman, and she fit your description."

"It was all I could think of at the time. At least you've got a name."

"That's all it is. There's not a real live Trevor Gorman who fits the dead guy's profile in the entire United States. We did find a fake Facebook account in Gorman's name, and the private messages he sent Kreski. He painted himself as a PWA sympathizer and convinced Kreski he and some compatriots were going to blow up the center, but he was sure the Feds wouldn't give them credit. He promised to pay Kreski five thousand dollars if he took the photos and leaked them to the press."

"You can't trace the account?"

"No. The original IP address is a pay-as-you-go hotspot on a burner phone."

"Then you really have nothing?"

Tony's eyes twinkled. "I didn't say that. I have…a feeling."

"About what?"

He handed me his cell phone. It was a video clip of a bearded man dressed like our arson suspect wearing a backpack and coming out of a rest stop on the Florida Turnpike. He dumped what looked like an empty black plastic garbage bag in a trash can and climbed into the passenger seat of a tractor trailer. Tony reached over to the screen and scrolled backwards.

"There."

A clean-shaven man in a polo shirt and shorts, about the same build as the arsonist, was walking into the rest stop carrying a bulky black plastic bag in both hands. The time stamp was fifteen minutes earlier.

"You think that's the backpack?"

He nodded. "Yeah, that's my guess. He goes in, changes, puts his nice clothes in the backpack, then hitches a ride to the Jog Road exit. From there he walks down to the VA hospital and catches the bus. This video is from the rest stop a few miles south. I talked to Turnpike security—they have a rental sedan that's been parked there since Monday. No one noticed until I asked them to check their cameras."

"Did you trace it?"

"I did." He pulled out his notebook. "It was rented by a Joseph Perry, age forty-two, owner of Perry Fire Consultants, a private firm in Fort Myer. Dad was a firefighter. Undergraduate degree in chemistry, graduate research into advanced construction of non-combustibles. Did three years with LP, Inc., developing fire retardant building materials, before he started his own company. I guess chemistry didn't pay enough. According to the website, the company does fire investigation work for insurance companies and individuals suing for damages from combustible products."

"What was he doing at the center?"

"Not investigating, that's for sure. If he's our arsonist, and I'm sure he is, he's got the perfect résumé for it. We should have a warrant for his home and office before the FBI descends on us. Since I'm lead on this, I plan to drive over to Fort Myers and serve them myself." He paused.

"That's great! Congratulations," I said, handing back his phone. "So what are you doing sitting here with me?"

"Waiting for the warrant. Also, I have a favor to ask. Right now all I've got is a rental car and a black plastic bag. If I'm wrong and Perry is living and breathing in Fort Myers, I'm going to look like an idiot. And even if he is the guy lying in the morgue, if he didn't leave a paper trail, it's going to be hard to prove. I'd like to feel out Mrs. Perry first, unofficially, without tipping her off."

"You think she knows what her husband was doing?"

"Maybe. She hasn't filed a missing person's report. Could be that he's there, could be she's in on the whole thing, or it could be that he wasn't due back yet. How would you feel about calling his house and asking if she knows where he went on Monday? I'd have a member of my team do it, but to be honest, none of them is very convincing. I don't want anything that could spook her into burning file cabinets."

I hesitated. Digging around on my own was one thing. Doing it at the behest of law enforcement was another, especially if there was going to be an intra-agency power struggle. Those were the kinds of actions that ended with subpoenas to appear in court. Ramirez must have read my mind.

"Look, don't do it if it makes you uncomfortable. The thing is, once I show up with a warrant and a badge, my chance of getting a straight answer goes way down. Add in the FBI, and she'll definitely lawyer up. But if she's worried now, maybe thinks something is off, she might confide in another woman. Then I wouldn't be going in there blind." He motioned to my open laptop, the screen on a medical website about recovery from burns. I'd been researching physical rehabilitation for Josh in my down time. "Besides, I think I know you. You want this guy as much as I do."

He was right about that.

We decided I would pretend to be a client seeking damages from the company that produced faulty laptop batteries that caught fire. It cast me as a victim, someone in need of Perry's help, which might get Mrs. Perry to drop her guard. The office answering machine listed his home as an emergency contact number, so it would be natural for me to call if I couldn't reach him any other way. I would use my real name if she asked. That way if she did get suspicious and look me up, she would have no reason to think I was involved with the police.

The best lies are the ones grounded in truth.

"Can we eat first?" I asked. I could smell the food and my stomach was growling.

"Yeah, sorry. I have kind of a one-track mind," he apologized, unpacking the Panera bag.

He had brought chicken Caesar wraps, chips, and bottled water. While we ate we chatted about other things—Tony's personal life (he said he didn't have one) and my history with Josh, which was a fairly short story. Ramirez expressed surprise that I had known Josh for just a few months.

"Why? You don't believe in love at first sight?" I teased.

"Me? Absolutely. I just wouldn't have guessed you did. You strike me as more the pragmatic, wait-and-see type."

I wasn't sure whether to be flattered or offended.

"Well, I'm not."

"Good to know," he said with a flash of white teeth.

There was an odd tension in the air between us. I turned my attention to the food, and we finished eating in awkward silence. I caught Tony looking at me thoughtfully once or twice, but I put it down to concern over how well I would play my part in the phone call. When we were done, he handed me his notebook with Perry's house number.

"What's her name?" I asked.

"Beth. But I'm not sure—"

The Perrys' phone was ringing. I held up my hand.

"Hello?" A woman's voice, children in the background.

"Hi. I'm trying to reach Joseph Perry."

"May I ask who's calling?" The tinge of suspicion was unmistakable. I made a quick decision.

"Is this Beth?"

Ramirez was shaking his head beside me, but I ignored him.

"Yes. And you are?"

"Sandi Beck. Joe told me all about you. He's looking into the fire at my house."

Her voice warmed considerably. "Oh. Sandi, I'm sorry, he's not here right now. He had to fly to Palm Beach for a case. Can I take a message?"

"Well, the company called and offered a settlement. It isn't much. I wanted to know what he thought. He was supposed to call yesterday, but I haven't heard from him. I hate to bother you at home. I didn't know what else to do. I tried his office and his cell phone and never could reach him."

"I wish I could help you, but I haven't been able to get in touch with Joe either," she said, and I could hear the worry in her voice. "Sometimes he goes undercover as part of his investigation, and he can't take calls. He promised he would be home yesterday afternoon. I checked—he didn't make his flight."

"He didn't make his flight," I repeated so Tony could hear. "Oh, my. Did you call the police?"

There was a pause. "No, I…Joe's work is very confidential, and sometimes he has a sudden change in plans."

I let her answer hang in the air for a moment.

"Oh. Well, I guess…I mean, I'd be worried sick, but you must be used to your husband's work, so if you think everything is all right…please just have him call me when you hear from him."

"I will."

She hung up the phone. I turned to Tony Ramirez.

"It's got to be him. Beth Perry doesn't trust her husband, and she has no idea what he's doing." I filled in the end of the conversation he couldn't hear. "When she heard a woman's voice, she was instantly suspicious, which makes me think she's worried about an affair. But I also got that he doesn't disappear like this very often. She was definitely anxious about the missed flight."

Tony frowned. "She's going to be a lot more than anxious when she finds out he's in the morgue. I hate when this shit happens. When I go there today, I'm going to ruin this woman's life, and her kids' lives, and she has no idea what's coming."

"It's not your fault."

He sighed.

"Right. Tell that to Beth Perry."

Chapter 14

When I got to the hospital that afternoon, I heard laughter coming from Josh's room. The door was partially closed, and when I pushed it open, I saw Vianca Baptiste sitting on the edge of the bed.

"Sandi!" She jumped up at once, a flush creeping into her cheeks.

I'm not the jealous girlfriend type, but I knew what I saw. It shouldn't have been surprising. Josh was a good-looking guy, and he had saved Vianca's life. Under the same circumstances, I would have fallen for him, too.

"Hey, babe," Josh said, holding open his good arm. I hugged him a little longer than usual, marking my territory. I wasn't worried about harmless flirtation, but I didn't want to encourage it, either. My own past is proof that vulnerable people can do foolish things.

"Josh told me you got caught up in the riot last night. I'm so sorry that happened to you, Sandi," Vianca said. "We had no idea the memorial would become violent."

"It doesn't sound like it was anyone from the memorial. I saw Tony Ramirez this morning. He said it was a small group of teenaged agitators."

Josh gave me a curious look. "Where did you see Detective Ramirez?"

"He brought lunch by the boat."

A shadow crossed Josh's face. It was just for an instant, but my own face colored in response. I continued, talking slightly too fast, annoyed with myself for feeling guilty when there was no reason for it.

"He did it as a thank you for finding Kreski," I said, briefly explaining to Vianca how I had seen the man inside the center. "I told Tony about the kids who attacked my car last night. He said my description matched other reports they'd gotten."

Just then the nurse came in to change Josh's bandages and remove his IV, explaining that he would be taking oral medications for his last few days in the hospital. Vianca and I went out to the hallway and sat on a bench by the window to wait.

"The attack must have been terrifying," Vianca said, shivering. "I didn't even know the riot happened. Keesha took me home before the memorial was over…I was just so drained. I hope this doesn't ruin our chances to rebuild. I know that sounds selfish—I should be thinking about Talie."

"Is that the girl who was murdered?" I asked. It was similar to the name I had heard.

"It was her nickname. Her full name was Nephtalie Esther Aristide, but my mother called her Talie. She was a hard worker, focused—not like Angelina and some of the other girls. She was saving money to go to college. She wanted to teach math."

"You were close?" I asked, hearing the emotion in her voice.

"Yes and no. We talked, but Talie was reserved. She kept her thoughts to herself. I liked her, though."

"Why did she leave Saint Agnes?"

"She got a job at Playa del Lago. It's a country club on Ocean Boulevard, very upscale. She could make more in one night's tips than Mamá could pay her in a week."

"And that was it? Just the money?"

Vianca looked at me oddly. "No. It wasn't. How did you know?"

I made a calculated guess.

"Someone told me—I can't say who—that she might have had a problem with the Reids."

"Yes, she did, but I didn't think anyone else knew about it. I mean, even we didn't really know," Vianca said. "Talie wouldn't tell anyone what happened. Not even when Mamá pushed. She just said she wasn't comfortable cleaning there anymore and asked to be assigned to a different client."

"Did Talie work there with any other girls from Saint Agnes?"

"No. Melissa—Mrs. Reid—has her own cleaning staff, but she wanted someone to do certain rooms, like her bedroom. My mother only scheduled one girl twice a week while the rest of the team did a job nearby."

"Why would she hire a separate service to do just one or two rooms?" I asked.

"I'm not sure Melissa entirely trusted her staff. It's not unusual," she hastened to add. "In her business, my mother saw that kind of thing a lot."

"And Talie never said what made her uncomfortable?"

"No...."

"But you have a theory," I prompted.

She bit her lip. "I don't like to repeat gossip, but I'd heard David Reid could be kind of...touchy, you know? He never did it with me, but a friend of mine has an interior design firm, and she said when she was working on Julian's room last summer, David would come up behind her and put his hands on her shoulders. I mean, they weren't alone—she said Julian was in the room, so he probably didn't mean anything by it. Still, it kind of creeped her out. She said there was a weird vibe there. I just thought maybe Talie had the same experience."

That fit with what Julian said, though I had trouble seeing someone as image conscious as David Reid intentionally flaunting his misbehavior in front of his little brother. Still, family dynamics can be twisted in unhealthy ways.

"How is your investigation into the fire going? Are you still working with Detective Ramirez?" Vianca asked, interrupting my musings.

I nodded. "Yes. He has a lead on the second body that he shared with me, but it's too soon to say any more," I responded cautiously. "I am confident the investigation is moving forward, though."

"But you'll keep working on it, won't you?" she pleaded. "Without you, he wouldn't have found Kreski."

"If you want me to, yes."

Vianca's phone began vibrating loudly. She pulled it from her brightly colored purse.

"It's Alice Peerson," she said. She answered the phone, and I watched as her eyes widened in shock.

"You're kidding! Oh my God.... Oh, Alice, that's amazing! Thank you so much!"

When she ended the call, Vianca Baptiste was beaming.

"The foundation set up a Go Fund Me page for the center. After the memorial was on television, a piece about it ran on the NBC Nightly News. It's up to a hundred twenty-six thousand dollars in donations—in just twenty-four hours! I can't believe it. Alice is certain we'll be able to get the funds to rebuild after all." She glanced at Josh's closed door. "I need to contact my staff. Could you tell Josh I'll see him another time?"

"Sure."

As she left, Cynthia popped out of the door.

"Your boyfriend's all yours. If you could come the same time tomorrow, I've asked the occupational therapist to meet with you both. Josh will need the scar tissue on his back massaged three times a day to prevent a loss of flexibility. The PT guy is scheduled to come on Monday morning at nine."

When I returned to Josh's room, it was obvious he had heard the exchange.

"If you'd rather not do this—"

"Don't be ridiculous. I look forward to having you flat on your stomach," I joked, but he did not smile back. "Are you okay? Is something bothering you?"

"Yeah. Something's bothering me. This." He raised his cast off the bed, then gestured to his head with his good hand. "And this is bothering me. And Tony Ramirez is bothering me."

His voice stung me with its bitterness.

"I don't understand—"

"Of course you don't," he broke in. "You're not the one lying in the damn bed."

The outburst was so unlike Josh that it froze me. I stared at him, unable to think of a single word to say. He glared at me for a moment, and then the scowl melted from his face.

"Jesus. I'm sorry, San. Come here."

I moved to the side of the bed. He took my hand and kissed it, then pointed to the chair.

"I need to talk to you."

I sat.

"When I got out of the military, I thought I had it all figured out," he began. "I would do the nine-to-five gig, buy a house, get married—be the good son, you know? I felt like I owed it to my mom, after all those years of worrying about me. But I hated it. Going into that office every day felt like walking death. And that threw me, because I had a plan, you know? And being miserable wasn't part of it."

I nodded. He had told me this before. Where was he going with it now?

"I thought I needed time to kind of acclimate, maybe get my head together before I tried to join the civilian world again. So I bought the boat. I spent all that time refitting her, and I took off thinking I'd find myself—and I found you. And that wasn't part of the plan either, but it felt right. Like a good thing."

I waited for the next sentence.

"But then this happened. And I take full responsibility, San—I'm the one who ran into that building. But the thing is, no matter what plans I made, no matter what I told myself, I always knew I could go back. If civilian life didn't work for me, I had an out. Before I was discharged, the Army offered me a spot in OTS—Officer Training School. They promised it was good for two years."

"You told me you got out because you couldn't continue to take lives," I reminded him.

Josh ran his hand through his hair, pulling it as if the pain helped him to continue. "No. I said I couldn't get close to anyone, be a husband or a father, and do what I needed to do as a soldier. And now I'm questioning whether I can ever be as good at being a civilian as I was at being a soldier…and the choice is gone. I can't go back with these pins in my arm."

"You don't know that. I'm sure there are waivers—"

"For doctors and nurses, yeah. Not for Special Forces. The only future I have now is outside the military. And I don't know what that is. I've got no career, a boat I can't sail, and a fiancée who isn't sure she wants to get married."

He looked at me, waiting for a response. I took a deep breath.

"I love you, and I'll support you in anything you want to do," I said slowly. "But I told you from the beginning it would take time for me. We've only been together a few months. I'm sorry, Josh. I can't say I'll marry you just to make you feel better."

"I'm not asking you to…. I don't know, maybe I am," he admitted with a ghost of a smile. "This time was supposed to be a chance for both us to start fresh, get to know each other, but I feel like your focus is always on something else. And I get it, I do," he said when I opened my mouth to protest. "I see how animated you get when you're working on a case. You've found what you love to do, and I don't expect you to give it up. But it feels a lot like it did growing up, trying to get my dad's attention. Even when he was there, he wasn't, you know? At least he never replaced me with someone else."

"What is that supposed to mean?" I asked, rising.

"Nothing. Sit down. I'm not saying there's anything going on between you and Tony. But while you're off trying to find who blew up the center, you're doing it with him, and I'm here, and I have no idea what I'm doing with my life. All I have is you, and now I'm not even sure about that."

I took a deep breath to calm myself.

"I don't know what you expect me to say, Josh. There is nothing going on with Tony. I love you. You've got as much of me as I can give right now. But I can't be all you have. You have to find some purpose for yourself. This trip was just a vacation. You knew we couldn't sail around forever."

"I guess I hoped we might."

"It's not real life."

He looked at me with sad eyes. "I know. But I only know how to do one thing, and that's be a soldier. I'm not sure where I fit in real life…or your life. I don't want to lose you while I'm figuring it out."

"I'm not going anywhere," I said, reaching for his hand.

He pulled me to him, and I lay on the bed beside him, curled in his arm. He kissed the top of my head.

"It'll be all right," I whispered.

But my heart ached.

Chapter 15

I sat in the trawler in the darkness, watching the lights of Singer Island across the lagoon. It was after eleven on Saturday night, the waterway quiet but for a single ship entering the inlet. It was my first night on the boat, and I had woken after a half-hour, confused about where I was. Now I could not sleep, thinking about what Josh had said.

He was right. Working, searching for answers—these made me feel alive. At the same time, I had promised to spend this trip building my relationship with Josh, yet I had been pulled into cases ever since I left Virginia. I told myself it wasn't my fault—it wasn't like I went looking for them. Clients came to me. Now I admitted to myself it was more than just chance. It was choice. While Josh was pouring his energy into us, I was constantly focusing my attention on everyone else. No wonder I reminded him of his father. It wasn't fair to him.

But I was thirty-six years old, and it had taken me years to find what made me whole. I could not be solely responsible for his happiness, too. He needed to find that for himself. He would never be satisfied with our life together until he did.

A sharp knock sounded against the side of the boat, jarring me from my thoughts.

I rose and crept to the stern window, peering through the glass at the dock. Tony Ramirez stood there, a brown bag in his hand. I stepped out onto the deck.

"Hey," he said with a crooked smile.

"What's wrong?"

"A guy can't visit a beautiful woman without there being something wrong?" he joked, but his words were slurred.

"Have you been drinking?"

"Yes ma'am, I have. And I brought some for you," he answered loudly.

I saw lights flicker on Carlos's boat.

"Great," I said, pitching my voice lower. "Come aboard. And keep your voice down."

"Quiet as a mouse," he agreed, stumbling onto the boat.

Once inside the cabin, Ramirez collapsed onto the settee. "I brought bourbon. You look like a bourbon girl."

I took the bottle from him.

"What's going on, Tony? How did things go with Beth Perry?"

"T'rrific. Awesome. She slapped my face. Can't say I blame her." He started up, then fell backward. "Pour me a drink, Sandi."

"Did you drive here?" I asked.

He wagged his finger at me. "I see where you're going' with this. Yes. And I didn't have a drop till I got in your parking lot."

"How long were you in the parking lot?"

He squinted at his watch. "Two, three—three-and-a half-hours."

I stared at him. "You've been sitting out there since eight o'clock?"

"Yes ma'am."

"Why?"

"Because I didn't know if you were home," he said, as if it were the most obvious answer in the world.

I started to ask why he didn't just knock earlier but decided against it. You can't expect to have a rational conversation with someone who has been drinking for three-and-a-half hours. I opened the bag and was surprised to find most of the bourbon was still in the bottle.

"Is this all you drank?"

"*Si.*" He started to laugh. "I have a problem. A big problem. The alcohol, she doesn't like me." He winked.

"What do you mean?"

"It's simple. I can't drink!" he said in a loud voice that ended in a fit of laughing. That went on for a minute or two before he had to stop to catch his breath. "I mean, I can," he added, "but this is what happens."

It finally dawned on me. "You're alcohol intolerant."

"I am," Tony agreed, grinning broadly. "One shot, I'm the life of the party.

Two shots, I am *una cabra*." He twirled his fingers in circles on either side of his head.

"What happens at three shots?"

"I pass out!" he said, dissolving into giggles.

I looked at the bottle. That was about right.

Just what I needed.

"Let me call an Uber. Or let me take you back to your hotel."

"I could just stay here. You're alone, I'm alone—could be fun."

"I don't think so."

"Are you sure? 'Cause I think you might want to," Tony wiggled his eyebrows lecherously.

"Trust me, I don't," I said, thinking of my difficult conversation with Josh. "I'm calling an Uber."

He gave a mock sigh. "All right. Fine. We'll Uber. You can stay at my place."

I didn't bother to argue. I called and arranged a ride, arriving in fifteen minutes. Then I made Ramirez a cup of strong coffee while he put his head back and closed his eyes. He seemed marginally more sober when I woke him and handed him the cup. I could tell he had no memory of anything he'd said just before he fell asleep.

"You were right. Beth Perry didn't know what old Joey was doing," he muttered, taking a sip with a shaky hand. "She still won't believe it. She says I'm lying, he was on a job, he stopped fires, he didn't start them."

"But you're sure it's him in the morgue?"

He bobbed his head up and down. "Oh yeah. We subpoenaed his dental records—got the call they matched the body while I was there. That's when she slapped me."

I decided the best approach was to keep him talking about work. It seemed to clear his mind.

"Did you find anything in the house?"

He waved his arm in a negative gesture, nearly spilling the coffee. "Nothing. Zip. Zilch. *Nada*."

"What about the office?"

"Same thing. Techs have the computer. Maybe they'll find something. Doesn't matter. I'm done."

"It had to be Perry. He was the only person besides Vianca's mother who was there when it started."

"So what? He's dead. We have no proof what he was doing there, and you know what? I don't want any," Ramirez said. "Poor kids. If you'd seen their faces…."

I understood his dilemma and the reason for the bourbon. Perry was being paid by someone. He had no reason to set the fire otherwise. Catching that person was necessary to get justice for Mariana's death, but without hard evidence, the only people who would be punished by making Perry's name public were his wife and children. How was that just?

I got a text saying the Uber had arrived. I helped Tony to his feet and walked him out to the car. The movement made him dizzy. The driver, a young Hispanic man, looked at Ramirez dubiously.

"He's not going to throw up in my car, is he?"

"Of course I'm not!" Tony responded with great indignation. The driver looked at me.

"No," I assured him, hoping it was the truth. "He really didn't drink that much. He's just alcohol intolerant—it goes straight to his head. He'll be fine."

"I guess it's all right," the driver said, still unconvinced. "He's going to the Hilton near the airport? Room one seventeen?"

"Yes. Thanks. Could you make sure he gets inside all right? Please?"

The man sighed. "Yeah, all right. Ten bucks."

"I'll add it to the tip. I promise."

"You're not coming?" Tony asked as I strapped him in the back.

"No, I'm not. We can talk in the morning."

He reached for my face and pulled it down, kissing my mouth. His lips were warm and soft, and for a moment I could taste coffee and bourbon. Startled, I pulled back. Tony smiled and closed his eyes. I looked up to see the driver's grin in the rearview mirror.

"Take him to his hotel," I said grimly, shutting the door.

As they drove away, I saw Carlos and his wife staring out of the glass door of their cabin. I could only hope they wouldn't feel the need to share what they had seen.

I was barely inside when my phone rang. Thinking it was the Uber driver with a problem, I picked up without looking at the screen.

"Is this Sandi Beck?"

The voice was soft and trembling.

"Yes. Who is this?"

"Beth Perry. You called me this morning about Joe."

"Mrs. Perry, it's almost midnight—" I began.

"Please. Please just talk to me. I don't know what to do," she paused, and I heard her suck in a ragged breath. "I looked you up. Your website says you're a personal advocate. I saw the comments. You've done good things. You help people. I need help, Miss Beck."

"Mrs. Perry—"

"The police were here today. They said Joe blew up a building in West Palm Beach, and he died in the explosion. They tore up his office...our bedroom... the basement. Now the FBI wants to talk to me. I can't—I don't know what to think. Please. Please help me."

"Mrs. Perry—"

"Call me Beth, please. You knew Joe. You said he was trying to help you. He'd never do something like this."

I hesitated, torn. If I played along, she might share information Tony couldn't find in Perry's records. Beth might be privy to more than she realized. But pretending to take her on while working for Vianca was an ethical violation as well as a moral one.

"Mrs. Perry, I can't help you," I said. "When I called today, it was on behalf of a client. She's the director of the community center that was burned."

There was a long silence on the other end.

"She hired me because she needs to know why it happened. Her mother was killed in the fire."

Mrs. Perry sounded more shaken than before. "You really think...Joe did this?"

"I do."

"Oh my God."

I expected her to end the call, but she stayed on the line, crying softly. When she finally spoke, it was no more than a whisper.

"I want to know the truth about my husband."

I sighed. "What did Detective Ramirez tell you?'

Ramirez had been sparing on details when he spoke with her, saying only that her husband's body had been found in the burned building and that they had evidence he started the fire. I understood he was fishing to find out whether she was involved, but now that seemed unlikely.

She deserved the truth—all of it.

I told her everything I knew. When I got to the description of Perry's disguise, I could almost feel her shudder.

"He used that…a lot. He said no one notices homeless people."

"Beth, if there's anyone he was in contact with who might have hired him to do this, tell me. I don't think your husband knew anyone was in the building. I don't believe he wanted to harm anyone. I think this was just a job for him, and it must have involved a lot of money if he would risk his life and his family to do it."

Perry's wife started to cry again. In between sobs she choked out the words "Edward Hale."

"Who?"

"Ted Hale," she repeated, voice still shaking with emotion. "He's a state senator."

I waited as she gathered her composure. There was the sound of sniffling and crinkling of tissues. When she spoke again, her voice was stronger.

"Joe doesn't usually mention his clients' names, but he told me Hale hired him to do a small job. Joe didn't like Hale, but he promised Joe's company a contract to analyze the fire safety of his commercial buildings on the Gulf Coast. Joe just had to do this one thing first. We've been struggling, and it would have doubled Joe's business. He could have cut down on travel. He was looking forward to being home more…."

I grabbed a pen from the kitchen drawer and scribbled the name on a paper towel. It looked familiar.

"He didn't say what the job was?"

"No."

"Thank you, Beth. If you think of anything else, please call me."

She stifled a sob. "He was a good man, Sandi," she said, and the call ended.

I stared at the name. Ted Hale.

Then I remembered where I had heard it—at Alice Peerson's on the night of the foundation meeting. A Mrs. Edward Hale was on the board of the Jerome P. Garrison Community Center. I couldn't remember her face, but I was sure of the name. As tired as I was, I knew I wouldn't be able to sleep until I was certain Mrs. Hale's husband and Perry's employer were the same person. I pulled out my laptop and typed in Hale's name. The state senator's bio came right up.

A native son of Florida, he bought his first commercial building in 1980 at the age of twenty-nine and was a millionaire by his thirty-first birthday. His genius seemed to be anticipating where growth would occur, then buying up old buildings cheaply, tearing them down, and replacing them with multilevel complexes that included upscale shops, restaurants, and residential housing. He was on his third marriage, no children. Two years ago he was elected to represent District 30 in the Florida Senate. At the time a local newspaper uncovered his brief stint as a member of the Lake Worth Improvement Society. However, he had resigned from the organization well before the story broke about one member's connection to white supremacists, and he swore he never personally opposed the Garrison Center.

The public believed him. After all, his wife had a seat on the center's board. He ran on a platform of bringing opportunity to the community and improving the lives of those in need. It played well enough to win votes among the liberal portions of his district (he already had the conservatives and businessmen) and he took the state senate seat by a comfortable margin. The most recent photo of him showed a tall, well-built, good-looking man with blond hair and aviator glasses.

Hiring Perry to burn down the center was a dangerous move for a man in Hale's position. The payoff would have to be big to take that kind of risk.

A quick search of Florida property tax maps showed Hale bought many of the dilapidated warehouses near the center around the same time Garrison bought the old school. Several had been along the waterfront, and those had already been bulldozed and rebuilt as condominiums—including the Ocean Breeze Marina and Apartments and the dock where *Tortoise* and *Andromeda* were tied. As for the rest, he still owned two city blocks of underdeveloped property. Hale's net worth would skyrocket if the center's commercially zoned land became home to restaurants and other waterfront attractions.

It really was all about the money.

I lay awake until after two a.m. in the trawler's wide bed. My mind was a jumble of competing thoughts. It wasn't the information I had about Hale, or even the kiss. It was the hollow sound of Beth Perry's voice and the way Josh looked at me when I left his room. Both lost and needing my help.

There was little I could do for Beth Perry. Perhaps there would be proof that Hale had coerced Joseph Perry or threatened him—something to keep her belief in her husband's goodness intact. I hoped so.

As for Josh, he had been trapped in a hospital bed twenty-four hours a day, with little else to do but contemplate his future. He needed to know he still had value, that even if he could never go back to his old life, there was a life in front of him. There was something I could do for him.

I could agree to marry him.

My memories of Ryan were slowly fading. I no longer dreamed he was still alive. It had been almost a year since I had played a video to hear his voice. After Ryan's death I had clung to the belief that we were soulmates, that I would never find that kind of connection again. Now I could look back and admit to myself that as good as it was, it had not been perfect. It was a young marriage, and he had been gone almost four years now, nearly as long as we'd been together. We had never gotten the time to work things out. Even the thought felt like a betrayal.

Perhaps I wasn't afraid I would love Josh less than Ryan. Maybe I was afraid I would love him more.

I owed it to Josh to find out. It might be time to set a date.

That was my mindset when I fell asleep. In the darkness, I dreamed of a wedding in a garden by the water. I was dressed in flowing white, walking down a grass aisle, toward a man's outstretched hand. But when I took it and looked up at him, the face was not Josh's or Ryan's.

It belonged to Tony Ramirez.

Chapter 16

When I woke the next morning, I chalked the dream up to the stress of the previous day. I had almost managed to forget it happened when a sheepish Anthony Ramirez appeared on the dock.

I was finishing my morning coffee on the upper deck, talking to Josh on the phone. He sounded upbeat, and there was no trace of our previous conversation in his voice. As I hung up, I saw Tony walking toward *Tortoise*. He was freshly showered, hair still damp, though his face was unshaven.

"You look much improved this morning," I said, putting on a smile to cover a sudden feeling of awkwardness. "Come on up."

He climbed the steps slowly, then stood at the top and gazed at me through bloodshot eyes.

"Then I look better than I feel. Sandi, I'm sorry for last night. I don't remember much, but I know from the receipt in my pocket you're the one who got me the ride to the hotel. I owe you twenty-eight dollars."

"Don't worry about it. In the last week you've bought me breakfast and lunch. Plus, you left me three-quarters of a bottle of expensive bourbon," I joked.

Tony looked at his feet. "Yeah. I really am sorry about all of that."

"Apology accepted. Do you want coffee?"

He shook his head. "No. I can't chance it. My stomach feels like a washing machine. I just came to apologize and get my car."

He turned to leave when I remembered Beth Perry.

"Tony, hang on. Something happened last night after you left." I told him about her call and her claim that Joseph Perry was on a job for Ted Hale.

"*The* Ted Hale? The state senator?" he asked.

"Yes. The same Ted Hale who was a member of the Lake Worth Improvement Society, the same Ted Hale who owns this marina and most of the unimproved property in this area, and the same Ted Hale whose wife is on the Garrison Community Center Foundation Board."

He whistled. "I can see how it fits, but nobody is going to like it, and I mean nobody."

"Why not?"

"Hale's a popular guy, and he's well-connected. He's got friends in the White House and the DOJ. The FBI is not going to go after him on the word of an arsonist's wife. They are going to want something rock solid."

"Maybe there will be some record in Perry's computer. At least you know whose name you're looking for."

"True. So far, the computers are still in the hands of my tech guys, but I'll have to share this with Andrew Culliver, and he'll probably grab them. The FBI has the best chance of finding a money trail from Hale to Perry." He paused. "You know, I'll have to tell him where the info came from. Hope that doesn't get you in hot water with your boyfriend's father."

"Me too," I said with a grimace. I could just imagine Andrew Culliver's face when he heard the information on Hale came as a result of my role-playing on the phone with the alleged arsonist's wife. "Good luck."

"Thanks." He started down the steps, then stopped and looked back at me. "Like I said, I don't remember much about last night, but if I offended you in any way, or if I did anything out of line, I didn't mean it."

I remembered the taste of his mouth.

"It's okay. No harm done," I assured him, but we both knew it was a lie. The casual ease between us was gone.

Tony gave me a sad smile. "Yeah. Good. See you around."

He did not look back as he walked to his car. I drank the rest of my cold coffee and went below to change.

I left a little later to do some shopping at the mall on PGA Boulevard that Carlos had told us about. I wanted to pick up a peace offering before I went in to see Josh. He had sounded fine on the phone, but maybe a get-well-soon gift would be a tangible reminder that I did care, even if I hadn't yet made a permanent commitment. I had just pulled into the parking lot and switched off the engine when my phone rang. It was Wayne.

"Hey, how's sunny Florida?"

"Hot," I said, getting out and locking the doors. "How's D.C.?"

"Cold. Do you have a couple of minutes?"

"Sure. I'm on my way into the mall. How's Kylie?"

"She's good. She's great, actually."

He sounded embarrassed. I stopped walking. "Wayne, are you sure everything is okay?"

"Yeah, it's fine. I've just got…kind of a problem. I thought maybe you could help."

"Anything for you," I replied, worried now. "What's up?"

"How would you feel about being in the wedding?"

I almost dropped the phone.

"Wayne, I've never even met Kylie."

He sighed. "I know. The thing is, her closest friend is a guy. She wants to flip tradition and have him stand with her, as her man of honor. So I need a best woman."

I had been in one wedding besides my own, and the memory of the bright lavender tulle dress I had been forced to endure still haunted me.

"Don't you have a sister in Wisconsin?"

"Yes, and we haven't spoken in ten years. You know that."

"What about Kylie? Doesn't she have a sister or a niece or someone you can borrow?"

He sighed. "Yes. Four sisters and nine nieces, and if I ask one of them, the rest will never forgive me. Kylie either has to have all of them or none of them. She wants a small wedding, low key, not a three-ring circus. C'mon, San. I'd do it for you."

I imagined Wayne standing beside Josh at the altar and almost burst into laughter.

"Not necessary. I don't suppose you know what kind of dress she has in mind?"

"Not a clue. But if it makes you feel better, Kylie dresses like you. She wears the same turtlenecks and jeans everywhere."

It might have been an insult, but it did make me feel slightly better. "All right. Fine. I'll do it."

"I'll have her call you. She's handling the details," he said, sounding relieved. "How's everything going down there? I heard yesterday the Feds are investigating the fire as a hate crime."

I shared the basics of the investigation. When I got to Beth Perry's call, I could hear him searching for a notebook.

"Stop," I warned. "This is just between us. The last thing that poor woman needs is for her husband to end up on the cover of the *Washington Post*."

"I didn't say I was going to report it," he protested.

"You didn't have to. I know you."

"My pen's down. I promise."

I told him what she had said about Hale, and how Tony was concerned there would be pushback on the investigation.

"You know, this would be a great story," Wayne said. "And your detective friend is right. Hale is definitely connected. Word here is they're grooming him to take over as the director of HUD when Bronson retires this spring."

"Isn't that like putting the fox in charge of the hen house? This guy has made a fortune converting low income housing into high rent districts."

"Welcome to Washington, San. That's how the game is played."

Apparently Wayne's engagement had done little to change his cynical nature.

"Well, it's wrong."

"All depends on where you're sitting. Hope your detective friend has thick skin. At least you should be out of it. The case is solved. You can tell your client none of it was her fault, and there was nothing she could have done to prevent it."

He was right, but I didn't feel out of it. I wanted Ramirez to take down Hale, and I was not good at minding my own business. Wayne must have read my thoughts.

"I gotta' go, San. Try not to get involved in anything else catastrophic between now and February fourteenth," he cautioned. "I don't want to have to find a replacement."

"Your concern is touching," I responded drily. "I'll do my best."

I spent the next two hours wandering through the Gardens Mall. I picked up some shirts, a set of exercise bands, and a *Sports Illustrated* for Josh, then calmed my angst about our relationship with a box of Godiva truffles, which I promptly ate. Under the influence of chocolate, I even looked in a store window at wedding dresses.

On the way back to the hospital, I got caught in a back-up from a fender bender on the interstate at the Northlake exit. While I sat in traffic I scanned for local music. The first radio station that tuned in was a news station, and I was about to move on when I heard the name Nephtalie Arisitide.

The police have released the approximate date, time, and cause of death for Nephtalie Aristide. She is believed to have been killed on or about the tenth of

January. According to an autopsy by the Palm Beach County medical examiner, the eighteen-year-old had traces of the drug alprazolam as well as alcohol in her system when she died that may have contributed to her inability to fight off her attacker. The official cause of death was listed as asphyxiation. While police have not released the names of suspects, a source close to the investigation tells WJNO that a Palm Beach lawyer connected to the Garrison Community Center, site of last week's racially motivated protest, has been taken in for questioning in the girl's death.

I stared at the radio. There was only one Palm Beach lawyer connected to the center, and that man was David Reid.

Chapter 17

Melissa sat across from me, her eyes hidden behind huge dark sunglasses. We were seated on the wide porch of Al Fresco's overlooking the golf course. She had sent me a text late Sunday night, requesting a change of venue for our Monday lunch date. One look at her and I understood why. She was outfitted like someone in the witness protection program.

Mrs. Reid wore a shapeless navy dress and her hair was hidden beneath a wide-brimmed blue-and-white hat. She was already at the table when I arrived, nervously rearranging the silverware. She started when the host pulled out my chair.

"Thank you for coming. I hope you didn't have trouble finding it," she said, so softly that I had to lean forward to hear.

"No, not at all."

She glanced around, then said in a low voice, "Too many people know me at Chez Jean-Pierre. You heard about David."

I nodded. "Yes."

She opened her mouth to speak, but the waiter came to take our drink order. She asked for a vodka tonic. I ordered a club soda. As soon as he left, Melissa began wringing her napkin.

"The police kept him for six hours. It's ridiculous. He told them he was at the golf course all day and then home the entire night that they think that girl was killed."

"As long as you can confirm that, there should be nothing to worry about," I assured her.

She made a sudden movement, nearly upsetting her water glass.

"Melissa? You can confirm it?"

She looked at the tablecloth, lips moving without sound.

"Melissa?"

"I told them I could," she whispered, taking the sugar packets out of the silver bowl one by one, as if in a trance. I reached over and laid my hand over hers.

"Melissa, was David with you all night?"

She shook her head, just the slightest movement. I drew in my breath.

"You have to tell the truth. If you lie to the police, you could be charged with obstructing justice."

"I know," she said, biting her bottom lip. "But he thinks…he thinks I don't know. We went to bed at ten. I heard him get up after midnight. Hours went by, and when he didn't come back, I got up to look. He wasn't in the den. He wasn't in the office. Then I heard the car. I…I went back to the bedroom and pretended to be asleep."

"What time did he come back?"

"Four a.m."

Nephtalie's time of death was estimated at between one and three a.m.

"He wouldn't do it, Sandi. He would never kill anyone. I swear."

I couldn't help but remember another wife, Beth Perry. She had said much the same thing, and she was wrong.

"Did you ask him about it?"

"No. I'm…afraid." Melissa shivered.

"Of David?"

"No. I'm afraid…of knowing…of losing everything. It's not…the first time."

I understood then. It wasn't that she believed David Reid had killed anyone, but she did believe that whatever he had done instead that night, exposing it would destroy their marriage. Some women prefer to look the other way.

The waiter returned with our drinks. I watched as Melissa bent her head and slipped the napkin under her glasses, wiping her eyes.

"I have a friend who works for the police—" I began. Her head snapped up.

"No. I'm sure I have the dates wrong. There's no point." She pulled open her menu, her voice sharp. "Forget I said anything."

I murmured my agreement, but I knew I wouldn't.

Melissa turned the conversation to the center's successful fundraiser, her words coming at breakneck speed, leaving no room for me to do more than nod and smile. She continued in the same vein after we placed our orders, and while we ate, she moved on to a charity garden tour she was sponsoring. It wasn't until the check came and she placed her card on the bill that her façade cracked.

"What I said before...please don't tell anyone," she said, grabbing my hand. "I really could be wrong. I have trouble sleeping, and sometimes I take a Xanax. The medicine can confuse me. I probably have the dates mixed up."

Her palm was wet with sweat. I slipped my hand from hers gently.

"I won't say anything. But Melissa, you need to talk to David. Secrets like this—they don't keep. It will bother you until you find out what happened."

She shook her head. "You're wrong. We live with secrets all the time. We always have."

It was not a compromise I would make, but I felt a tug of sympathy for her.

"Take care," I said, rising. "And thank you for lunch."

She stayed behind at the table, finishing her vodka tonic. As I pulled out of the parking lot, I saw her walk toward a black BMW convertible, head down, shoulders slumped.

I spent a few hours at the hospital Monday afternoon before returning to *Tortoise* to make final preparations for bringing Josh home. He had just finished a grueling round of physical and occupational therapy, and I could see he was frustrated. Despite my best efforts, I couldn't lighten his mood. He was scheduled to be discharged at ten a.m. Tuesday, and both his nurse and occupational therapist gave me a printout that afternoon of what he might need as he continued his recovery. I had already filled his prescription for mild pain meds and picked up additional gauze and wound cleaning supplies. Most of the burns on his hand and back had healed over with tender pink skin, but there was an area between his thumb and forefinger that was still open, as was a half-dollar-sized spot on his back. Those could take another week to close up, and I would be responsible for caring for them. Josh listened as they went over everything orally, his expression strained. He looked relieved when I said I had a lot to do and would see him in the morning.

Once back aboard the trawler, I removed three artificial potted plants and hauled them up to the marina office, where Willy agreed to find a place to store them. Josh's surgical stitches wouldn't come out for another week, and he continued to wear a sling whenever he wasn't doing the low impact exercises he'd been assigned. Given his current dizzy spells, the more open the space, the less likely he was to bump against a giant plastic palm and do additional damage.

After that I stocked the fridge with the foods Josh loved, crab cakes and shrimp and plenty of fresh fruit. I bought fresh pasta and pesto for Tuesday's dinner, along with a nice bottle of pinot noir. I even bought a smiley face helium balloon and a welcome home card and set them up on the table. Then I baked a loaf of homemade bread in the trawler's propane oven.

No matter how busy I was, I couldn't stop thinking about my promise to Melissa Reid and wondering what other secrets she and David kept.

Around ten Josh called to say goodnight. If the afternoon had been his low, he was now on a high, tense with anticipation, eager to get out of his hospital bed and see *Andromeda* again. I reminded him that the doctor had warned about climbing up and down the sailboat's ladder.

"Don't make me sic Doctor Kristofferson on you," I warned half-jokingly.

Josh laughed. "I just want to look at her. I promise I won't go beyond the cockpit. Besides, what I really want to do involves you and that big trawler bed."

It was the first time he had even hinted at sex since his injury.

"I'm not sure that's such a good idea, either," I teased. "You might break something."

"I'll take my chances. Love you, San. Sleep tight, and I'll see you in the morning."

"Love you, too. Goodnight."

Talking to Josh cheered me, even as I felt a tingling in my stomach about the conversations we would have—needed to have—when we were finally here together. I was certain his bouts of moodiness in the past week would dissipate as soon as he could feel water beneath his feet, and that my own uncertainty about the future would be eased when we resumed some semblance of our normal life.

I showered, poured a glass of Chardonnay, and dimmed the lights. From the trawler's u-shaped settee I stared into the darkness, watching flashes of lightning offshore dance across the sky. There is a comforting security to being docked in a sheltered port, safe from the tempest but still spectator to its power.

And yet, sometimes I longed for the storm.

Chapter 18

The FBI publicly identified Joseph Perry early Tuesday morning as the man killed in the Garrison Community Center fire, and they released transcripts of Facebook private messages in which he posed as Trevor Gorman and hired Kreski. The latter had been arrested and charged with conspiracy to commit a hate crime and conspiracy to commit murder. A task force spokesman said that the investigators believed Perry knew a woman was in the center and set off the explosion anyway. The report made no mention of Edward Hale.

I tried to call Tony, but there was no answer. I sent him a text, carefully worded, asking if he had looked into what we had discussed. I got a call back just as I was leaving to get Josh from the hospital.

"I've only got a minute. Sorry, San, I tried. I questioned Hale myself, and he says he contacted Perry's company about doing a risk analysis, said he had no idea why Perry was in Palm Beach. There's nothing on the computers. The FBI is going with Perry as a closet white supremacist."

"But that—"

"I know. I agree, there's nothing in the guy's entire life to support that except the messages to Kreski. But there's also nothing to tie him to Hale. It's a done deal. My boss wants to see me tomorrow in Tallahassee, and I got the definite impression Hale reamed him out about my visit. I'll be lucky to keep my job."

"Tony, I'm sorry—"

"Nah, no sweat. You gotta' do what you gotta' do. It was nice working with you. *Adiós*, Sandi Beck."

He ended the call as I was saying goodbye.

That was it, then. Yet I was convinced the spray-painted slurs and the hiring of Kreski were a cover for the real reason Perry started the fire—Ted Hale.

But a feeling isn't proof, and without something more substantial, there was nothing more I could do. On the drive downtown I thought about Beth Perry and her children, and how the FBI's conclusion would change the trajectory of their lives. It is one thing to commit a crime for money; it is another to do it out of unreasoning hatred.

At least Josh's departure from the hospital cheered me. It was a triumphal procession to the exit. He had managed to make friends with every volunteer, orderly, nurse, and doctor on his floor, and all of them lined up to cheer as an attendant wheeled him out. A local news crew waited there, reporting on the recovery of the brave Garrison Community Center explosion hero, and Josh smiled disarmingly for the camera and assured everyone he was just glad he'd been there to help. It wasn't until we were alone in the car that the energy melted from him and he leaned his head back against the seat.

"Are you okay?"

"Yeah," he answered, closing his eyes. "I'm just beat. You wouldn't think a week of lying in bed could set you back this much."

"It's not like you were on a beach in Saint Thomas, Josh. Your body has been healing."

"Then it didn't get the memo. I still feel like I was run over by a truck."

"Is it that bad?" I asked, concerned. He hadn't complained about pain since his first day in the hospital.

He grinned, eyes still shut.

"Okay, maybe not a truck. A moped. I feel like I've been run over by a moped." The last word faded into a yawn, and then he was asleep.

Willy, Carlos, and Carlos's wife all came out to greet us when we got to the marina. Standing on the dock, Josh looked thinner and more fragile than I had realized. I let them chat for a few minutes, then insisted he get inside and rest. He agreed, and though he cast a longing look at *Andromeda* as we passed her, he didn't mention going aboard. As we stepped on *Tortoise*'s back deck, Josh teetered momentarily, steadying himself by grabbing the railing with his left hand.

"Have you got it?"

"Yeah," he said, smiling ruefully. "I guess I need to get my sea legs back."

We went into the cabin. When he saw all the green and the turtles, he started laughing.

"You weren't kidding. This is really something."

He slid into the captain's chair and put his hand on the polished teak helm wheel, looking out over the water.

"You know, except for the fact there's no sail, this isn't bad."

I put my arm around his shoulder. "Don't let *Andromeda* hear you say that. Are you up for the full tour?"

"Sure."

We went below to the galley and the forward berth, then back to the saloon and down the stern cabin steps to the master berth. Josh sat on the end of the island bed and leaned back, looking drained.

"Why don't you lie down and rest awhile. When you get up, I'll make some lunch."

"I'm sorry, San. It's hard to get real sleep in a hospital," he apologized.

"It's okay. We've got no schedule. I'm just glad you're here," I assured him, kissing the top of his head. "Now close your eyes."

I grabbed my laptop and headed for the upper deck to answer some emails. It was a comfortable eighty degrees with a northeasterly breeze, and I breathed in the salt air as I stepped outside the saloon. I heard someone call my name and turned to see Arthur and Alice coming down the dock. They carried a large basket and a wine bag.

"Alice made you some comfort food for lunch," Arthur explained as they reached *Tortoise*.

"We thought it might be nice for y'all to just enjoy each other's company this afternoon without havin' to fix anythin'," Alice added with a wink. "Where is your young man?"

I explained that Josh was resting.

"Then we'll just drop this off and leave," Arthur said. "We don't want to wake him."

"No, please. This was so sweet of you. Let me put the food in the fridge, and we can sit on the deck and visit."

They followed me inside and waited while I stored the crabmeat casserole and biscuits. I poured us all glasses of iced tea and we climbed up to the top deck. They asked if I'd heard from Wayne, and we talked about the upcoming wedding and my spot as best woman, a concept Alice found hugely amusing. Then our conversation turned to the girl whose body had been found.

"Ah' can't believe the police suspected David Reid," Alice said. "He's tighter than a bull's behind at fly time, but no one would take him for a killah. You know the police announced today he was no longer a person of interest in that po' girl's murder. Speakin' of which, have you spoken to Vianca?"

"Not recently. The last I heard, the foundation's Go Fund Me page was doing well."

“It’s up to three-hundred eighty thousand,” she said with a broad smile. “If David Reid thought he was goin’ to make a pretty penny off that land, he’s fixin’ to be gravely disappointed.”

“That’s wonderful! Have you started looking at plans for the new building?”

Alice snorted. “We should be. We’d like to update the design, make it look more in keepin’ with the neighborhood, but Vianca liked the interior layout. We thought we could save time and money by usin’ the blueprints from the renovation, but our copies are gone and the company that did the work went out of business the year after we opened.”

“That’s too bad. Were the blueprints burned in the fire?”

She shook her head. “No. Our secretary was in charge of keepin’ all the foundation’s documents at her home office from the beginnin’, and we never bothered to move anything from before the openin’ into the center. But when we asked her for the blueprints, she couldn’t find them to save her life. I went over to help her look, and I tell you, that woman’s desk looked like a trailer park aftah a tornado. She swore that wasn’t how she usually left it, but I know bettah. That woman could lose the nose off her face. Why, just last month we had to cut her a new key!”

I had been laughing at her description, but the sound died in my throat.

“A key for the center?”

“Yes indeed. Can you believe it? Not that she evah uses it. She just likes to say she has one. It makes her sound like she knows what’s what.” Arthur raised his eyebrows at his wife, and she held up her palm. “I know, I know. Arthah’ thinks I shouldn’t be so hard on her.”

“Alice, what is the secretary’s name?”

She looked at me curiously. “Sharon Hale.”

Sharon Hale—Ted Hale’s wife. Edward Hale must have gotten the key and blueprints from his wife’s office. That explained how Joseph Perry got into the center and how he was able to plan the explosion and know the layout once inside.

“Now, Alice, the woman is nearly eighty. You might want to give her some grace,” Arthur remonstrated.

“Oh, she’s no spring chicken, but it has nothin’ to do with age,” Alice responded with spirit. “She’s not that much oldah than I am. The truth is, she’s flighty and always has been. You can’t blame that on age.”

“Do you know her husband well?” I asked.

“A gold digger if you ask me. She’s old enough to be his mother—”

“Alice,” Arthur broke in, “Sharon’s only ten years older than Ted, and he wasn't exactly a pauper when she married him."

"That's because he could sell hay to a farmer." Arthur's face reddened at his wife's continued attack on the Hales. "I know, I know, darlin'—be nice."

"How long have they been married?"

Arthur answered before Alice could pile on any additional insults. "Five or six years, I'd say. He met her at a fundraiser for the center before it opened. And you have to admit, Alice, he made a generous donation to the youth program back in December."

Alice sniffed but held her tongue. I didn't say anything—I was thinking about what I had heard. Arthur misunderstood my silence and stood up.

"Sandi, I'm sorry, darlin'. We said we weren't goin' to stay. You've got enough on your hands without entertainin' us. Alice, let's go, honey."

His wife rose and hugged me. "Now y'all call if you need anything, you hear?"

I promised I would. I waited until they were off the boat, and then I dialed Tony Ramirez. He never picked up, so all I could do was leave a message.

"Tony, it's Sandi. I was just talking to the Peersons. Alice told me Sharon Hale, Ted Hale's wife, had blueprints and a key to the center, and both of them went missing. Give me a call."

"Who was that?" Josh had come up the stairs from the bedroom just as I was putting down the phone. He looked a little more alert, though he still had shadows under his eyes.

I told him about the Peersons' visit and explained what I had heard. I hesitated. "I just left a message with Detective Ramirez."

If hearing Tony's name bothered him, he didn't show it.

"You think Ted Hale took them and gave them to Perry so he could trigger the explosion?"

I nodded. "It would make sense."

Josh looked unconvinced. "It still seems a little risky for a state senator to get involved in something like this. Even the allegation could destroy his career."

"He had a huge financial incentive," I argued. "With the center gone, his adjoining property could be worth millions. And remember, he didn't expect anyone to get hurt."

"Didn't you say the guy is already rich? Why would he jeopardize all of that?"

"Money can be addictive. It doesn't have to make sense."

"Okay, you've got me there," he agreed. "Have the investigators questioned Hale yet?"

"Ramirez did, but Hale claimed he was hiring Perry for a legitimate risk assessment of his properties. The FBI closed the case."

"But you haven't." He said it matter-of-factly, without judgment.

"I just don't believe it, Josh. And now this thing with the layout and the key…."

"I get it. Did they find a key in the fire?"

"I'm not sure."

Josh rubbed his shoulder absently, and a grimace of pain flashed across his face.

"What's the matter with me? You're supposed to be resting," I said at once.

"Not your fault," he said, sliding into the u-shaped settee. "I'm just tired of being in bed. I thought maybe I'd keep you company."

I checked my watch. "It's almost lunchtime. Do you want me to heat up the casserole Alice brought?"

"That would be great."

When I came back up from the galley, Josh was propped against a green turtle pillow, gently snoring. I wrapped up the casserole and put it back in the fridge, then curled up in one of the club chairs with a book, banishing Ted Hale from my mind.

It was a slow, lazy day, just what we both needed. Josh slept until nearly five, and when he woke we took a short walk along the docks. He did climb aboard *Andromeda*, but he waited in the cockpit while I went below and got the ship's log and a couple of his books. We went back to the boat and had an early dinner of Alice's fabulous reheated crab casserole for dinner, and later we stood on the bow with glasses of wine to look at the stars.

"This was a good idea," he said.

"Which part?"

"All of it. You were right—I'm not up to moving around the sailboat. This is the next best thing. Thank you," he said, pulling me to him.

"You're welcome," I said as I kissed him.

That night we made love in the way you do after a loss—tenderly, time slowing as you try to hold each moment. Afterward we lay together in the wide bed, skin to skin. Josh leaned up on his good arm, looking down, his eyes serious.

"Can I ask you something?"

"Sure."

"When you and Ryan were married, what was your plan? What did you want for your future?"

We had never talked about Ryan apart from his death. I hesitated.

"If you don't want to tell me—"

"No," I said. "It's just…I don't know. We thought we had time. The first few years we did whatever we felt like. We bought the boat, we sailed, we went skiing…we were planning a trip to Europe the summer of the year he was killed."

"Did you talk about kids?"

"Yes." My eyes stung with memory. "After we bought the house, we said in maybe three, four years…we were still having fun. And he hoped he wouldn't have to travel so much after the next promotion. We were still so young… there was no rush."

"What about you, your job? Was it what you wanted?"

I gave him a weak smile. "I thought so. I liked teaching. I thought I would do it till I retired. It's a good job if you plan to be a mother."

"But not anymore."

"No. I used to love those long literary discussions about what a poem meant, what the writer was thinking. When Ryan died it seemed pointless. What difference does it make when you can be alive one minute and dead the next?"

Josh's eyes were troubled. "Yeah. I know what you mean."

He lay back against his pillow, and I wondered what he was thinking but didn't ask. Instead I snuggled against him and waited till his breathing slowed before I closed my eyes and let myself fall asleep.

Chapter 19

Tony sent a text Wednesday morning, short on words and curt in tone. No key had been found in the wreckage of the center. He was being transferred to another district. Nothing else.

We spent the next week in and out of doctors' offices and rehabilitation centers as Josh's healing was evaluated and therapists worked to strengthen his arm and keep the new skin on his hand and back from becoming thick and inflexible. I attended every session, learning how to do the exercises and massage so that his visits could decrease. On the twenty-sixth of January his stitches were removed, and more aggressive rehabilitation of the arm and shoulder began. Josh was also given a green light to do more physical activity, and the first thing he did was get back on *Andromeda* to do some work. He discovered a slow leak somewhere on the deck and spent hours laboriously re-caulking the toe rail. I offered to help, but Josh insisted on doing it himself, saying it helped to feel useful. I thought he might be anxious to move back aboard the sailboat, but he said he wanted to use his recovery time to get the little jobs done that he couldn't while sailing her. What he didn't say was the dizziness still bothered him. He avoided talking about any future beyond the next few months, and I did the same.

***

The Peersons invited us to a party at their condo Saturday night. They were celebrating Alice's seventy-second birthday. I had a watercolor of their creek in Irvington shipped from an art gallery in Kilmarnock, and we brought it, along with my crab dip, to the event.

The condo was crowded with people we didn't know. A few I recognized from the foundation reception, but I couldn't remember their names. The

Reids were there, but aside from a quick greeting, Melissa avoided talking to me. Josh found a retired army general who was thrilled to meet a fellow soldier, and he proceeded to regale Josh with his exploits in the Gulf War. I listened politely for as long as I could, then excused myself under the pretense of refilling my wine glass. Instead I slipped through the glass doors and onto the darkened balcony. I was dismayed to find I wasn't the only one there. A tall man with gray hair was leaning over the railing, staring out into the ocean. He turned when he heard the door.

"I'm sorry. I didn't know anyone was out here," I said, turning to go.

"No, please stay. I would appreciate the company."

His voice was deep and warm. I moved over to the railing next to him, looking out at the waves breaking on the shore.

"I never get tired of the sea," he said. "She changes minute by minute."

I smiled. "Why does everyone assume the sea is female?"

"That mercurial nature, the incredible mix of power and beauty—what else could she be?" he countered. "'Timid men desire the shallows, for they would drown in such great depths as hers. She is the untamed sea.' John Mark Green."

"But you're not a timid man?" I asked lightly. Though he was old enough to be my father, there was something compelling about any male who could quote poetry, and I found myself flirting.

"I am not. And I gather the word doesn't apply to you either, Miss…."

"Beck. Sandi Beck," I said, extending my hand. He took it and bowed slightly.

"Enchanted to meet you. My name is Ted Hale."

It was all I could do not to snatch my hand back from his.

He was considerably older looking than the photograph I'd seen, with little blond left in his hair, but he was still undeniably handsome. He had none of the smooth oiliness I expected. I would have pegged him as a writer or college professor, not a real estate magnate and politician.

"Do you live in Palm Beach County, Sandi?"

"No. We're just…passing through."

"We. Is there a Mr. Beck?"

"My fiancé is here. He's standing next to Colonel Bell."

Hale looked through the glass to where Josh was chatting. His expression changed. It was just a slight frown and a tightening of lips, barely perceptible, but I caught it.

"Isn't that the young man who pulled Vianca Baptiste from her car?"

"Yes. Joshua Culliver."

"Well, then," he said, "I owe him a debt of thanks. If you'll excuse me, Sandi."

He went inside, walking directly toward Josh and the colonel. By the time he reached them, he was wearing a broad smile.

I watched him as he spoke and saw the colonel's face light up. Josh's expression was more guarded, but he did laugh in response to some remark Hale made. The senator had a gift. He was the kind of man people followed and believed in. He was intelligent and attractive, and he made you feel as if you were the most important person in the room. No wonder Joseph Perry agreed to do a job for him.

Later that night, on the drive home, Josh mentioned he had met Hale.

"What did you think?" I asked.

"That he's good at what he does. Compelling. I believed him when he said he was grateful I'd saved Vianca's life."

I sighed. "So you still think I'm wrong about him."

Josh grinned. "I didn't say that. Hale's the kind of guy who could take your last dollar and convince you to thank him for it. No, if anything, I'd say you're probably right. But I don't think it makes any difference, San."

"Why?"

"Because I've known a lot of guys like Hale. They don't make mistakes."

"He made one when Mariana Baptiste was killed."

Josh shook his head. "No, babe. That was collateral damage. The mission was still fulfilled."

It was a cold way of looking at death. I stared out of the car window as we passed by the burned-out center, despairing, knowing Josh's assessment was accurate. Perry's death had simply tied up loose ends. Hale's only regret might be that Mariana died and Vianca lived. The former had garnered public sympathy, the latter public support. Without both, the foundation might have given up on the center altogether. For the moment, at least, it appeared Hale was not getting the development he wanted.

Perhaps that explained his expression when he saw Josh. It was difficult to read, but I was certain of one thing—it was not gratitude.

We spent what was left of the weekend exploring three of the nine different arts districts in Palm Beach County, bringing home a signed board painting of the sea by Wyland. It was three feet long, and we both knew there was no place for it on the sailboat, but we had fallen in love with it. We could always store it with Josh's parents until we had a place to hang it. Buying the painting together felt like a deposit on the future.

On Monday, the burn specialist gave Josh clearance to get in saltwater. In celebration, we grabbed our snorkel gear and headed to Phil Foster Park beneath the Blue Heron bridge. I didn't think Josh was ready for a full dive trip, but the underwater snorkeling trail, made of limestone boulders and prefabricated reef modules, spanned a two-acre area with an average depth of about fifteen feet. I had heard from locals that you could see as much marine life there in the harbor as you would offshore, and it seemed like a low impact environment for Josh to test himself.

It was a glassy day, mid-eighties, with no wind and little boat traffic. I put my phone in its waterproof case, and we stood in shallow water to strap on our fins and a few pounds of weight to make descents easier. We swam slowly out to where the trail map identified the first marker. The visibility was good, and as we passed over a small sunken boat, I snapped several photos of brightly striped tropical fish darting in and out of the hull. Josh motioned and pointed to a large, dark shape below us, lying in the sand. We took deep breaths and kicked downward, freediving, then came up laughing. Someone had a sense of humor—they had placed a sculpture of a nine-foot hammerhead shark on the lagoon bottom.

As we worked our way out to the edge of the trail, we swam through underwater piles of limestone with schools of angelfish, grouper, and parrotfish. We passed over three scuba divers, kicking up a cloud of sediment as they searched for spiny lobsters. The rocks created shallow caves, and a variety of sea creatures lived in those shadowy crevices. On the deepest dive, perhaps twenty feet, Josh tapped my arm. In between two boulders was an octopus, tentacles encircling the rock, blinking at us through horizontal pupils.

I noticed as we surfaced that Josh was favoring his right arm.

"Did you see his eyes? That was great!" he said, spitting out his snorkel and grinning.

"It was. How are you doing?" I asked, pulling off my mask to rinse the fog that formed on the inside.

"Okay. My head feels fine, but I think I tweaked my right shoulder. Not sure how."

I looked around. The sky was clouding over. "I think we're about at the end anyway, and we're going to lose our light. Want to call it?"

"Yeah."

We swam back to the beach and pulled off our masks and fins. After fetching our towels and the cooler from the car, we rinsed off in the park's outdoor shower, then sat on the top of a picnic table with cans of seltzer to let our bathing suits dry. Josh's face was relaxed and happy.

"Thanks, San," he said, putting his good arm around me. "This was a great idea."

In front of us the three scuba divers surfaced. All but one of their bags was empty.

"Any luck?" Josh asked as they pulled off their hoods.

"Nah. Didn't see a single bug," complained the oldest, a balding middle-aged man. The other two I took to be his sons, both in their teens.

"Bug?" I repeated.

One of the boys grinned. "It's what we call lobster down here. Dad, Sammy might have gotten lucky. He found a purse under that last rock."

The second boy walked to the picnic table closest to us and dumped out his mesh bag, revealing a water-soaked yellow cloth purse. He opened it, pulling out a hairbrush, lip gloss, and a wallet.

"Is there any identification?" the father asked as his son riffled through the wallet.

"No driver's license, but—Dad, look!" Sammy held up a wad of cash.

"See, I told you he got lucky!" his brother exclaimed. "How much is it?"

While Sammy separated the bills and counted them, his father came over and examined the wallet.

"Don't get too excited, boys. There's some kind of paper in here, looks like a pay stub." He unfolded it carefully and laid it on the table. "That's what it is, all right. I can make out the name. We'll need to turn this in to the lifeguard."

The boys let loose howls of outraged protests as Josh and I muffled our laughter.

Their father hushed them, frowning. "Sammy, Brian--I raised you better than that. Suppose you were this Angelina Torres? How would you feel?"

I stopped laughing.

"Excuse me. Did you say Angelina Torres?"

The man looked at me curiously. "Yes, why? Do you know her?"

"Can you see the company name on the pay stub?"

"The ink ran, but it looks like Saint something."

Josh and I exchanged a glance.

"Sir, you need to call the police. Angelina Torres has been missing since January thirteenth."

The boys didn't protest as their father dialed 911.

We waited by the table as the family went up to the restrooms to change. The police had promised to send someone within fifteen minutes.

"What do you think?" Josh asked after they left. "Any way this is related to the fire?"

I paused, considering. "I don't know…I can't see any connection. There was no benefit to Perry to kill her—even if he knew she worked in the afternoons, she would have been gone by the time he got there. And he already had a key from Hale."

"Angelina worked for Saint Agnes. So did that other girl who was killed," Josh observed. "Do you think they could have been victims of the same person?"

"You mean Talie Aristide. Besides, she used to work for Saint Agnes, but she didn't anymore. I don't think there's a killer out there targeting cleaning women."

"Still, one person dead, one missing, both girls of color, both with a connection to the same company—that doesn't sound suspicious to you?"

"You've watched too many movies. Serial killers account for less than one percent of murders."

Josh shook his head, amused. "You know, the average person doesn't have that statistic readily available."

"I personally find it comforting."

He laughed.

The female detective who arrived a few minutes later didn't seem particularly concerned about serial killers either. "Probably drowned," she said cheerfully, taking the wallet from the father, whose name was Reggie Bosch. "That's usually the case when we find a wallet or a purse."

"What about the money?" Sammy asked.

She gave him a sympathetic smile. "I'm afraid I'll have to take that, too. It goes to the next of kin."

The boys' faces fell.

She asked Sammy for the specific location of the purse, and whether it appeared to be caught on the inlet side of the rocks. "Stuff washing in gets caught there. Stuff washing out usually gets caught on the other side," she explained.

He thought for a moment. "It was on the side facing the bridge."

The detective sighed. "Well, that's great. I guess we'll have to do a sonar sweep of the whole lagoon." She turned to Mr. Bosch. "It was good of you to call, sir. Not everybody would."

She carefully placed the purse in an evidence bag and tossed her gloves in the trash can on her way out. As we left, Mr. Bosch was promising his sons a night at the arcade to make up for the loss. Neither of them seemed concerned about the girl whose purse they had found.

"Not very empathetic," I noted as we walked to our car.

"Don't be hard on them," Josh said, putting his arm around me. "Death doesn't seem relevant when you're young."

Late that afternoon we heard two helicopters flying low over Lake Worth. They did several passes over the bridge and the lagoon in front of the marina, then swooped slowly northward, following the Intracoastal Waterway. A marine police boat with a diver on the stern followed a few minutes behind. Josh followed their progress from the trawler's stern deck, his green eyes pensive.

"I hope they find her," he said.

I thought of his aunt, drowned last year in the Chesapeake, her body washing ashore, and of a client whose husband had gone missing, his body not found until weeks after his death. Nothing was worse than the waiting because it allowed you hope.

As we stood there, the sun set behind a low bank of clouds in an overcast sky, pale pink seeping through like a stain. The air was stagnant, a faint westerly filling the harbor with the sounds and smells of the hundreds of thousands of people who lived along this crowded coastal corridor. I felt a sudden longing for the little dock in Irvington.

Josh must have sensed my thoughts. He curled his fingers around mine.

"One way or another, everyone finds their way home."

Chapter 20

It was still dark when the phone rang. I rolled over and reached across Josh, grabbing it from the bedside table.

"'Lo?" I mumbled.

"Hello. I'm trying to reach Sandi Beck." The woman's voice on the other end was unfamiliar.

"Speaking." There was a pause. I suspected a telemarketer, and my finger was already on the screen to end the call when she spoke again.

"I'm sorry—I woke you, didn't I? I don't know why I called so early. I do this all the time—think everyone is on my schedule and forget that most people don't go to work at five a.m. This is Kylie. Wayne's fiancée."

She sounded both impossibly young and breathless.

"No, it's fine," I said, easing out of the bed. "Hold one minute." I grabbed my robe, slipped from the cabin, and closed the door. "Is everything all right?"

"Gosh, yes. I didn't mean to scare you. I'm calling about the wedding."

I glanced at the clock on the wall. Six-thirty in the morning.

"Go ahead," I prompted, trying to keep the grumpiness out of my tone.

She launched into her speech, talking at breakneck speed. "Wayne said he told you about our problem. I really appreciate your doing this. I know it's kind of untraditional, but it's been crazy enough without having my whole family in the wedding, you know what I mean? I'm texting you a picture of the dress. I need your size, and the shop will do a fitting when you get here. I hope you like it—I tried to pick something you wouldn't be mortified to wear. I hate it when bridesmaids wear those huge poofy gowns."

She stopped to catch her breath, and I took advantage of the break in her monologue to ask when I was supposed to be in Virginia for the fitting.

"Oh, right, you don't have the schedule. I'll text that, too. The fitting is the eleventh, because she has to have time to get it done before the wedding, and if possible, she'd like you there before noon. I'll be trying on my wedding dress at ten-thirty, so if you get there by then maybe we could visit or go to lunch. It would give us time to get to know each other. The rehearsal dinner is on Thursday the thirteenth, and the wedding is Friday evening. Wayne and I reserved a room for you and—Josh, right?—Josh at the Inn in Irvington for the eleventh through the fifteenth. Wayne went ahead and rented out the whole place, because I've got four sisters and their families coming in, and then my friend Kirk and his partner, so we thought it would be fun to have everyone in one place. Kirk's my man of honor, lol. Does that sound okay?"

I had no idea. She had lost me in the first sentence. Yet it was hard not to smile at her headlong exuberance.

"Sure. Just, um, text me everything."

"Great!" she said, sounding relieved. "I was so worried this wouldn't work out. I know you mean the world to Wayne, and I can't wait to meet you. I don't know if he told you, I have a new research project starting in April, and I'm trying to finish up the grant I'm on now, but the weather's been bad and we've had trouble getting out to do the oyster surveys. Wayne tells me you're a diver, so you can imagine—twenty-eight-degree air temperature and a thirty-mile-per hour wind! It's been a challenge. Anyway, I'll let you go, and I'll text those things over as soon as I get off the phone. Otherwise, knowing me, I'll forget. Thanks, Sandi. I really appreciate it."

"You're wel—" I began, but she'd ended the call.

Not only was Wayne Kremm marrying a girl who sounded like she was sixteen, she also talked nonstop, and unless I was mistaken, did not have a sarcastic bone in her body. Opposites might attract, but they don't make for peaceful relationships. No wonder Wayne needed Arthur to write a prenup.

I made a cup of chai and settled into the captain's chair. There was a misty rain falling, the water and the sky the same shade of steel gray. I turned on the television, keeping the sound low so as not to wake Josh. I watched a few minutes of a morning show, then flipped through channels, looking for something more interesting. The headline of a local news broadcast didn't register until I was a half-dozen channels away, and it took a few minutes to go back and find it.

They were rolling video of the search late yesterday on Lake Worth. The voiceover explained that the body of Angelina Torres, missing since January 13th, had been found a mile north of the Blue Heron Bridge in fifteen feet of water. According to authorities, the body had been weighted with concrete from a nearby housing construction site. For obvious reasons, it was being treated as a homicide. Police were also looking into a possible connection between Torres's death and the murder of Nephtalie Aristide, noting that both girls were once employed by St. Agnes Maid Service.

Perhaps serial killers weren't as rare as the statistics led me to believe.

I watched the remainder of the news, then switched off the T.V. Josh had a rehab appointment at nine, and with city traffic it could take forty-five minutes just to get there. I was about to go wake him when I heard the sound of his footsteps on the stairs. I made him a cup of coffee and told him about the police finding Angelina's body. He shook his head.

"Man, that's too bad. I'm sorry. Did they give a cause of death?"

"Not yet, but they said the body was weighted down, so it couldn't have been an accident."

"Aren't you supposed to meet Vianca for lunch today?" Josh asked.

"Yes, but if you aren't sure about driving—"

He had just been given permission to drive this week, but he had only gone to and from the grocery store.

"No, I'm good. I was just wondering if the police were going to talk to her. Both girls worked for her mother."

"Probably not. Vianca wasn't really involved in the cleaning business. But they might go to Keesha. Why?"

"No reason. I just feel like Vianca's got enough to worry about."

According to my last phone conversation with Alice, the foundation had raised nearly $500,000 so far and had hired an architect to create plans for the new facility, but several city council members had come out against the project. The same fight from years ago was being waged all over again, but this time there seemed to be more money and muscle behind the campaign to move the center's location. The city was offering to help locate property and even fund the construction if it was moved farther inland. The decision needed to be made soon—with the arson investigation closed, the site was being cleared this week. Alice thought the whole "move" push was being orchestrated by David Reid, though she admitted she couldn't prove it. She supported keeping the center where it was, if just to spite him, but she thought Vianca was being swayed toward moving.

"I guess I'll hear what's going on today. I'm supposed to meet her at the center at eleven-thirty. You're sure you don't mind going to rehab alone?" Josh's sessions had been lasting two hours, and I wasn't sure I could make it back in time.

Josh grinned. "Are you kidding? Have you seen that cute blonde therapist?"

"Very funny. Seriously, Josh."

He came over to where I was sitting and kissed the top of my head. "Seriously, I'm fine. The dizziness has been better and there isn't much for you to do if you do come. Afterwards I was thinking of dropping by the army unit here. A guy I used to serve with is in town. He sent me a text this morning."

I felt a twinge of concern about whether being around an active duty soldier would make Josh feel better or worse.

"I need to get going. It's eight-fifteen now. I'll grab something to eat on the way. You're sure you're good to walk to the center? It's raining."

"Sure. I've got an umbrella, and Vianca's driving us to lunch."

"All right. I'll see you this afternoon. Love you, babe," he said, grabbing the keys and his wallet. I watched as he jogged down the dock in the falling rain.

I got a bowl of cereal and read the *Washington Post* on my Kindle, noting Wayne's byline at the top of two front-page stories. One was about a fired presidential aide, the other about whistleblower complaints surrounding the attorney general. Both were solid pieces of reporting, so at least his engagement hadn't affected Wayne's work. As promised, Kylie sent a photo of the dress she wanted me to wear, and to my relief it was a very plain red sheath. The schedule for the wedding week was also attached, and I saw that in addition to the Tuesday fitting there was a family gathering on Wednesday at the Irvington Yacht Club, a rehearsal dinner on Thursday, and pre-wedding photographs on a historic skipjack Friday morning. It seemed like a lot of fuss for a low-key wedding, and I had trouble imagining Wayne participating in any of it.

By the time I sent back a text thanking Kylie for the information, showered and dressed, the rain stopped and the sun was peeking out. I decided against the umbrella and had a pleasant walk to the center. A bulldozer was taking down the remaining walls and pushing debris into a pile. Vianca, watching from the open hatchback of her new car, waved me over and rose to give me a hug.

"It's hard to watch," she said. "I'm glad Jerry wasn't here to see this. It would have broken his heart."

"I heard you've raised a good bit of the money you need to rebuild."

"We have," she agreed. "But I'm not sure what we're going to do with it."

"Why?"

"It's a long story. I'll tell you about it at lunch."

We got in the car and Vianca drove us north on Route 1. She pulled into a nondescript strip mall and parked in front of a small Mexican café.

"I know it doesn't look like much, but the food is incredible," she promised. "That's why I wanted to come so early—the place packs up at lunchtime."

There were already a few customers, and by the time our iced teas arrived and we placed our orders, nearly every table was full.

"I see what you meant."

"I know. My mother loved the enchiladas here. That's what I was bringing her the night...." Her eyes filled with tears.

I reached across the table and touched her hand.

"I'm sorry. It gets a little better each day, and then I remember something, or I go someplace she loved, and it's like it just happened all over again."

"I understand." And I did. For months I avoided the places I'd gone with Ryan, unable to bear the pain of the memories.

"Did you hear about Angelina?" Vianca asked. "They found her body. They're saying she was killed."

I told her about the boy who unearthed Angelina's purse the day before. Vianca sighed.

"I feel horrible about what I said. It's a bad habit, judging people, and I try not to do it. Most of the families I work with have been judged enough."

Our food came then, and Vianca was right—it was amazing. As we ate, she filled me in on what was happening with the center. It was basically the same story Alice told me, but Vianca was more upbeat, in part because the county's department of health had called that morning to offer the foundation another facility.

"It's on Avenue H. It was a fitness center, but it went bankrupt. They owed a bunch of back property taxes, so the county took possession. They were looking into setting it up as a free health clinic, but someone suggested donating it to the foundation. All we have to do is agree to fund seventy percent of the renovation. The city and county are willing to pick up the rest as long as we include them in the planning and coordinate with them on some health programs. It's a big facility, and the location is more central. Plus it already has some of the big-ticket things on our wish list, like a gymnasium and an indoor pool."

"Does the board know about this yet?" I asked.

"No. I sent Alice an email and asked her to call a meeting. I only hope it's all right with Melissa. I know how she feels about carrying on her father's legacy."

I didn't know about Melissa, but I guessed her husband would be thrilled. So would Ted Hale. But there was no point in ruining the moment for Vianca. She had no idea that I suspected either of involvement in the fire. I had told her I was satisfied with the official findings, and she believed the explosion was the act of a few extremists. That was better than always wondering if her mother was killed to make room for a waterfront mall.

As we were paying our checks, Vianca got a call from the foreman of the demolition crew. They had found a few things they thought she might want to keep and asked that she stop by and pick them up.

"I can't imagine there's anything left worth keeping," she said. "Do you mind? I can take you back to the marina first if you'd rather."

I assured her I didn't. There was a roll of thunder as we got into her car, and by the time we pulled up to the center's parking lot, it was pouring. A man in a yellow slicker and hard hat came up to her window, holding a blackened metal box.

"We found this. It's locked, and we thought it might be important."

"Thank you! I forgot all about that," Vianca said at once. "It's the petty cash box—not that it ever has much in it."

"Oh, and we found this," he said, digging in his pocket. He pulled out a fragment of tile flooring. "Looks like it melted right in. Don't guess you'll be needing it."

Embedded in the heavy vinyl tile was a key.

Chapter 21

I waited until she closed the window to ask.

"Is that your key?"

"No. All my keys are on my key ring," Vianca said, pointing to the ignition.

"Could you show me your door key? The one for the center?"

She looked at me curiously, but she pulled her set from the ignition and flipped through them, holding up a silver key.

"Here it is. Why?"

I compared the key in the tile to the one in her hand.

"Do they look the same to you?" I asked.

"I guess so. Why?"

I ignored the question.

"Do the keys have numbers on them or any way to tell whose they are?"

"No. I mean, there are only six of them to begin with. What difference does it make?"

"Vianca," I said carefully, "the investigators never found out how Joseph Perry got inside the building. That had to be the key he used."

She looked at it with revulsion. "Oh."

"The question is, how did he get it?"

Her face paled. "I think Sharon Hale's key went missing. Do you think he broke into her house and stole it?"

I seriously doubted that.

"We need to get this to Tony Ramirez."

"I mean, it's scary to think that man was in Sharon's house, but does it make any difference now? He's dead."

I didn't want to name Edward Hale without more to go on, but there was a slim chance some DNA evidence could be found on the key.

"Suppose there was someone else involved, someone who took the key?" I suggested. "It could even be someone in the Hales' household or someone who works for them. I think Tony would want to know."

She shrugged. "Okay, if you think it's important. Do you want me to call him?"

I thought about his last text. It had been more than two weeks ago. I was beginning to wonder if he blamed me for his transfer. "That's probably a good idea. Do you have his number?"

"It's on my desk at home. I'll call him when I get there."

"I have it. Why don't you do it now."

She did, but there was no answer. Vianca left a brief message explaining why she was calling.

"Okay?" she asked when she was finished.

I nodded. "When you get home, put the piece of tile in a Ziploc bag, and try not to touch the key."

I could see from her expression that she thought I was acting strangely, but I didn't care. My mind was on Ted Hale. We drove to the marina in silence.

"Tell Josh I said hi," she said as I got out of the car.

"Sure. And don't forget about the key," I repeated.

Vianca gave me an odd look. "Sure. Okay."

It was still raining. I ran down the dock, and she waited until I reached the safety of *Tortoise*'s cabin before she pulled away.

I hadn't seen our rental car in the lot, which meant Josh wasn't back yet. I went down to the head and grabbed a towel to dry off my damp hair and shirt. There was a buzzing from my purse, and I remembered I had turned off my ringer in the restaurant. I half-expected it to be a call from Tony Ramirez, but instead it was Wayne Kremm. He didn't even bother with a greeting.

"Is there a murder in Florida you're not involved in?"

"What do you mean?"

"I was just reading the AP story on the death of Angelina Torres. The reporter interviewed the kid who found her purse while he was diving. He says a couple on the beach told his father it belonged to the missing girl. Didn't you post pictures on Instagram of you and Josh snorkeling that same day?"

"That's hardly involvement," I contended. "That was just chance."

"With anyone else, I'd agree. But this is you we're talking about," he rejoined. "Remember how I asked you to avoid trouble between now and the wedding? You're killing me here. You're making me a nervous wreck, wondering what story you'll show up in tomorrow. You're—"

"Did you call just to harass me, or do you have a purpose?" I broke in.

Wayne gave a short, barking laugh. "Both. I talked to a guy at CNN covering the story. A source inside the investigation leaked him some information I thought you'd find interesting. The Torres girl was drugged, just like that girl in the park, and the killer tried to strangle her, but she was still alive when she went in the water. And one other thing. The source said they have surveillance video from the construction site. It shows a black BMW driving in and out of the entrance. They have a partial plate, just the first two letters: JY."

The car sounded familiar. So did the plate. I closed my eyes, trying to visualize where I had seen it.

The parking lot of Al Fresco's. Melissa Reid's car.

"I've got to go, Wayne," I said, not trusting myself to continue the conversation. "I'll call you later."

I flopped back on the closed lid of the marine head. There were plenty of BMWs in Palm Beach. Probably half of them were black. And I could be wrong about the plate.

But it felt right.

I knew from experience that women were capable of murder. In the right circumstances, even Melissa Reid might kill, but I couldn't picture her dragging concrete from a construction site or hauling a body to the water. No, if her BMW was the one used in Angelina's death, to me it meant one thing.

David Reid was the murderer.

It didn't take the police long to come to the same conclusion. When Josh got back to the boat that afternoon, I was glued to the four o'clock news, watching in real time as the Reids' life disintegrated.

"What's up?" Josh asked, coming into the cabin.

I pointed to the television. It showed police taking David Reid into the West Palm Beach headquarters. This time he was in handcuffs.

"Isn't that the foundation lawyer?"

"Yes," I answered as the show went to a commercial break. I told Josh about the surveillance video of the black BMW, and how I remembered seeing

Melissa get in a similar car after we had lunch. "The police have a warrant to search his car and his house. They haven't charged him yet, but the police chief says they plan to hold him for seventy-two hours while they wait on the complete results of the autopsy and the search."

"Wow. That's crazy," Josh said, sitting beside me. "You've got to feel bad for his wife. You said their marriage didn't seem very happy, but there's no way she could have expected this."

"No. But I think she expected something. I got the impression he had done some running around on her, but that's a far cry from murder," I said, switching off the television as the anchor moved on to another story. "How was your day? How was rehab?"

"Good. Kelsey said I was progressing on schedule. My next appointment isn't until the seventh."

Since we hadn't had much of an opportunity to talk this morning, I filled him in on the wedding plan schedule. His mouth turned up at the corners.

"You look miserable just talking about it."

"I am. But the dress isn't too bad." I pulled up the photo on my phone and showed it to him. "And we do get a free room at the inn for four nights. But it looks like I'll be busy for most of it."

"That's okay," he said cheerfully. "I figured I'd go up to D.C. and see my family for a day or two. Now you don't have to come. I'll get back for the rehearsal dinner and the wedding."

It sounded even worse to spend two days in the company of Wayne and forty or fifty strangers, but I couldn't blame him. Plus, it would get me off the hook from spending any time with Joanne Culliver.

"Oh, how was your visit with your friend? What was his name?"

"Lieutenant Colonel Thomas Elliot, but the guys call him Elly. It was good to see him. He's taking a secondary command position at SWICK this fall."

"Swick?"

Josh explained that the nickname stood for the U.S. Army John F. Kennedy Special Warfare Center in North Carolina. It was a training school for a number of specialties, including civil affairs, or as he put it, "hearts and minds stuff."

"I'm really happy for him," Josh added. "It's a big step up, and Elly's a great guy."

He sounded like he genuinely enjoyed the visit, and I saw no trace of the depression he exhibited a few weeks before.

"I want to shower up. We were out on the range for a couple of hours. Then let's go out to eat."

"Sounds good."

When he went below, I turned the T.V. back on and flipped through the local channels for any additional information on Reid. It was the big story of the day, but no one had any additional details. I switched to a jazz radio station and poured us each a glass of wine, listening for the shower to turn off. The trawler's water pump was loud enough to be heard throughout the cabin. As I was taking a sip, Tony Ramirez called.

"*Hola*. Did I catch you at a bad time?"

"No. It's nice to hear from you. I guess you got Vianca's call?"

"Yeah, I just got off the phone with her. She told me you were the one who convinced her to call me. I had her take the key to a crime scene investigator I worked with at the Palm Beach County Sheriff's Office."

"Oh," I said, disappointment evident in my voice.

He made a noise that sounded like a cross between a groan and a sigh. "Sandi, I understand you believe Hale was involved in the fire. He probably was. But I can't get anywhere near him—it is *prohibito*, as in, forbidden. Period. Otherwise, I need to find a new career. I called Adebayo and told him Vianca was coming. He said he'd have his lab look at the key, and he promised to question Hale. But I wouldn't expect too much. Hale will say it was stolen, along with the blueprints. He'll claim to be Perry's victim, and no one's going to believe Beth Perry over a state senator." There was a pause while he let me ponder that reality.

"All right," I muttered. "I understand."

"Good. I'm sorry about disappearing on you. But I was in some seriously hot water."

"I figured as much," I responded. "Hey, did you see the news?"

Ramirez hadn't heard about Reid. I gave him the detailed version, though I did not share my conversation at Al Fresco's with Melissa Reid.

"I guess he was the boyfriend Angelina was talking about. I wouldn't have pegged him as a killer, though. He just doesn't seem like the type," Tony mused. "But then, that's what the neighbors always say about serial killers. How's your boyfriend doing? Is he getting around okay?"

I gave a glowing report about Josh's rehab.

"It sounds like everything there is looking up. Now you can relax and enjoy your vacation."

"That's the plan."

“Terrific. Take care, Sandi. It was a good time… working with you. I wish—” His voice broke, betraying some deeper emotion, but he covered it with a cough. “*Adios.*”

“Goodbye.”

The Reid arrest was the lead story in every news report that week. David Reid maintained his innocence, and the police released no new information. Reid’s lawyer insisted his client was being held without cause, and there was no evidence tying him to any crime. The DA agreed, and David Reid was released.

Five days after Angelina’s body was pulled from the water, David Reid stunned everyone by turning himself back into police. Waiving his rights, he confessed to the murders of Nephtalie Aristide and Angelina Torres.

Chapter 22

The confession came less than twenty-four hours after Reid was initially released. At that time, the district attorney was saying publicly her office didn't have enough to take Reid to trial. The search of the home turned up traces of the DNA of both girls, but they had worked there, so that proved nothing. The BMW had been fully detailed a few weeks before, and again just before Reid's arrest, and it contained no conclusive evidence.

What the district attorney could have said—and didn't—was that bloodwork showed that at the time of her death, Angelina Torres was seven weeks pregnant. Her office was quietly waiting for DNA results from a water glass Reid had been drinking from during questioning.

On Sunday, February 9th, two detectives showed up on the fifteenth green at the Playa del Lago golf course. According to Reid's caddy, an eighteen-year-old college freshman who was more than happy to speak on camera, they informed David Reid that a DNA paternity test confirmed he was the father of Angelina Torres's unborn child.

"He just went totally white, man," the kid explained. "Then they told him they also had a video of his car near where that other girl was killed, you know, the one with the weird name? And they were on to him for that murder, too. Mr. Reid got this really freaked expression, man. Like he totally zoned out. He just held up his hands and told them they could go ahead and arrest him. He said they didn't need to investigate anything because he did it."

Josh and I were having lunch at a bar on Singer Island when the story broke. It was a touristy place, and no one showed much interest in the television blaring out Reid's guilt above our heads. It was a local problem, not of interest to vacationers pursuing winter tans. The sound was muted, but the closed captioning was on. In addition to the caddy, reporters interviewed Angelina Torres's sister, who wanted Reid to pay for what he'd done, and Talie Aristide's mother, who broke down and blamed herself because she encouraged her daughter to accept David Reid's help in finding a better job.

"Maybe that is how he lures the girls in," she sobbed. "And I trusted him. Such an important man. Why would he hurt my little girl?"

Reporters camping out at the Reids' driveway entrance captured footage of Melissa Reid as she left in the back seat of a gray sedan, huddled behind tinted windows. The family's lawyer read a prepared statement in front of police headquarters, asking the media to respect her privacy, reminding them that she was a victim, too.

"You've got to feel bad for her," Josh declared. He was surprised when I disagreed.

"She knew something was wrong, and she didn't want to face it. Maybe if she had, one of those girls might be still alive."

"You think she suspected her husband of being a killer?"

"No…" I hesitated, wishing I had kept my mouth shut. I had never shared the details of my conversation with her at Al Fresco's.

"Then what?"

"She told me something that day we had lunch. She thought he was having an affair. He snuck out late at night—possibly the same night Talie was killed—and she lied to the police. She never asked her husband about it. She didn't want to confront him. She just pretended everything was fine."

Josh looked at me but didn't comment.

"What?"

"Nothing. It's just…you might want to cut her some slack, San. Relationships are complicated. We all avoid confrontation, and we all pretend sometimes."

I wasn't sure if he was talking about the Reids or us, and it wasn't something I wanted to explore. Which I suppose made me a lot like Melissa Reid.

We ate in silence.

"There's something I've been meaning to talk to you about," Josh said when the bartender took our empty plates. "I realize now I should have brought it up sooner."

My stomach turned over. Had Carlos mentioned Tony's late night visit? Or was this another replay of my refusal to commit?

"Do you remember the guy I was telling you about, the one I met last week? Lieutenant Colonel Elliot?"

"Yes."

"He's coming by this afternoon. He, uh…he offered me a job."

The relief I felt must have shown in my face.

"What did you think I was going to say?"

"I didn't—nothing. It just sounded serious."

He sat back on his barstool. "It is kind of serious, San. It's my life."

"Right. Of course," I agreed, mentally kicking myself. "So tell me about it."

He searched my eyes for a moment, and whatever he saw seemed to satisfy him. "Elly didn't go into specifics. It was just an idea he had, and he needed to run it by his next in command before he said any more. But he sent me a text this morning. He'll be at the boat at one-thirty to talk to us about it."

"Is it at that school you told me about? SWICK?"

"Yeah. It's an instructor position. That's all I know. I'm sorry—I should have said something the day he told me about it."

I wanted to agree, but given my own glass house, throwing stones was probably not advisable.

"That's okay. You're telling me now," I assured him, laying my hand on his arm. Josh's expression was guarded. I added lightly, "It can't hurt to think about it, right? It might be a great opportunity."

He covered my hand with his. "The school's in Fort Bragg, San," he explained gently. "It's two hours from deep water."

When you're a sailor, that's how you think. I managed to stifle my initial reaction, but Josh knew me. He understood that tidewater now ran through my veins. There was no way I could live a hundred miles inland on some landlocked army base.

"Oh," I mumbled.

"What are you thinking?" he asked when I didn't say more.

I chose my words carefully. "I think I'd miss the water. But I'm willing to listen to what he has to say."

It wasn't much of a concession, but Josh's face lit up. "That's my girl. Thanks, babe."

By the time we finished our drinks and started home, it was one-fifteen. There was a bulldog of a man in uniform waiting for us when we reached our dock.

"Sorry to keep you waiting, sir," Josh called as we got out of the car.

"No, you're right on time," the lieutenant colonel reassured him, striding toward us. An inch or two taller than I was, he carried an extra hundred pounds of muscle, and he had a brow that could cut stone. I guessed his age to be mid-forties.

"Lieutenant Colonel Elliot Thomas, this is my girlfriend Sandi."

Girlfriend, not fiancée. It was a telling slip, I thought, as the officer extended his hand. Up close I saw his face was softened by large, expressive blue eyes.

"Nice to meet you. And call me Elly, please. Everyone else does."

"Nice to meet you, too, Elly," I said, shaking his hand.

"Did your boy here tell you I'm trying to make a pencil neck out of him?" he asked with a hint of a smile.

"Not the words I used, sir," Josh cut in. "The boat we're staying on is down this way."

"Where's that sailboat you wrote me about?"

"That's *Andromeda* there," Josh pointed to where the sailboat floated at the dock. Elly gave it an appreciative look.

"She's a pretty boat all right. You did a fine job."

Josh led the way to *Tortoise*, and we all went aboard. Once inside the cabin, I offered the lieutenant colonel a drink.

"Iced tea if you have it," he said, sitting in one of the club chairs. "J-man here did not acquaint you with his affection for pencil necks, did he?" he added.

"He did not. What exactly is a pencil neck?"

Elly laughed. "Your boyfriend is prejudiced against people who fight with words instead of guns. Which is ironic, because J-man here was as good or better at talking to the local population than he was at shooting his rifle. And let me tell you, your boyfriend was really good with a rifle, Sandi. The Army misses him. Hell, I miss him. Remember that time you—"

"Let's not bore Sandi with any war stories, Elly," Josh broke in quickly.

Lieutenant Colonel Elliot shrugged. "If you say so. But they're good stories."

"I'd love to hear a few."

"Maybe another time, Sandi, when the big guy here isn't feeling so modest. If he takes a job at SWICK, we'll have plenty of opportunity to chew the fat."

"Josh said you wanted him to be an instructor?" I asked, handing him his glass.

"Yes ma'am. I'm with the U.S. Army's Civil Affairs and Psychological Operations Command. All our soldiers already know how to wage war. But the success of our operations in places like the Middle East depends on post-conflict stabilization. That means reconnaissance of possible destabilizing factions within a population, and to do that we have to build trust. The sergeant here was the best I've ever seen at connecting with people. He had half the women in Fallujah bringing him hot meals, and he personally brokered a cessation of hostilities between two rival clans."

"Lieutenant Colonel Elliot exaggerates," Josh assured me.

"Bull hockey," Elly said to me. "Your boyfriend here can speak three languages and a dozen dialects. He's still a legend at SWICK."

"I told him we're on vacation," Josh noted.

"And I heard you. But I won't be there officially until May, and the position I want you in won't come open until fall. It's a civilian position, federal government. With your experience, I can bring you in as a GS-14 and offer you on-base housing."

Josh glanced at me. "We hadn't really considered moving away from the coast."

Elly nodded, his eyes on my face as he talked. "Gotcha'. But don't count it out right off the bat. There's some pretty country thereabouts. I bought a lakefront house west of the base, property's dirt cheap compared to the coast." He paused. "But, hey, Mary's easy to please. I know it's not for everybody. A lot of the civilian instructors do a four-day workweek and go home to Jacksonville or Wilmington, so that's an option."

Neither Josh nor I commented. Elly smiled.

"I'm not asking for a decision today, son. I'm just asking you to both give it some thought. Now, Sandi Beck, why don't you tell me the story of how you ended up on a boat with this character."

The rest of Elly's visit went pleasantly enough. He was a warm and friendly man with a gift for conversation, and it wasn't long before I was listening spellbound to his description of his and Josh's exploits. The bond between the two was palpable, and I began to understand just what it was that Josh missed about being in the military.

At four, the lieutenant colonel looked at his watch and announced it was time for him to leave. He politely refused my offer of dinner, saying he had to hop a flight back to Fort Benning, Georgia. He embraced Josh and shook my hand again before he left.

"I'm not gonna' rush you, but the job closes on the twentieth," Elly said on his way out. "Let me know one or way or the other before then."

Josh promised he would. When the lieutenant colonel was gone, he turned to me. "What do you think?"

What am I supposed to do on an army base in the middle of nowhere?

I did not give the thought voice. Instead I put on an encouraging smile.

"You said you were worried about not having options. It's an option. You don't need to make a decision right away."

"Yeah," he said, and I couldn't tell if he was relieved or disappointed by my answer.

I hesitated. "I guess what really matters is, what do you think?"

Josh looked out of the window. "I think I might take it."

It wasn't what I expected.

He turned back to me. "You said it yourself—I've got to find purpose for my life. Elly's right—this position is made for me. And the money is good. A GS-14 starts in the six figures."

What about us? I wanted to cry, but I was the one who refused to make a commitment. Did I really think he would continue to sail around with me, waiting until I was ready to move on?

"It's not like I've made up my mind," he said quickly. "But if we pick up our trip in April and do the Leeward Islands, we'd want to be back on the ICW before hurricane season starts. We could sail up to North Carolina, maybe find a long-term slip on the coast a few hours from Fort Bragg. We both liked the area around Wrightsville Beach."

I felt my face heat up. "So I'm going to hang around on the sailboat four days a week and wait for you to come home?"

"No," he corrected me quickly, "that's not what I meant. I thought maybe we could rent out a place in town, either in Fayetteville or on the coast, with some office space for you. You know, open up an actual agency, with a sign on the door and everything."

I had never once considered having a real office. For three years I had worked out of a sailboat with files in milk crates and a computer on my lap. I liked it that way, though to be honest, it was unprofessional, and some of my clients were hesitant to write retainer checks to a woman without a permanent place of residence.

"What about my boat?"

I was referring to *Serenity*, on blocks in a boatyard in Havelock, North Carolina.

"If you decide you want to open your office along the coast, I understand you'd probably rather live aboard *Serenity* than in an apartment. And if you decide to stay with me in Fort Bragg, *Serenity's* still a more comfortable weekend boat than *Andromeda*, so we could put her in the water somewhere along the Outer Banks and put *Andromeda* up in the yard until we want to cruise again."

He had obviously thought this out.

"This isn't a permanent choice, Sandi. I'm just saying we can try it out, and if it works, we can go from there. If it doesn't, we do it until the lease is up on your office, and then we make a new plan."

He watched my face, like he was trying to gauge my reaction. It was a compromise of sorts, with a commitment that didn't require walking down the aisle. And it was only for a year.

"And you won't be hurt if I'd rather stay on the coast?"

"No. You know what they say about absence. It will be like having a romantic getaway every weekend," he grinned.

"I'll think about it," I said at last. "I guess it could work."

"It would work," he corrected, coming over and putting his arms around me.

But that night, as I lay beside him in the trawler's wide bed, I was not so sure.

Chapter 23

I was packing my bag Monday afternoon for our early Tuesday flight to Richmond when Alice stopped by. She had a small box she wanted me to take to the bride and groom.

"It's a gift card," she explained. "Ah don't trust the post office."

I slid it into the pocket of my duffle.

"Honey, has Melissa called you yet?"

I stopped what I was doing and turned to her. "No. Why would she?"

Alice flushed guiltily. "Ah may have mentioned you were flyin' to Virginia. That poor girl is a wreck, between bein' married to a man who's crazier than a soup sandwich and worryin' about that boy who, Ah might add, is not even her relation. Julian has barely said two words to her on the phone since his brothah decided to unburden his conscience. Of course, you can't keep a thing like this quiet. It's psychologically damagin' to the boy, make no mistake."

"Alice, what does this have to do with me?"

"Well…I may have suggested you look in on Julian at school. It would settle her mind some."

I groaned. "Alice, I barely know the kid. I talked to him one time, and I wouldn't say we bonded." Not to mention the fact that he tried to smash in my car window. "I have no idea what to say to him."

"I have faith in you, dear. You were born to help people."

"I get paid to help people, Alice. It's not the same thing."

"Bless your heart, Sandi Beck. Ah know you would nevah' bring up money at a time like this," Alice reproved. "Now I'll let you be so you can get on with your packin'. Take plenty of pictures at the wedding. Ah can't wait to see what Wayne's gotten himself into this time."

I hoped Melissa would think better of calling, but my phone rang just minutes after Alice left. Her voice was weak and shaky, and if I hadn't been told to expect her call, I would never have recognized it.

"I'm sorry.... I know this is a terrible imposition," she said haltingly. "Julian got into some... trouble at school. I think he's...acting out, you know, talking back...because of David. The dean won't discuss it over the phone, but he says...if Julian has another incident...they'll expel him. I can't leave right now...with everything that is going on. But if you could talk to him...."

"Melissa, I really don't think I have enough of a relationship with Julian—"

"I'm not asking you to counsel him. I just need to know exactly what's going on. I'd like to hire you to...investigate. Alice and Arthur speak so highly of you...please. There's so much, I just can't—" she choked, and her sentence ended in a sob.

I thought about what Josh had said, that I needed to cut her some slack. I had been judgmental, and he was right. The only crime Melissa Reid had committed was lying to protect her marriage, and she hadn't known the extent of her husband's evil. No one had.

"All right," I said. "But you'll need to contact the school and give permission for them to share confidential information with me. And it's probably a good idea to give me a written authorization as well, in case the school is concerned about privacy laws."

"I'll have my lawyer draw up a letter and send it over to you this afternoon. Thank you so much, Sandi."

I gave her the marina address and told her the messenger could leave it at the office if we weren't here. When I hung up the phone, I was already wishing I had said no.

The letter came a few hours later. Josh, who had been replacing some worn lines on *Andromeda* in the hope of sailing again, was coming back to *Tortoise* for lunch and intercepted the messenger. I was making us taco salads when he brought in a large brown envelope and laid it on the counter.

"This just came for you. Were you expecting something?"

I revealed how Alice had volunteered my services and described my conversation with Melissa Reid. It made me sound like a better person than I felt.

"I'm proud of you. You did the right thing," Josh said.

I opened the envelope. Inside was an official-looking letter giving me full authority to act as the representative of David and Melissa Reid and granting access to any materials or individuals pertinent to Julian Reid's academic, physical, and social well-being as it related to his residence and enrollment in St. Timothy's School. Paperclipped to the document was a note with the dean's email address so that I could write to set up an appointment at my convenience on Wednesday. Behind it was a check, drawn on Melissa's own account, for two thousand dollars.

Josh frowned. "That's a lot of money to check on a kid and maybe meet with his guidance counselor. What exactly did Julian do?"

I had the same reaction. "I don't know, but I'm beginning to think it isn't just talking back to a teacher."

"Guess you'll find out on Wednesday."

We went out for an early dinner at the same Mexican restaurant I had eaten in with Vianca. Back at the boat, we put our bags in the car, left a note on the office door reminding Willy we'd be gone, and were in bed by nine.

The six-fifteen flight to Richmond was nearly empty. I mentioned this to the flight attendant when she brought our complimentary cup of coffee.

"This route is never that busy," she said, "but some of our passengers go on to Baltimore and transfer flights for California and Washington state. I think we're seeing some slacking off in travel there because of concerns about the virus."

Josh and I seldom watched anything but the local news. I knew about a pneumonia-like outbreak originating in China that had been carried to the West Coast, but there were fewer than a dozen cases, and everything I'd heard suggested they were contained.

"We've heard the same thing, but one of my friends works international flights, and she said people across Asia and Europe are worried. There are something like forty thousand cases overseas, and it has killed a thousand people so far."

Josh, who had been reading the in-flight magazine, looked up at the number. "I thought they weren't even sure it could be transmitted between people."

The stewardess made a face. "Well, they're sure now."

After she left, I gave Josh a wry smile. "This year isn't turning out too well so far. I say we go back and start over."

"Think happy thoughts," he admonished. "We're on our way to watch two people get married. What could be more positive than that?"

If I had said it, the line would have been sarcastic, but there was a hopeful naiveté about Josh, especially when it came to topics like love and marriage.

I bit back a response about this being Wayne's fourth wedding, and instead patted his hand and drank my coffee.

We arrived in Richmond just after eight a.m., picked up a rental car, and drove straight to Kilmarnock. The air was cold, and the sky was overcast with thin, high clouds that bled the sun of its light. I knew from Facebook friends in Virginia that this January had been mild, but the past week had seen record low temperatures. When we passed over the bridge in West Point, where the Mattaponi and Pamunkey rivers join to form the York, I saw a thin crust of ice over the surface of the water.

I had forgotten how desolate winter can be. After spending the past month in Florida, the bare trees and brown lawns we passed seemed naked and forlorn.

We pulled in front of the dress shop on Main Street just after nine-thirty. The sign on the door said it didn't open till ten, and Kylie's fitting appointment wasn't for another hour. We decided to drive the extra three or four miles to see if we could check into our room early.

The memories crowded in as we turned on to Irvington's uncrowded streets. I had wandered them in the years after Ryan's death, numb to the world. More recently I had found purpose there, had touched the lives of men and women in unexpected ways. It was last fall, in the doorway of Nick's restaurant, that I had gazed up into Josh's face and realized I was in love.

I looked over at him and smiled. Happy thoughts.

We parked in front of the Old Town Inn, a sprawling Victorian bed and breakfast along Tavern Road in downtown Irvington. In addition to the house itself, the tall white privacy fence hid two acres of quaint cottages connected by stone paths winding through gardens of eclectic outdoor art. I had never stayed there, having lived only a few blocks away on my boat, though I had walked in the gardens. The inn's chef served dinner to the public on weekends, and I had eaten some memorable meals in its small, intimate dining room, followed by drinks outside.

I also knew the owners—you can't live for more than three years in a town with a population of four hundred-and-four people without knowing most of them on a first-name basis. But Douglas and Pamela were not there, and instead we were greeted by Charlene, whom both Josh and I knew from her job as an ER nurse at the local hospital.

"When I saw your name, I told Douglas I had to be here today," she said, coming out from behind the ornately carved bar that served as a front desk and wrapping us both in hugs. "I've been helping them out this winter part-time so they could take some weekend vacations before it gets busy again. It's a nice break from the hospital."

Our cottage was already cleaned and made up for us, she said, leading us out the rear door. There was a propane fireplace we could use, and there were outdoor gas firepits with wrought iron chairs in conversation circles throughout the grounds. We passed by a wooden enclosure with a mermaid on the door.

"That's the outdoor shower. It has candles and a propane porch heater inside, but we can't turn on the water if it's below freezing," she explained. "Not that you'd want to use it in this weather, but it's supposed to warm up tomorrow. Here you are—the Green Cottage."

The cottage was indeed green, with a tin roof and its own little front porch. The interior was decorated with a mix of antiques and comfortable white slipcovered furniture, set against a backdrop of red, white, and black artwork.

"Do you want to stay here while I go back to Kilmarnock?" I asked after Charlene was gone. "The fitting is sort of a girls' thing."

Josh glanced at the T.V. "If it wouldn't hurt your feelings."

"Not at all. I think Kylie wanted to take me to lunch after, so you'll be on your own."

He grinned. "I know my way around Irvington. I might visit Debbie at the café."

I laughed. Debbie was the owner/manager of the Back Porch Café, and she bossed everyone around, customers and employees alike. Everyone but Josh, over whom she absolutely fawned.

"Have fun!" he called as I left.

Right, I thought. Because what could be more fun than standing in a room full of perfect strangers while someone sticks pins in your dress?

I made it back to the Kilmarnock dress shop with a few minutes to spare and parked next to a battered Ford truck. As soon as I opened my door, a girl in jeans and a khaki jacket got out of its rusted driver's door and bounded toward me.

If people were puppies, Kylie Kennedy would have been a golden retriever. She had long, flyaway strawberry blonde hair and gangly limbs, and she moved in bursts of excited energy. She hugged me, jumping up and down.

"Oh my God, I'd know you anywhere. You look just like Wayne said. I'm so glad to see you!" she said in a rush. "You look amazing—that tan is awesome. The dress is going to be incredible on you! I can't wait for you to see it. Phoebe's already here, so we can go in."

She grabbed my arm and propelled me to the door.

"I'm so glad to finally meet you. Wayne told me so much about you. I love women who are adventurous, you know? I think it rounds you out as a person. Here's Phoebe."

A thin, gray-haired woman in a tweed jumpsuit came from the back.

"Sandi, right?" she asked. "I think I've seen you at the gym."

I had a vague memory of seeing her in my Zumba class once or twice last fall. She was a spare, stern woman, and if I remembered correctly, she had no sense of rhythm. I murmured a polite greeting.

"Kylie, your gown is in fitting room one. Please be careful this time. I don't want to have to sew anything else back on," Phoebe warned, casting a severe look at the girl. "Sandi, your dress is in fitting room two. Call me in when you've got it on."

I followed her directions, slipping on the sleeveless red sheath. I was relieved to see there was an accompanying shawl. If the weather on Friday was anything like today, we might all freeze to death. I called out Phoebe's name, and she came in with a sewing box, followed by an exuberant Kylie skipping behind in a flowing white gown.

It was a simple dress with bell sleeves, a bodice covered in tiny white pearls, and a low V-neck, but it softened her angular frame and brought out the creaminess of her skin. Kylie was not beautiful in a traditional sense, but she was healthy and wholesome-looking, and in that dress she looked young enough to be Wayne's daughter.

"I knew you would look amazing in it!" she exclaimed, grabbing my hand and twirling me around with her. "So what do you think of your dress? Do you like it? I tried to pick out something you wouldn't hate wearing—"

Phoebe stepped in front of Kylie and stared her down. "No skipping in that gown. No spinning around in that gown. No fast walking in that gown. You can do what you want at the wedding. I don't care if every single pearl flies off. But my job is to get that dress there in one piece. Do you hear me, Kylie? One piece."

Her tone was threatening enough to subdue the girl somewhat. Kylie moved to the chair in the corner and started to sit down, a move that drew another round of scolding. She gave up and stood in the corner, but her eyes gleamed with mischief.

"I love the dress. It's perfect," I said as Phoebe began pinching fabric and pinning.

"You said size six, but you're muscular," she stated bluntly. "Eight in the shoulders and chest, but six in the waist and buttocks. Fortunately, I ordered an eight. I can take dresses in, but I can't conjure material out of the air. We'll need to do two tucks, here and here."

I stood motionless as she moved expertly around me, sticking long pins millimeters from my skin. Kylie kept up a constant stream of chatter, telling me about her sisters, her nieces, and the menu for the reception. Fortunately, she never required a response. When Phoebe was finished, she turned to Kylie.

"Turn around. Let me see how it looks."

The girl started to whirl, then thought better of it and turned slowly. Phoebe nodded approvingly.

"That will do. Now take it off and hang it up carefully. Very carefully. You can pick it up Thursday when Sandi comes back to get her dress."

Phoebe followed Kylie out, and I began the painstaking process of removing the dress without impaling myself on the pins. When I stepped out of the dressing room, Kylie was already waiting.

"There's a new Thai place down the street; I thought we could go there. They do this thing called shabu, where they bring you this boiling broth and you cook your food. It's really cool. Wayne hates it. He thinks if you have to do the work, there's no point in paying to go out, but I think it's an aesthetic thing. You really experience the food."

It was only a block away, so we walked up Main Street. A cold wind chilled our faces, and I was glad to get inside. The lunch itself was delicious, served family style with a mix of seafood and vegetables, including leeks and bok choi that we submerged in hot liquid. The mechanics of cooking slowed Kylie's conversation, allowing me to almost relax.

"Tell me how you and Wayne met," I suggested as the waiter took our empty plates.

"Well, he was doing a story on overfishing and menhaden regulations for the *Post*, and they sent him to interview me. I thought he'd understand better if he saw it firsthand, so I took him out on the skiff to watch the big ship with its nets. That was December, and it was windy and sleeting, so the boat was pitching up and down and we both were coated in ice. I guess he was so grateful to be alive when it was over that he asked me out. We went to dinner, and it just felt like we'd known each other forever, like I could tell him anything, you know what I mean? A couple of days later he asked me out again, and then he invited me up to his place in D.C., and that was wild. I'm not a city person, if you know what I mean. I grew up on a farm. My parents are right out of *Mother Earth News*. When I was a little girl, we had solar panels for electricity, a woodstove, and an incinerating toilet. They eventually moved away from some of that—you can take sustainability too far, and I think my parents finally figured that out—but it was crazy to be in such close quarters with people. D.C. is not my thing, but fun to visit."

Her breath control was amazing. When she paused, I jumped in. "What are you going to do after you're married?"

"You mean, like, where will we live?" she asked. "I have no clue. I'll be in Alaska for a year, and after that I'm hoping for a grant to study algae blooms in Florida. So, I mean, we'll work it out as we go. We talked about buying a place around Asheville, near my folks. Kind of a part-time home. But right now Wayne's going to come stay with me when he can, and I'll fly to D.C. and stay with him when I can."

It was a dizzying plan. Here I was, hesitant to stay two hours from Josh, while Kylie seemed unfazed about marrying Wayne when the two would be separated by thousands of miles. The more time I spent with Kylie Kennedy, the less I understood why she and Wayne were getting married at all.

The waiter brought the check, which Kylie snatched out of my hand. "Oh no. I promised Wayne I'd pick up the bill. Do you want to come out drinking with us tonight? We're doing the family thing tomorrow night, and the rehearsal dinner is Thursday, but tonight we're going to try and sneak out for dinner all by ourselves. We thought maybe you and Josh could meet us for drinks after."

We settled on eight-thirty at Nick's, which had a nice bar and was one of the few places open on weeknights in winter. The wind was still brisk on our walk back, but at least it was no longer blowing in our faces. When we reached my car, Kylie hugged me again.

"Thank you for coming. You don't know what a lifesaver you are. My sisters would have pulled each other's hair out if I had to choose just one or two of them, and by the time I put in all the other kids, we'd have more people in the wedding than on the guest list."

I told her how glad I was to help, and after a final squeeze she released me. I got in the car and watched as she started the truck and roared away, never once checking the traffic behind her. It seemed she and Wayne did have something in common, after all.

Chapter 24

Josh and I went to Nick's early, sat at the bar in our old spots, and had the day's special: scallops and eggplant over linguine in a light garlic and white wine sauce. The place was vacant, and Nick, the owner, pulled up a stool on the other side of the bar while we ate and asked questions about our trip south.

"You've been good for her," he pronounced to Josh as he cleared our plates. "She's finally put on some weight."

Josh stifled a laugh. Nick was a traditional Italian-American male from a bygone age who believed all women were improved by additional meat on their bones.

We ordered another glass of wine. Wayne and Kylie were a few minutes late, and I got the impression they'd had a disagreement. Her cheeks were bright pink and she was quieter than I thought possible. Wayne looked stiff and tense, and there was an awkwardness between us as he took the bar stool next to mine.

The conversation was superficial, moved along only by the questions Josh and I asked about the wedding and their honeymoon. They were flying to Napa Valley on Sunday to tour wine country for a few days before Kylie had to be in Anchorage for a meeting. Josh asked Kylie about her grant, and she warmed considerably, going into detail about the climate change study she was co-conducting with a colleague at the University of Alaska. We each had a couple of additional drinks, and then Josh mentioned his job offer. I felt my own face tighten. Wayne looked at me, then at his watch, and suggested we call it a night.

Back in the cottage, I mused about their relationship.

"I just don't get it. They are so different. She's so, I don't know—enthusiastic. She's got this wide-eyed wonder about life. Wayne is nothing like that."

"Opposites attract," Josh noted, rubbing my shoulders.

"I know people say that, but do they really? You and I have a lot in common. We like the same things. What do Wayne and Kylie have?"

He kissed my neck. "Great sex?"

I gave up on serious conversation and turned off the light.

***

Josh left early Wednesday morning to visit his parents. I took a walk around town, feeling the need for exercise, and stood for some time on the dock where *Serenity* was once berthed. Afterward I stopped in to visit Debbie at the café and have lunch. Kylie had offered to loan me her truck later that afternoon, and while I was skeptical it would make the trip to St. Timothy's school, there was no local rental car agency. I stopped by her room at the inn to pick up the keys, but she wasn't there. Charlene caught me in the lobby and handed me an envelope with the Ford's key, explaining that the rest of Kylie's family had come into town, and they were all off sightseeing. Given the possibility of a breakdown, I left the inn at two to make my three o'clock appointment.

My fears were unwarranted. Despite its appearance and lack of muffler, the truck made it to Urbanna without incident. Once on campus, I followed the signs to Wellesley Hall, home of the school's administrative offices. I was ushered into a side room, where Karen Stern, PhD, met me. The assistant dean of student affairs, she was my age or younger, with long auburn hair, serious gray eyes, and a permanently compassionate expression.

"Dr. Langstree asked me to see you. The situation surrounding Julian is delicate. Because I was most closely involved, he felt I would be the better one to discuss what happened and where we need to go from here to best meet Julian's needs and the needs of our community."

"I don't know anything about the situation," I said honestly. "Mrs. Reid said the dean wouldn't discuss it over the phone."

A puzzled frown briefly flitted across Dr. Stern's forehead. "I see. That is true. But I did have a long conversation with Mrs. Reid in December, when the situation escalated, and again when Mr. Reid was…." Her professional vocabulary failed her momentarily. I waited.

"Unexpectedly detained," she finished.

"I'm afraid she didn't share any specifics with me, but she had a lot on her mind when I last spoke with her," I said.

Dr. Stern nodded sympathetically. "I'm sure this is a stressful time for her. I appreciate your stepping in to help with Julian. He is expecting you, by the way. I asked him to wait in his dormitory when he got out of class, and I said I'd walk you over. He seemed pleased you were here."

That seemed unlikely, but I smiled in response.

"Let me see if I can summarize what has happened," Dr. Stern began, glancing at an open folder on her desk for reference. "On November fourth of last year, a student came to see me. I can't give you her name, but I can tell you she was very upset. She and Julian had become friendly. We don't allow dating off campus here until the second semester of the junior year, but obviously we know the students form romantic attachments. We strive to keep those as platonic as possible."

I appreciated her innocent optimism, but I wondered just how effective that was. I had a more realistic view of human nature.

"Julian violated those guidelines?" I guessed.

"Yes. He became…more intimate than this student felt was comfortable, and when she tried to break it off, he became verbally and psychologically abusive. He followed her between classes, sent her texts, and when she continued to ignore him, he began posting some very…well, inappropriate and hateful comments on social media. We called Julian in and he admitted he had done everything she said, but he showed a concerning lack of remorse." She paused there and closed the folder.

"Miss Beck, are you familiar with bi-polar disorder?"

"Not personally. I did have students who were bi-polar. I spent eight years as an educator."

"To be clear, I've never received a copy of Julian's clinical diagnosis. I am just aware that he has a prescription for a drug that is typically prescribed for that disorder. In my opinion, Julian also falls somewhere on the autism spectrum, though the symptoms he exhibits could come from trauma as well, and I know he lost his parents at a young age. But I believe he could benefit from testing. I spoke to Mrs. Reid about the possibility, but she rejected the idea. Julian is very bright, very witty, but he has difficulty reading more nuanced social cues or understanding the purpose of social norms. There have been other incidents involving academic dishonesty, and though he accepted responsibility, I never felt like he thought he had done anything wrong. It was the same with this girl. We told him if the behavior continued, we would expel him."

"How did he react to that?"

She shrugged and shook her head. "He didn't. But the behavior stopped, and so we thought perhaps some time at home and then starting a new semester would change that. He also had some work he had to complete over the break, and when he came back with everything done, I hoped…."

Dr. Stern looked out of the window.

"He started harassing the girl again?" I asked.

"Not at first. But about the same time we heard about his brother being questioned, Julian began trying to contact this student. She didn't return here—she transferred to a private girl's school about forty miles away. We tried to convince her to stay, but children can be cruel, and some of the other boys here picked up on the things Julian posted about her. They were disciplined as soon as it was reported, but she just didn't want to have to deal with it anymore. I didn't blame her. Then the guidance counselor at her new school called me to say it had started again, and the administration there threatened to call the police. Apparently Julian hitched a ride to the girl's campus and was waiting for her across the street from her dormitory. It frightened her, especially given…what his brother was accused of doing."

I had a sudden impulse to tear up Melissa Reid's check. Julian's behavior repulsed me, and my revulsion must have shown on my face. Dr. Stern backtracked quickly, softening her tone.

"I thought she was overreacting, to be honest, Miss Beck. Boys do this all the time—they fall in love, and they have a hard time letting go when that love isn't returned. They think if the girl just understands how much they care for her she'll change her mind. Our students also tend to come from wealthy families. They are good-hearted, but they are used to getting what they want. That is one of the reasons we stress moral values and teamwork here. We aren't just trying to build better students, but better people," she said earnestly. "I believe we can help Julian, but with what is happening at home, he may need more support than we can give. I'd like permission to set up an appointment for him with a pediatric psychiatrist I know. He's very good."

"I'm not sure—"

"Mrs. Reid authorized you to make decisions in her stead," she reminded me.

The trapdoor closed. No wonder Melissa Reid was paying me two thousand dollars.

"All right."

"You can talk to Julian and introduce the idea to him, and then I'll set something up," Dr. Stern said, smiling warmly now that she'd shifted her burden to me. "I'll walk you over there now. I'll call you tomorrow with a more detailed plan for Julian going forward."

She rose, pressing a business card into my palm. We put on our coats, and I followed her outside and down a brick path that crossed a wide manicured green. The campus looked like something out of Oxford, all acorn lamp posts and archways, with ivy-covered walls and boxwood gardens. The air had warmed into the fifties, and in the distance, the Rappahannock River glittered in the low winter sun.

A few students passed us, wearing the same blue jackets, button down shirts, and maroon ties. They ducked their heads respectfully, greeting Stern as "Doctor Karen" or "Ma'am." She called each one by name.

"Here we are," she said, stopping in front of one of the residential buildings. She punched a key code into the pad on the door. "Most of our students are in activities now. We strongly recommend participation in extracurricular clubs and sports, and practices run until sunset. Julian was temporarily removed from the sailing team, but we have every intention of reinstating him as soon as this situation is resolved."

"The girl was a teammate?" I deduced.

"Yes. Some of her friends were…adamant about Julian's removal. I've been talking with them, and I believe if he apologizes to the former student and modifies his behavior, they will accept him again." She pulled open the door and we went inside. We were standing in a common area with two sofas, some chairs, and game tables.

"This way," she said, leading me down the hallway. We stopped at the last door on the left and she knocked softly. "Julian? It's Karen."

"Come in," a boy's voice called.

Dr. Stern pushed the door open and motioned for me to enter. It was a typical institutional room, bland cream-colored walls and tile floors, two nondescript dressers, two desks under identical cork boards. There were sports posters on one wall, video game posters on the other. Julian, dressed in his school uniform, sat on one of two twin beds. His face was unreadable.

"Julian, your guest is here. Please remember to walk Miss Beck to her car when you've finished visiting."

"Yes, Doctor Karen."

She waited, perhaps hoping for some additional sign of welcome, then cleared her throat. "Well then. Enjoy your visit."

She left the door ajar as she departed.

Julian and I looked at each other silently as the click-clack of Dr. Stern's heels faded down the hallway.

"How much did she pay you?" he asked.

I didn't pretend to misunderstand him. "Two thousand dollars."

He smirked. "Should be easy money. You can tell her I'll leave Sofia alone."

Something about his directness irritated me. "I'm afraid that won't be enough. The school wants you to see a psychiatrist."

I caught a flicker of concern in his eyes. "So? Tell them no."

"I don't think they'll take no for an answer. Unless you want to be expelled."

"I don't want to go to some head doctor. There's nothing wrong with me. Ask Melissa," he said, his voice cracking, betraying his fear.

"She left it up to me."

His eyes became hooded. "Fine. Whatever."

I tried to stir up some semblance of empathy. Julian was a product of his environment, and the death of his parents and the acts of his brother were events he could not control. He was struggling to maintain some power over his own life. I would have done the same.

I slipped off my jacket and sat on the opposite bed without invitation. "It might help to talk to somebody," I said.

"Yeah, right."

"I mean it, Julian. Sofia is not the only issue. You must be upset about your brother."

"You don't know shit about my brother," the boy snapped.

"This isn't about me and what I think or feel. It's about you."

"I gotta' take a wiz," he said, rising abruptly and walking out the door. "It could be a while."

Two minutes passed, then five. He was probably hiding in a doorway, waiting for me to give up and leave. I stood, looking at my watch. I'd give him ten minutes, and if he didn't come back, I would go. With nothing else to do, I looked at the cork board over Julian's roommate's desk. It showed a dark-haired boy at various ages, wearing soccer uniforms and posing with his parents. There were newspaper clips and a few photos of pretty girls.

I moved on to Julian's board. There was a photograph of Julian as a child beside an older man and woman whom I took to be his parents. There were also a half-dozen photos of Melissa, but none of David. The rest of the board was covered with pencil drawings of game avatars. My attention was captured by the sketch of a powerful monster with two faces. One was human, one a fanged and terrible demon, but it was the human face that disturbed me. Its countenance was distorted by pain. I was about to turn away when I noticed the two silver chains looped over a pushpin, hanging behind the drawing. I lifted the paper to see underneath.

Two St. Agnes medals dangled against the cork.

I dropped the paper and stepped backward.

"See something you like?"

Julian's voice came from the doorway. I turned to face him, forcing myself to regain composure.

"The drawings. Are they yours?"

"Yeah."

"They're good." I picked up my jacket from the bed. "I need to be going, Julian."

He opened the door wider. "I'll walk you out."

"No need. I know the way."

"Doctor Karen said to, and we need to do what Doctor Karen says." Julian's voice was singsong, his tone mocking.

I brushed past him and into the hallway. "Up to you. But I have someplace I need to be."

He followed me to the dormitory door and down the path to the parking lot. I walked quickly, but he stayed at my shoulder, just a step behind.

"Why are you here?" he asked.

"I told you. Your sister-in-law paid me to come," I said in a clipped voice.

When we reached the parking lot, I unlocked the door and slid into the seat, then shut it firmly behind me. I opened the window a crack. Julian crossed his arms across his thin chest.

"What are you going to do?" he asked.

"I'm going to tell Doctor Stern to make the appointment."

He shrugged as if to say it didn't matter.

"Goodbye, Julian," I said, and I put up the window. He stepped back as I started the Ford, then stood motionless in my rearview mirror, watching as I drove away.

I pulled over at the first gas station on the main road, trying to make sense of what I'd seen. The Reids weren't Catholic, and there was no reason for Julian to have two necklaces of the patron saint of young girls—unless they weren't his at all. Both Nephtalie and Angelina would have had St. Agnes medals, given to them by Mariana Baptiste. Serial killers often kept mementos of their victims.

Had he taken them from David? Or was Julian Reid the murderer?

I thought about the drawing he tacked over the saint's medals; the creature that was all monster save one tortured human face. Is that how Julian saw himself?

I dialed Wayne's number.

"Hey, San. Everything okay with the truck?"

"The truck is fine. You did a story on DNA testing and criminal convictions, right?"

"Yeah, last summer. Why?"

"Could a paternity test mistake one brother for another?"

I heard Kylie's voice in the background.

"No, she's fine," he said, talking to his fiancée. "The short answer is no. But brothers share a lot of the same DNA markers, so you'd have to have both of their samples to compare to the baby's to positively establish paternity. If you only had one brother's sample, you'd need to do a more extensive analysis using additional markers. What's going on?"

I ignored the question.

"Would the police routinely do that kind of testing?"

"No. Not without a reason. It's more expensive and takes longer to produce a result. They just do a basic test. What are you thinking?"

I heard Kylie in the background again, along with a cacophony of other female voices.

"San, sorry, I've got to go. We're taking Kylie's family out to Merroir for oysters before we go to dinner at the yacht club. She said to remind you you're welcome to come." After more commotion, the call was dropped, but it didn't matter. I had my answer.

If David Reid hadn't killed those girls, why confess to crimes he didn't commit?

For Julian.

David had professed his innocence until the DNA test came back. He must have realized then that Julian fathered Angelina's unborn child. He must have guessed his little brother killed both girls, and he did what might have been his first truly selfless act—he confessed so that Julian would not be caught. I had seen on the internet this morning that at yesterday's arraignment Reid pled guilty to the charges. His sentencing hearing was next week. The police had no reason to look further.

Except that serial killers don't stop. If my theory was correct, David Reid's selfless act could cost more young women their lives.

I wasn't sure if Julian saw me look underneath his drawing, but if he did, the necklaces would likely disappear. The only way to get anyone to listen to the possibility David Reid was the wrong man was to get the police to order a more extensive paternity test. That would be up to the district attorney.

I did a quick Google search of newspaper articles about Reid's arrest and found the name of the D.A. in charge of the case. It took seconds to locate an address and phone number, but unfortunately, there were two secretaries and an assistant who ran interference for the D.A.'s office, and it took twenty minutes in the gas station lot before I got to the most senior one. He informed me that Mrs. Gershiwitz was currently in a briefing, but I managed to sound urgent enough that he gave me her private email account so I could contact her confidentially. I spent another ten minutes carefully summarizing my theory about David Reid's innocence on my iPhone with my thumbs before pressing SEND. When I finished, my hands were shaking.

I put my head back against the seat and breathed.

The sun was setting as I drove into Irvington. The inn had only street parking, and much of it was full with Kylie's family's vehicles. Wayne had rented a half-dozen limousines for the night, effectively employing every limousine driver in three counties. I found a spot along the unlit alley at the back end of the inn property, near a gate in the fence that turned out to be locked. The adrenaline rush was gone, leaving my arms and legs like water. I walked the block back up to the inn entrance slowly and slunk around the outside of the building to our cottage, avoiding conversation with Charlene at the desk.

Once inside, I poured a glass from a bottle of Bordeaux we'd bought, turned on the propane fireplace, and lay on the couch. I switched on the television and caught the end of the Richmond weather report. A warm front was moving in, bringing with it spring-like temperatures that would increase to near sixty degrees overnight and reach the upper sixties Thursday and Friday. Good news for the wedding, and for the sleeveless dress I was supposed to be wearing.

I must have dozed off because I started when my phone rang. I didn't recognize the number, but it was a Florida area code. The caller, who sounded rushed and a little peeved, identified herself at once as Leslie Gershiwitz.

"Miss Beck, let me get this straight. You have evidence suggesting we put the wrong man behind bars, and the real killer is still at large?"

"Yes."

"I'll need to hear it if you expect me to initiate further investigation on a case that's about to go to sentencing."

I described Julian's history and told her about the St. Agnes medals in his room. There was a long pause on the other end.

"You were at the school on the behalf of Mrs. Reid?"

"Yes."

"Anything you saw there probably wouldn't be admissible."

"It doesn't matter," I said. "David lied to protect his brother. If you do the new paternity test, and he isn't the father, that all but proves it was Julian. He's the only other person with similar DNA markers."

"I'll see what I can do."

That wasn't good enough. She didn't sound convinced, and it might be politically expedient to take a gamble I was wrong and move on. I pulled out the only other card I had.

"Mrs. Gershiwitz, my closest friend is a *Washington Post* reporter who also appears frequently on CNN. If you don't do something, and another girl gets killed, I will give everything I have to him. Then your office can explain why you refused to spend a few extra dollars for a better test."

There was another pause in which I thought I heard Gershiwitz curse under her breath.

"Fine, Miss Beck. I'll authorize the test. If you're correct, you'll see it on the news. Either way, I don't expect to hear from you again."

She hung up the phone.

I didn't take it personally. The Reid arrest was a career-maker, and I just tarnished what was a foolproof case.

I took my half-finished wine to the front porch. Solar fairy lights twinkled from the tree branches. The sky was clear and starry, the air noticeably warmer. I went back inside and rang the front desk.

"Charlene, is the outdoor bath on?"

"Yep. And there are no other guests except the bride's family, and they're all out. They said they wouldn't be back until nine at the earliest. There's a lighter in the drawer under your microwave for the candles. I'll go start up the propane heater if you'd like."

I thanked her, refilled my wine glass, grabbed the lighter, a towel and shower gel, and put on one of the thick white waffle robes hanging in the bathroom. The night was still, the only sound the low tones of piped in jazz from the inn's outdoor deck. Once inside the wood-fenced enclosure, I lit the dozen cream-colored candles and slipped off my robe, feeling the contrast of the propane flame and the cool night air on my skin. I turned on the shower, waited for the hot water, and stepped underneath.

The rough, wet stones beneath my feet, the smell of dead leaves and vanilla candles, the swirl of the Milky Way against velvet blackness—these were sensual, intoxicating. I reached for my glass and took a deep drink. The wine was bitter in my mouth. I swallowed it down and closed my eyes, letting the cascading warmth of the water wash my mind clean of the day.

There was a rustling somewhere outside, a squirrel or a bird. I put my glass on a weathered wooden shelf engraved with nymphs that hung from the fencing, opened the shower gel, then soaped and rinsed. Afterward I stood for several long minutes under the falling water, draining the last of my Bordeaux, then rested against the bench. My limbs felt heavy, my mind clouded, and I was surprised at how quickly the wine went to my head. Time to call it a night. I turned off the faucet, toweled off, and slipped on my robe, then turned off the heater and blew out the candles, letting my eyes adjust to the dark before I opened the door.

Julian Reid stood on the path in front of me.

Chapter 25

I opened my mouth to ask what he was doing there, but my tongue was thick and refused to cooperate. I felt myself slipping to the ground, and he stepped forward and caught me, his wiry frame surprisingly strong.

"Not too fast. You don't want to fall," he breathed in my ear.

I tried to pull away, but no part of my body seemed to be working. I could barely hold my head erect. I thought of the wine glass, the bitter taste, the sounds outside the fence. Drugged…the wine. Like Nephtalie and Angelina.

"Don't worry. I've taken care of everything," Julian said, putting my arm over his shoulder and locking his around my waist. "We're going this way."

He half-dragged, half-carried me through the now open back gate and out to Kylie's truck. His head darted from left to right, but the street was empty. Then he opened the passenger door and shoved me in, face first, lifting my legs and swinging them behind me. He went around to the driver's side, climbed in, and pushed my body upright in the passenger seat. All of this happened in such slow motion that I knew I should be moving, trying to escape, but my limbs were paralyzed and useless.

Julian dangled the key in front of my face before putting it in the ignition. "You should lock your cottage when you leave."

He pulled out on the main road and headed east.

My vision blurred, and I struggled to stay awake. Julian looked over at me and smirked.

"Bet you didn't expect to see me tonight."

I focused my eyes on the dash, the panic rising in my throat. He continued talking, an excited edge to his voice.

"Do you know the whole story of Saint Agnes? No? I didn't think so," he said as if I had answered. "She was this Roman bitch who came on to guys and then wouldn't put out. They turned her in as a Christian, and she was dragged naked through the streets, burned at the stake, and beheaded with a sword. Pretty sick, huh?"

He took out his phone and plugged it into the USB on the stereo, then scrolled through and touched a button. The cab filled with the slow, haunting sound of an acoustic guitar.

"Sting. My dad loved him. This is "Saint Agnes and the Burning Train." It's all instrumental. Like, the notes are the words. I played it for Angelina, but she didn't get it." He laughed, a harsh, hollow sound. "Guess she gets it now."

My eyelids drooped shut. I concentrated on willing them open, but they seemed disconnected from me. The music died, and the last thing I heard was the muffled hum of the engine, followed by silence.

I don't know how long I was unconscious, but when I woke we were traveling on a bumpy gravel road through a scrub pine forest. My head had fallen to the side, so Julian could not see my eyes. My mind was still fuzzy but clearing. I kept my breathing slow and even, testing my arms and legs for movement. My wrists and ankles were bound. I shifted slightly so I could see the wide duct tape.

"You're awake. Good. I wasn't sure about the dosage. I've never given anyone rohypnol before," Julian explained.

I struggled to form a sentence, managing only a few words. "They know... about you."

"I figured. That's why we're here."

He came to a stop on a gravel pad, opened both of our windows, and turned off the ignition, leaving the headlights on. The forest ended here, turning into a thin strip of marshland. Perhaps a hundred yards farther the grassy swamp became a sandy shoreline. A narrow boardwalk led from the gravel to the beach. I recognized where we were—the Hughlett Point Nature Preserve. Julian must have taken the park ranger's access road.

We were in the middle of two hundred acres of wooded wetlands.

Julian got out of the truck and went around to the bed, where I could hear him drop the creaky tailgate. Then he walked to the front, into the high beams, carrying a red five-gallon gas can. He put it on the ground, then came to my window.

"What do you think it feels like, to be burned alive?" he asked.

Fear gripped me. I struggled to loosen the tape as he reached in and draped the two St. Agnes medals over my neck. "Julian...no," I croaked.

"I didn't hurt them," he continued. "I just wanted to touch them, make them feel what I felt. She never gave me a choice. But I didn't care. I loved her."

He stood on the truck's step and reached inside toward the glove box, his hand brushing against my leg where the robe had fallen open. He fumbled around for a moment in the darkness before finally pulling out a lighter. He held it in front of my face. I closed my eyes.

"Look at me, Sandi," Julian said angrily. When I didn't open my eyes, he slapped my cheeks. I forced myself to stare into his eyes.

"I don't want to hurt you, but you have to do what I tell you. Do you understand?"

I nodded.

"Good. Don't be afraid, Sandi," he said, flicking the lighter on and off. "This isn't for you. You're only here as a witness. You're going to keep looking at me, and you're going to tell her everything you saw. Can you do that?"

I nodded again.

"That's all I want."

He put the lighter in his pocket and walked back to the front of the truck, positioning himself in the middle of the light. Then he pulled the stopper from the gas can nozzle and looked directly at me.

"I would have done anything for her. You tell her that."

Julian raised the gas can to his shoulders and tipped it, pouring the liquid over his shoulders and torso, letting it soak through his clothes and run down his legs. Then he lifted it over his head and closed his eyes, drenching his hair and face. He felt blindly in his pocket and found the lighter. He held it up and flicked it once, twice, and nothing happened. I opened my mouth in a soundless scream.

He must have seen me, because he smiled at me and flicked it again. There was a spark and then a bright flash of light, and the fumes around the boy ignited.

The flames jumped from the air to his gas-soaked clothing like a living thing. He stood motionless, arms outstretched, as they raced over him, his mouth still twisted in a smile. I saw the moment when he felt it, the searing pain of the burning. Julian's eyes widened, and he shrieked and began to run back and forth in the light, waving his arms. He fell to the gravel, rolling and writhing as the fire consumed cloth and melted flesh. Still screaming, he rose again and stumbled toward the passenger door.

In a frenzy of panic I kicked and bucked, pushing myself upward, into the driver's seat. Julian fell forward, moaning as his body pitched against the metal and slumped to the ground.

My vision closed in a tight circle, and I heard nothing more.

I woke to the sound of voices. The driver's door opened, and I saw Wayne's face against a backdrop of flashing blue light.

"Oh, thank God," he breathed, touching my face. "Sandi? Are you hurt?"

I shook my head, my eyes filling with tears.

Kylie was standing behind him. She reached under the seat and pulled out a leather pouch. Inside was a pocketknife. Wayne stepped back as she knelt beside me, cradling my ankles and wrists as she gently cut the tape.

"Don't try to move yet," she said, putting her hand against my chest as I struggled up. "Rub your arms and legs to get the circulation back."

"Was it Julian Reid?" Wayne asked.

"Yes."

"Where did he go?"

I raised one hand and pointed to the right side of the truck, but the police were already there. As Wayne lifted me from the car, they trained their flashlights on the smoldering heap of what had once been a sixteen-year-old boy.

"Holy shit," Wayne muttered, but Kylie put her arms around me, pressing my face into the soft whiteness of her sweater while I cried.

An ambulance took me to the hospital. The emergency room doctor had my blood drawn and stitched a cut on my leg that I couldn't remember getting before declaring me fit to go home. I knew better. Julian's burning body had permanently etched itself in my retinas.

One of the police officers came in then, a friendly, broad-faced local deputy whom I'd seen before. He was careful and kind, but the tears ran down my face anyway as I described what had happened.

"You said he talked about a girl before he died, that he said," he checked his notes, "quote, 'Tell her everything you saw. I would have done anything for her. Tell her that.' Do you have any idea who he was talking about?"

"There was a student at his school last semester. I don't know her name. The assistant dean said he got upset when she wouldn't see him anymore. She transferred to the girl's school in Tappahannock."

The officer looked down at the report thoughtfully. "I don't think I know the assistant dean over there. Do you by chance remember her name?"

"Stern. Karen Stern."

He seemed about to ask another question, but instead he closed the lid on his clipboard and put his pen back in his pocket.

"That'll do it for now, Miz Beck. You're going to be in town a couple of days, is that right? Well, if you think of anything else, give me a holler, and if I need anything, I have your number."

He handed me his card, folding it into my limp fingers.

"You take care now."

I was given a mild sedative and released soon after. Kylie and Wayne took me back to the cottage and sat on the sofa, waiting and watching as I curled tightly on the bed and fell into a deep sleep.

I woke at three a.m., my heart racing, my mouth dry. The dream, whatever it had been, was hovering just at the edge of my memory. Kylie was beside me at once, a water glass in hand.

"It's okay. I'm here," she said softly, pressing it to my lips.

I drank too fast and gagged. She patted my back, waiting while I caught my breath.

"I'm sorry," I choked out.

"You have nothing to be sorry about."

"Your family…your wedding."

"The wedding isn't till Friday, and my family is used to drama. They're the ones who raised an environmental activist. I've chained myself to a tree, had my boat rammed by a whaling ship, and called them three times to bail me out of jail, so I'm pretty sure they can handle this." Despite the light tone, she looked at me with serious eyes. "I guess Wayne didn't mention that I get in trouble a lot. That's why he loves me—I remind him of you."

I moved uncomfortably.

"Sorry. I guess that didn't come out right. I mean, he's really fond of you, and he admires you. He told me about you on our second date. I think he was trying to scare me off, but it didn't work. That's—we had a talk about it the other night. I guess you noticed we were kind of pissy with each other. But it's okay." Kylie looked at me, her lips turned upward in a half-hearted smile. "I understand you can love more than one person in your life."

I started to say something, but it ended in a cough. She gave me the water glass and steadied my hand while I drank.

"You're probably wondering why I'm marrying Wayne," she continued. "I know my parents are. I get that he's older. But guys my age, they either want no commitment or they want to know where you are every minute of the day. I'd rather have someone with some baggage who has been around, do you know what I mean? Like you and your boyfriend. You aren't going to magically turn into someone else, and neither is he, but you accept each other. I'm cool with Wayne being Wayne, and he's cool with me being me. "

She looked both very young and very old all at once, and I couldn't help but wonder if she believed what she said or only thought she did. Feeling suddenly dizzy, I lay back against the pillow.

"Gosh, I'm so sorry," she said. "I know I talk too much. It comes from spending all my time alone in the field. I can't shut up when there's another human actually listening." Kylie rose and pulled the sheet over me. "I'm out on the sofa. If you need me, call me. The doctor did prescribe a stronger sedative. Wayne picked it up for you. I can get it if you want it."

I shook my head.

"I wouldn't want it either. Sometimes it's better to just deal with things yourself." She started for the doorway, then turned back to me. "I'm sorry for what happened, but I'm really glad you're here, Sandi," she said. "Try to get some sleep."

I lay there listening as she went to the sofa. A few minutes later I heard her breathing deepen and slow. Feeling oddly comforted, I closed my eyes and fell back asleep.

Chapter 26

The sun was bright when I awoke. I grabbed my watch by the bed and saw that it was after ten o'clock. I pushed myself up on one elbow, testing, relieved to find the heavy sensation gone from my head. I heard a rustling in the next room, and Josh came in. His chin was covered in dark stubble and he had shadows under his eyes.

"Hey, babe. I thought I heard you getting up."

He came to the bed and opened his arms, and I melted into them, pressing my face in his neck.

"I'm so sorry, San. I shouldn't have gone to Maryland. I shouldn't have left you alone," he lamented, pulling me back and searching my face.

"It's not your fault. There's no way you could have known."

"Yeah, I keep thinking about that. He was just a kid. I've seen kids in desperate situations do some pretty rough things, but this…man. I don't understand how his family could have missed the signs here."

"They didn't miss them. They ignored them, and then they lied about them," I said bitterly. "Because of them, three people are dead."

"I know, babe. I know." Josh lifted his hand and stroked my cheek. "What about you? Are you all right?"

"No," I said honestly. "I don't know how you do it…see what you've seen and let it go. I'll never forget how he looked…when he was burning."

"You don't forget. You make a choice not to dwell on it. And sometimes it still comes back to bite you." He leaned over and kissed my lips gently. "You want to talk about it, I'll listen."

I shook my head.

"So what do you think is going to happen now?"

I told Josh about the call with the district attorney and my suggestion that she do a paternity test.

"What Julian said to me amounts to a confession. If she does the paternity test and David Reid isn't the father of Angelina's baby, the only thing she can charge him with is obstructing the investigation and making false statements. Since he was doing it to protect his brother, a jury's going to be sympathetic. She'll probably negotiate a deal with his lawyer for a fine and probation, or maybe home confinement."

There was a knock at the cottage door. Josh left to answer it while I stood shakily, trying out my legs.

"You're awake. That's great," Wayne said, coming to the doorway.

"More or less," I said, dropping back on the bed.

"Kylie sent over some scones. They're on the counter. She wants you to know if you're not up to the rehearsal, it's no big deal. She can go over it all with you tomorrow morning."

"No. I'm fine."

Josh came back in, carrying a cup of coffee and a plate.

"She just needs sugar and caffeine," he joked, handing them to me.

Wayne came over and sat on the edge of the bed. "I thought you might want to know--the Palm Beach County D.A. has called a press conference at eleven. I gave her name to the deputy last night and told him to fax her the report about Julian. I said it was an active murder case. My guess is she ran the paternity test first thing this morning."

I looked at the clock. "That's in about fifteen minutes. I wish we could see it."

"You can. I brought my computer in. We can stream the news report."

While Josh and Wayne went into the sitting room, I worked my way out of bed and took a quick shower. My wrists and ankles were chafed, and the stitches itched, but other than those minor injuries and a head full of frightening images, I felt okay. I dressed in jeans and a turtleneck and joined them on the sofa. Wayne's computer was set up on the coffee table in front of us.

Gershiwitz came to the podium in front of the courthouse at exactly eleven. She got right to the point:

"Last night in Kilmarnock, Virginia, Julian Reid, age sixteen, confessed to the killings of Nephtalie Aristide and Angelina Torres before taking his own life. This morning, a detailed DNA analysis concluded that Julian Reid, not David Reid, was the father of Angelina Torres's unborn child. Mr. Reid has since admitted that he lied to police in an effort to protect his brother, who suffered from mental health issues. He maintains that he had no prior knowledge of the crimes, and he based his assumption of his brother's guilt on conjecture only. He has expressed his regret for hindering the investigation that could have saved his brother's life, and perhaps provided the help he so seriously needed. We are currently working with the Lancaster County, Virginia police and other authorities to determine the motivation behind the killings of Ms. Aristide and Ms. Torres, but given the suspect's death, we understand some answers may never be forthcoming.

"At this time the charges against Mr. Reid are being dropped. He was released from custody at nine-forty-five this morning. We are investigating the possibility of bringing future charges but wish to allow Mr. Reid and his family time to bury their dead and deal with their loss. Thank you."

She declined to take any questions and left the podium. Wayne shut his computer.

"So that's it, then. Case closed."

"It looks like it," I agreed.

"One thing the D.A. didn't mention—David Reid's wife filed for divorce yesterday. I guess she jumped the gun, since the guy is innocent."

I remembered Julian's face when he spoke of his brother.

"No one in that house is innocent," I said.

Wayne patted my shoulder and left.

Josh drove me to the dress shop, where I picked up the altered bridesmaid's gown. Phoebe must have heard some rumor about what happened—Kilmarnock is, after all, a small town—because she didn't even insist that I try it on. Afterward we drove out to Reedville for lunch. Josh told me about his visit with his parents, who were enthusiastic about the job offer in North Carolina, though his mother mentioned more than once that there were plenty of positions at the Pentagon. He said they asked about me, but I doubted it was with the same affection he conveyed.

After we ate we went back to the cottage. The day was warm, and we sat out in the garden and chatted with one of Kylie's sisters and her husband. Wayne and Kylie had not shared the previous night's ordeal with her family, so I was spared any awkward conversation. Instead we heard about their children at length and answered questions about Wayne, whom I tried to portray in the best possible light, until Josh caught me yawning and excused us. Once inside the cottage, he insisted I take a nap. He spooned beside me, and I slept soundly against his warmth.

By the rehearsal, the immediacy of the horror had faded, replaced by a strange sense of euphoria. I was alive, and colors seemed brighter, fragrances more intense, music more moving. I felt my eyes tear as Kylie walked down the vineyard's porch steps to the arbor where Wayne stood. I caught Josh's worried look as I wiped my cheek.

The entire run-through of the marriage service took less than forty minutes. The rehearsal dinner followed, held at the large waterfront hotel down the street from the inn. It was a raucous affair with a disc jockey and thirteen children (nine girls and four boys, aged three to twelve) racing around the banquet hall. Without warning the noise overwhelmed me, and I locked myself in a stall in the empty bathroom, weeping. It was Kylie who eventually found me.

"I don't know what's wrong with me," I said, blowing my nose.

"You went through a pretty traumatic experience," Kylie pointed out. "You can't expect to feel all better just like that. I think you've done pretty amazing as it is."

"I usually handle things better than this."

"Then you must be superhuman," she joked. "Go back to the inn. Cuddle with your boyfriend. Or I'm going to send my grandmother in here after you."

It was the threat that did it. Kylie's grandmother was a tiny Irish woman with an opinion about everything and no apparent filter. She had already told me I'd look better with longer hair and I was getting "long in the tooth" and better hurry and have a baby if I didn't want my womb to dry up.

"If you're sure you don't mind."

"I'm sure. Unless you'd rather sit on the toilet with Nana Margaret all night."

Josh looked relieved when I said we could go. All of Kylie's nieces had decided they were in love with him, and the girls were taking turns dragging him onto the dance floor.

We ambled along the dark sidewalk, illuminated only by the warm glow of windows in the houses we passed. As forecast, the night air felt more like spring than winter, and we passed a mailbox planter where daffodils were heavy with yellow buds. My head was on Josh's shoulder, his arm around me, as we drank in the smells of pine needles and damp earth.

We had not gone far when Josh's phone buzzed in his jacket pocket. He ignored it, but it no sooner stopped than it began again, vibrating incessantly.

"You may as well see who it is," I said. "It could be important."

He pulled out the phone and put it to his ear. "Hello?"

As the caller talked I watched Josh's face darken. "All right.... Okay.... Thanks for letting us know."

He slipped the phone back in his pocket.

"That was Charlene. There are T.V. reporters from Richmond outside the inn. They know about what happened with Julian."

"From which station?" I asked.

Josh looked at me grimly. "All of them."

Chapter 27

We pressed our bodies against the bank's wall and peered around the corner. The Episcopal church parking lot was crowded with news vans, and the sidewalk opposite the inn was littered with tripod spotlights, cameramen, and reporters holding microphones.

"What a circus," Josh muttered.

"How are we going to get past them?"

He gestured toward the pavilion in the middle of the open lot between the bank and the town's tennis courts. It was the site of the monthly farmer's market and local festivals, but it was day use only. There were no lights.

"If we can cross over here and get behind the tennis courts, we should be able to go down the alley and get in through the pool shed. Charlene was going to unlock it."

I followed his pointed finger to a small white outbuilding that blended into the inn's perimeter fence. It housed the pool's pump and filter, obviously not in operation in February. There was an exterior access door for maintenance workers which I had not noticed before.

"Stay low, but don't run," Josh advised. "Eyes are drawn to fast movement."

We made our way across to the pavilion, where we crouched to catch our breath. Then we slipped around the tennis courts and crossed the empty side street to the shed. I expected to hear shouting and running feet at any moment, but Josh was able to open the door just wide enough, and we squeezed inside. He fastened the chain behind us while I let out a shaky sigh.

Douglas, the inn's owner, was waiting for us on the cottage steps, a look of intense concentration on his face that eased once he saw us.

"Sandi, I'm glad you made it," he said, embracing me. "And you must be Josh."

He extended his hand and Josh shook it gratefully.

"I'm so sorry, Douglas. We had no idea—"I began.

"I know. Charlene told me all about it when we got back this evening. I just got off the phone with Larry at the hotel. When the party's over, he's going to shuttle everyone down in their courtesy bus and we'll meet them at the back gate. Pamela's brother is on the Town Police, and he's agreed to block off the back alley so we can get the guests in without having to go through the reporters." Douglas saw my eyes fill with tears. "Don't worry. We can handle this. You go on and get some rest."

He strode off, heading toward the inn's office as Josh ushered me inside the cottage, locking the door behind us.

"How did they find out so soon?" I lamented, sitting down on the sofa. "The local police agreed not to release my name until after the wedding."

"I don't know, San. Do you want me to turn on the T.V.? It's almost ten o'clock now."

I knew I wouldn't be able to sleep without knowing what was being reported. I nodded.

The local channels were still broadcasting their evening lineup, but we caught live video of the front of the Old Town Inn playing behind the anchor on CBS. Josh turned up the volume.

"In a bizarre twist on the murder of two young women in Palm Beach County, Florida, Virginia police are reporting that the killer, Julian Reid, age sixteen, of West Palm Beach abducted a family friend from a bed-and-breakfast in Irvington on Wednesday before killing himself in a state nature preserve. We turn to Brooke Varnus from our affiliate station in Richmond, WRIC. Brooke, tell us what you've learned."

The screen shot shifted to a young blonde reporter.

"That's right, Amanda. Sandra Beck, age thirty-six, was staying in the Northern Neck town of Irvington when she was allegedly drugged and abducted Wednesday evening from the Old Town Inn grounds by the teenager, who drove her to the Hughlett Point Nature Preserve about seven miles away. Once there, she told police he admitted to the murders of Nephtalie Aristide and Angelina Torres, both of Palm Beach County, Florida, before killing himself by dousing his body with gasoline and setting himself on fire. Reid's older brother and guardian, David Reid, had previously pleaded guilty to those murders, but officials in Florida say he admitted he did so only to protect his younger brother.

"CBS 6 has learned that Julian Reid was a student at Saint Timothy's School, a private upscale boarding school about thirty miles from here. Sources tell us Sandra Beck visited there Wednesday afternoon at the request of Julian's sister-in-law. In a CBS exclusive, we were able to locate and speak with Julian's roommate, Calvin Forester, who gave the boy a ride to a restaurant in the nearby town of Kilmarnock just hours before the abduction."

A tape rolled from earlier that day, showing the same reporter talking with a dark-haired boy that I recognized from his cork board photos. The teen fidgeted awkwardly as he explained that Julian came to him right after sailing practice and asked for a ride. He told Calvin he was meeting a girl, and she was supposed to give him a ride back to the campus. No, Julian hadn't acted like anything was wrong, but he was always kind of strange and kept to himself.

The screen switched back to the live feed, and the reporter told viewers police had determined Julian Reid never went inside the restaurant, but instead entered a Walmart in the same shopping center. Surveillance footage showed the boy purchasing a five-gallon gas can and a lighter, crossing the parking lot to a gas station where he filled the tank, then waiting outside Walmart for about ten minutes before boarding a local commuter bus.

"Police were able to question the bus driver for the Northern Neck Transport," the reporter continued. "He says the boy told him his truck had run out of gas and he needed a ride back to Irvington. He let Julian Reid off near the Old Town Inn where the boy said his truck was parked. Not long after, Reid abducted Sandra Beck in a stolen Ford F-150 truck owned by one Kylie Kennedy, the bride in the wedding Beck was in town to attend. In an interesting twist, the groom in that wedding is Wayne Kremm, a *Washington Post* reporter and CNN news analyst. We are hoping to speak to Ms. Beck or other members of the wedding party as they return to the Old Town Inn tonight from the rehearsal dinner, being held at a nearby hotel."

I switched off the T.V. "This is horrible, Josh. It will ruin Kylie's wedding."

"No. It will be all right," he assured me. "Douglas and Pamela sound like they know enough people that they'll find a way around it."

"I hope so." I rose from the couch as he turned out the light. "One thing's for sure. I wish we had never stopped in West Palm Beach."

Josh sighed. "Yeah. That makes two of us."

I slept fitfully, then woke at four a.m., unable to close my eyes, while Josh slumbered peacefully beside me. I finally gave up at six and dressed quietly in jeans and a heavy sweatshirt, then crept into the inn's dining room to get coffee. I was sitting in the garden, drinking it as the sun rose, when Wayne joined me.

"You left early last night," he said, sitting down on the bench beside me.

I gathered that Kylie hadn't told him about my meltdown, and I felt a surge of gratitude.

"I was just tired. Did you manage to get everyone into the inn without talking to the reporters?"

"Yeah." Wayne leaned forward, looking out at a metal sculpture of a heron perched over a flowerbed. "I'm used to telling the story, not being in it. Last night gave me an appreciation for all the people who slam doors in my face."

"How's Kylie?"

He gave me a weary smile. "Fine. She's resilient. Nothing bothers her for long. Douglas and Pamela have arranged a police escort to the vineyard, and the staff is blockading the driveway so that no one passes who isn't on the guest list. When the news crews realize they aren't going to get any sound bites, they'll leave."

"I'm sorry, Wayne. You asked me not to get involved in anything catastrophic, but I never thought…."

"I forgot about that. Maybe I was the one who jinxed it."

We both made a feeble attempt at laughter, but it died in our throats. The events of the last two days were not a laughing matter.

"So, what do you think, Sandi? Is this the right thing to do?"

It took me a minute to realize he was talking about his marriage.

"I admit I wasn't sure at first," I acknowledged. "But I really like her, Wayne. She's a truly nice person."

"Is that comment directed toward my previous wives?" he asked, looking faintly amused.

"Yes, it is. She's different, Wayne. She's young and idealistic, but she seems to know what she's getting into. And she loves you," I said with feeling. "I hope you realize that."

"I know. That's what scares me." He stood and paced in front of me. "What if I can't do it? We're looking at a lot of time apart. You know me. What if I screw this up?"

"Don't."

Wayne shook his head. "It's not that easy."

"Staying married isn't magic, Wayne. It's a choice you make every day." I sighed. "At least it should be. I just can't seem to make one."

His eyebrows shot up. "What do you mean? I thought it was all settled. You and Josh are engaged, and he's taking that job in North Carolina. He told Kylie you were getting married sometime this year."

"Wishful thinking. Nothing's settled."

"I thought…." He started, then paused and looked away. "Back in December, when I spoke to you, you seemed pretty definite about marrying him."

I shrugged. "Maybe I was. Maybe I am. Things have been…confused."

"I wish you'd told me," he said softly. "Is there anything I can do?"

Just then the cottage door opened, and Josh stepped out. His frown turned to a lopsided smile when he saw me.

"Yes," I said. "Live happily ever after for me."

Josh reached us just as Wayne stood up. They exchanged brief hellos, and Wayne excused himself. Josh watched his back with a bemused expression as he walked away.

"Everything okay?" he asked when Wayne was out of earshot.

"Just wedding day jitters." It wasn't the whole answer, but it was close enough.

Josh's studied my face. "So nothing serious? "

"No," I said, rising and taking his arm. "Nothing serious."

And it wasn't. Wayne and Kylie looked every bit the happy couple as we posed for pictures on the deck of a wooden skipjack after Douglas clandestinely ferried us to the dock in his catering van. Two of the news crews had already gone, unable to get to me and finding no other eyewitness to go on camera and comment on Julian's death. By the time the limousines came to transport us to the vineyard, a breaking story about a missing nursing home resident in Henrico drew off the others, and I passed out of the news cycle almost as quickly as I had entered it.

Despite a thin sheen of sweat on his forehead, there was no hint of uncertainty in Wayne's voice that afternoon when he stood in the arbor and repeated his vows. As for me, I went through the motions numbly, and it was not until I saw Kylie's lip quiver when Wayne slipped the ring on her finger that I remembered that heady feeling of leaping into the future, eyes wide open and unafraid.

The reception was an informal affair beneath a tent, with an open bar and heavy appetizers spread across several "standing" tables and no seating. A classical guitarist played in one corner, and guests stood in small groups, talking and laughing. Even Kylie's family seemed to have put aside their reservations, and her sisters nearly crushed Wayne with their exuberant embraces.

"You look happy," Josh said, coming up behind me on the vineyard's wide front porch.

“I am.”

He handed me my phone. “You left this on the table outside of the restroom. It looks like you have a message.”

I expected a reply from Alice—I had sent her several photos of the wedding throughout the day—but this was a Gmail notification from a contact I didn’t recognize: janus180. The subject line read “YOU NEED TO SEE THIS.”

“I thought Google was supposed to block this stuff,” I groused.

“You aren’t going to read it?” Josh asked.

“No. They didn’t even use a real name. It can’t be anything important,” I said, dropping it in my spam folder without a second thought.

That was my first mistake.

Chapter 28

David Reid stood at the trawler door.

I almost didn't recognize him. He had lost weight, and there was gray along his temples, but it was more than that. The arrogance that once defined him was gone. His shoulders slumped, and there was no challenge in his eyes.

"Can I talk to you for a few minutes?" he asked when I opened the door.

I let him in, and he dropped into one of the club chairs, as if the act of walking the dock had exhausted him. I sat opposite on the settee, waiting.

I had both dreaded and expected this moment since we flew back from Virginia last week. I expected the Reids to hold me accountable for Julian's suicide. They had written me a check to look in on their ward, a check I had cashed because I felt I earned it. But Julian had killed himself in part because of what I had uncovered in his dormitory room—not that I held any responsibility for the acts that led to the necklaces dangling from his cork board, but it is human nature to want someone to blame. Not legally, of course—any attempt to take me to court would have forced them to lay bare their own dysfunction. The families of the murdered girls were already considering a civil suit, citing the Reids' negligence, and rumor had it the Reids were negotiating a settlement. They were doing their best to salvage their own reputations, presenting a united front despite their separation. They released information about Julian's bi-polar disorder, something they said their pediatrician had recognized when he was a young teen, as evidence they had been caring and involved guardians. Melissa and David had gotten him treatment. If he refused to take his medication, what could they do? But they produced no other evidence of the boy's condition, and his pediatrician refused to comment other than to confirm he had prescribed lurasidone at Melissa Reid's request.

Knowing all of this, I had steeled myself for the accusations I knew would come, but the man in front of me was gaunt and drained, with no fight left in him.

David Reid leaned forward, elbows on his knees, hands clenched as if in prayer.

"You were the last one to see Julian…when he died," he said so quietly that I could barely hear him. "What did he say?"

I tried not to think about that night. I had no intention of replaying it now. "Just what was in the police report. Your lawyer should have it."

"He does." Reid looked at me with tortured eyes. "I just thought maybe there was…something else, something you didn't tell them."

I wondered what he hoped or feared to hear. Unfortunately, I had nothing to offer him.

"No. That was all."

He bowed his head.

"It was my fault," he murmured. "I let Melissa handle him. I didn't know what to do with Julian, he was…not like me…and she seemed to understand him."

He stopped, his shoulders shaking with dry sobs. When he spoke again, his voice was a toxic mix of bitterness and despair. "She wouldn't discipline him…always making excuses, and his behavior got worse and worse. I had to step in, and when I did, they both hated me for it. The way Julian looked at me…." David Reid recoiled at the memory. "I shut him out. I admit it. But I wasn't the only one at fault. When Melissa left that night, I realized things had to change. For all of us. But it was too late… too late."

The words focused inward, not for me to hear. I felt a stirring of sympathy for him. Despite the animosity he felt toward his wife, his remorse for Julian seemed sincere. But he was right. None of it mattered now.

When I didn't respond, he rose stiffly.

"I'm sorry to bother you," he said.

"It's all right."

I sat and watched as he let himself out.

***

The third message from janus180 came that night.

"I don't understand this," I said to Josh. "Is this some kind of a hacking scam?"

We were sitting on the settee. Josh was listening to a podcast, earbuds in, while I checked emails and updated my website. I turned my laptop toward him. The message from janus180 was on the screen. Josh pulled out the earbuds and looked at the screen curiously.

"This is the third one you've gotten?"

"Yes. I marked the first two as spam."

Josh read the message aloud. "And the subject lines were all the same?"

I nodded. "Yes. I opened the last one, but all it had was a link. I never clicked on it. I'm pretty sure this is the same one."

"Did this come to your business email? The one on your website?"

"Yes."

Josh copied the first few words of the link—darkcloudsecrets—and did a web search. It came up as an online file storage service for encrypted data, one that had a reputation for catering to conspiracy theorists and political extremists.

"It looks like someone wants to share their files with you." Josh opened my spam folder, found the other two messages, and moved them to my inbox. "The links are the same except for the numbers on the end. Possibly three separate files."

"So they can hack into my computer? Or my email account?"

"Maybe. Or it could be a new client, somebody worried about being exposed. If you're curious, you can copy the links in writing and open them on a public computer. That way you aren't putting your own data at risk."

"There's a computer up in the marina lounge," I suggested. "Unless you think I'll crash Willy's internet."

"Only one way to find out."

I copied the link on the notepad of my phone, then looked back at the other two messages. They had come five days apart. The links were identical to the new message with the exception of one letter. Josh, who had been doing his daily rehab exercises, took a break to walk up to the lounge with me.

The days were growing longer, and the sun had not yet set. The docks were slowly filling with snowbirds returning from the islands. Willy told us they would stagger in across the next month, then meander northward, chasing spring. By May they would be in the Chesapeake, enjoying warm sun and cool breezes, then move on to New England by July, when the summer heat set in.

We hoped to taste their experience. Josh was nearly healed, and his doctor had been pleased enough with his progress to allow him to continue physical therapy on his own. This meant we could move up our timeline. Josh had spent the last few days preparing *Andromeda* with the goal of moving back aboard on the first of March. Weather permitting, we would leave for Grand Bahama in two weeks. I looked out toward the inlet with rising anticipation. Seeing Wayne and Kylie get married had reawakened something within me.

"Janus sounds familiar," Josh said, disrupting my line of thought.

"It's Roman," I explained, making rare use of my years teaching World Literature 201. "The god of gates, passageways, beginnings and endings. He's usually depicted with two faces, one looking backward and one looking forward, past and future." A sudden image flashed in my mind, and I wondered why it hadn't occurred to me before. I grabbed Josh's arm. "Do you remember that drawing I told you about? In Julian's room?"

"Yeah, the monster with two heads."

"It wasn't really two heads—it was like one head with two faces. But it can't be from Julian. The first email came two days after he died."

"That doesn't necessarily mean anything. You can schedule emails to send on a certain date and time. Guys did it all the time before a mission. Then they could cancel it if they got back and didn't want to send it."

I was about to ask why when I realized—they had written final goodbyes, last words in case they didn't come home.

The lounge was empty. The computer, an ancient Hewlett Packard, was running an antiquated version of Windows. I opened the browser and carefully typed in the link.

The screen immediately went black, displaying a single illuminated file. I clicked on it. There were two documents inside, but when I went to open them, rows of letters, numbers, and symbols appeared.

"Encrypted," Josh said.

"Can you decode it?"

"I can't, but I know a guy who can."

He explained that he had a friend in the army who was a computer coder and encryption expert. Unfortunately he was currently stationed in the Middle East, so it could take a few days to get a response.

"If you don't think he'll mind," I said.

"Are you kidding? Hijack lives for puzzles like this."

"Hijack?"

"He stole a Humvee once," Josh replied, grinning. "Long story."

Josh copied all three links and sent them on his own server, along with a request to decode. That was the last I thought of it until his phone rang at one-thirty in the morning a few days later.

"What the hell, man! What are you into?" The voice on the phone was loud enough to be heard clearly from my side of the bed. Josh sat up.

"Hijack?"

"Yeah, man. I been lookin' at your files. That's some crazy shit, man."

Josh glanced over at me, and I nodded. "I'm going to put you on speaker, Hijack. My girlfriend's here. The emails came to her. She's a private investigator."

The soldier's voice and language altered immediately. "Uh, sure man. Yeah. Put her on."

"Hi, Hijack. This is Sandi Beck. Were you able to decode the files?"

"Oh, yeah, no problem. It's a pretty basic encryption program, comes with a subscription to the site. Each file has two documents. One is a screenshot of emails, and the other one has images."

"Can you send them to me?"

"Not the photographs, man. They are pretty twisted, and Uncle Sam has some strict views on child pornography."

Josh and I exchanged looks.

"What kind of child pornography, Hijack?" I asked.

"Some of it's pretty standard T and A, ma'am, cell phone shots of a teenager and a couple of different girls. Looks like they're stoned, don't know what's happening. But the earlier ones…well, ma'am, it looks like the same kid, but younger, maybe ten or eleven. They're pretty blurry, poorly lit, and you can't see who he's with, but he's naked, and it looks like he's tied up." Hijack cleared his throat uncomfortably.

My God.

"The police are going to want those photographs," I said.

"You can give them the links. They won't have any trouble with the encryption. I'll shoot Josh an email with the other documents in a few minutes. They aren't related to the photos, as far as I can tell. Just some real estate stuff."

I thanked him.

"Yeah, no problem. But y'all watch yourselves. This is some evil shit."

Josh turned to me as soon as the call ended.

"Do you think it was David Reid?"

My stomach turned. "I don't know. He talked about disciplining Julian, how it made both Melissa and Julian hate him. If he sexually abused his brother, it could have triggered Julian's behavior. Josh, how could anyone do that to a child? And if she knew, why wouldn't Melissa Reid do something about it?"

"Questions for a higher power, San. What are you going to do?"

"I don't know. I'd like to see the emails first. But whoever abused that boy is responsible for his death and the deaths of those girls. They need to go to jail."

We waited by the computer for the email from Hijack, but it did not come. Josh noted there was often a delay of hours or even days between sending and receiving from outposts like Hijack's. His friend had been lucky to get a satellite call through.

"I can't wait that long," I insisted. "Who knows what this person is doing now? I'm going to contact the district attorney and give her the links for the photographs. Maybe the police can do something with the photos to provide clearer images."

D.A. Gershiwitz wasn't eager to take my call, but her attitude changed when I told her about the photos. Her animosity toward Reid was evident, and while she sounded repulsed by my summary of their content as reported by Hijack, there was a triumphant note in her voice.

"I knew we'd get the bastard somehow."

"I'm not positive David Reid is the abuser," I cautioned.

"Oh, he's the one all right. He fits the profile perfectly," Gershiwitz said confidently. "You just send the links. I'll take it from there."

Even without seeing the photos, the idea of them haunted me. That night I had a dream that I was walking through the woods in darkness, alone. There was a sound on the path behind me, and I turned. A young boy stood there, and though his face was shadowed, I knew it was Julian.

"You were my witness," he said, and he threw something toward me.

An object flashed in a shaft of moonlight and a red-handled hatchet landed at my feet. Dead leaves crunched as Julian ran toward me. I reached down and grabbed the hatchet and raised it as he slashed at me with sharp silver claws. There was a searing pain in my chest as I brought the hatchet down. His body fell and lay still, the hatchet embedded in his chest. It was no longer a boy or a monster, but a shapeless figure in a hooded black robe. I leaned down and pulled back the hood, exposing two pale, featureless faces.

Chapter 29

The D.A.'s office wasn't able to identify Julian's abuser from the photographs, but it didn't matter. Melissa Reid was cooperating with authorities, a source close to the investigation telling a *Sun Sentinel* reporter that she agreed to testify against her husband in exchange for immunity. David Reid was arrested again, this time for eleven counts of child sexual assault and child pornography, one for each photograph.

At the arraignment, Melissa Reid presented her sworn testimony to the court in writing as her physician judged her too psychologically fragile to speak in public. While the statement itself was not released, whatever was in it proved damning. The court denied Reid bail and set a trial date of March 25th. One day later David Reid hanged himself by the neck in the county jail using his own bed sheet—exactly two weeks after Julian's death.

There was an initial flurry of protest from Reid's lawyer, who said his client should have been on a suicide watch, but it fell on deaf ears. No justice activist was interested in taking up the cause of a child predator. Reid dropped from the news cycle, and that was the end of it. The outbreak of the virus, now called COVID-19, supplanted all other stories. Originating in China, the virus had spread to South Korea, Iran, and across Europe. There were still only fifteen cases in the U.S., all on the West Coast, but there was enough concern that travel bans were being considered for countries other than China. Josh and I watched the news with mild anxiety, wondering if it would complicate our plans to sail to the islands.

I saw Melissa Reid a few days after David's death. I was walking back from Publix and she was standing with several men in suits at the vacant center site. They were looking at plats, and I walked down the street and crossed at the shopping plaza to avoid running into her. Melissa must have seen me, because I got a call a half-hour later, inviting me to her house. She said she needed to talk with me.

I wanted to say no. The previous night was the first to pass without a nightmare since I'd learned about the photos. But she sounded so distraught that I gave in and agreed to meet her. Josh had gone to a marine consignment shop in Ft. Lauderdale with Willy, and I had nothing to do but wait for him to return. At least he'd left me the car. I sent him a text letting him know where I was going and drove out to South Ocean Boulevard.

There was no guard at the Reids' gatehouse, which surprised me. I waited a few minutes, then drove into the driveway, pulled into a spot by the pool, and walked to the main entrance. A matronly woman answered my knock. She spoke no English, but she understood the name Melissa, and led me out to the gazebo by the pool to wait.

My phone vibrated, likely a text back from Josh. But when I checked, the notification was for an email from a us.army.mil address. It had to be Hijack. He had promised to send the decoded emails, but they had never arrived. With David Reid's suicide, there hadn't been any point in pursuing them.

Hijack's email consisted of a brief greeting and two attachments. The first was the transcript of an email exchange between Melissa Reid and Ted Hale. Scrolling through it quickly, it was evident that although both writers were careful to avoid specific details, the topic was the Garrison Center.

Melissa was the one who initiated the exchange, asking if there was anything Hale could do to help her "derive financial benefit from the property." What followed was a veiled discussion of prospects and an offer of a development partnership with a 60/40 split of net profits. When Melissa asked about what could be done to force the Garrison Center to move or close, Hale wrote he was "looking into it." That's where it ended.

I looked up. No one was coming. I opened the second document. It continued the conversation. At one point, Hale wrote, "The problem has been solved." The date was January 9th. The next exchange was on January 14th at six a.m.

M- What happened???? They know this was no accident.

H- It's taken care of.

M- Two people were killed! An arson investigator wants to see me.

H- Calm down. We had nothing to do with that. It was an accident. Call me tonight.

I scrolled down. That was the last email.

The email exchange was proof that Ted Hale and Melissa Reid conspired to burn down the center. Why would Julian send this to me? According to David Reid, the boy was very close to Melissa. Why would he arrange to expose her after his death?

I thought back to Julian's last words: "I would have done anything for her. Tell her that."

I remembered Melissa's slip at the restaurant, only now it sounded rehearsed: "I heard David get up after midnight. Then I heard the car, the BMW."

I saw David Reid, sitting in the trawler chair. "When Melissa left that night, I realized things had to change."

I had assumed he was talking about when his wife left him, but now I understood. It all came together: the BMW at the construction site; the cork board with its many photographs of Melissa next to the two-faced monster and the St. Agnes medals; the username, janus180.

And I knew.

"I'm sorry to keep you waiting," a voice said at my shoulder.

I closed the screen and looked up into Melissa Reid's questioning eyes.

"That's okay. I was just texting a friend," I said, hiding my sudden nausea behind a too-wide smile.

She wrinkled her nose as if she smelled something she couldn't quite identify. Her eyes still on my face, she took the chair next to me.

"I've wanted to tell you how badly I felt about putting you in that situation with Julian. I had no idea what was going on with him. That poor boy. I wish he had come to me for help. If I had truly known what David was doing... how sick he was...." her voice quavered as she wiped at her eyes.

I had an image of Julian burning, the heat of the vision flushing my cheeks. My control snapped, and a reckless urge to hurt her overwhelmed me.

"Julian gave me a message for you."

Her head flew up at the harshness of my voice.

"What...what did he say?"

I stood up. "That I should tell you exactly what I saw. Do you want to hear how he poured the gasoline all over his body, and how he couldn't get it to light? Or what his eyes looked like when he realized what he'd done?"

Melissa rose abruptly and pushed her chair between us.

"What kind of a sick joke is this?"

"It's no joke. He tried to tell me, but I didn't understand. I thought he was talking about a girlfriend. But he was talking about you. How could you, Melissa?"

"You're wrong. I tried to help him," she insisted.

"By raping him?"

"That's a lie! I never did that!" she protested, voice rising. "Never! He came to me when David was away. He crawled into bed with me. We didn't do anything wrong. He was just a little boy, and he couldn't sleep. He had bad dreams. Sometimes he got violent, and I had to restrain him. Then I gave him one of my pills, and they helped him go to sleep."

"I know what was in the photos, Melissa. You abused him."

"I did not," she insisted. "I loved him! He didn't understand how to feel. I showed him. But he got older, and he wanted more. He lost control. That's when I told him we had to stop."

"So he did what you taught him—he drugged girls and assaulted them."

"I told him he should find a girl his own age. I had no idea he would do something like that," she objected. "Can't you see I was trying to help him be normal?"

"He killed two girls, Melissa. Because of you."

Her eyes flashed. "None of that was my fault. David is the one who caught him trying to put a Xanax in the maid's drink. He didn't even try to talk to him—David grounded him, took away his car keys, then sent the girl to work at the club and told Julian he could never see her again. Don't you see, that's what started all of this? Julian was still upset when he went back to school, and then he had that problem with a student there. He was crying out for attention, and David wouldn't listen."

"But you did."

"I tried to help him, but he was angry with me. He blamed me for not standing up for him with David. Then he came home for Christmas and saw that girl again, at the club when he went there with David. The next thing I know he calls me, crying. He had snuck out to meet her at the beach. He took some of my Xanax and put them in her drink, and then she stopped breathing. I told him to leave her there and walk away, but then she started choking and making noises and he panicked."

"Her name was Talie Aristide, and he murdered her."

"He didn't mean to—he got scared, and he wanted her to be quiet. Yes, I protected him. What else was I supposed to do? She was dead when I got there. I helped him bury her. But then he did the same thing with the next girl, he gave her some pills, and then he called me crying again, wanting me to tell him what to do."

"Except that he didn't kill Angelina Torres, Melissa. She was alive when she went in the water."

Melissa's face darkened. "Because she told him she was pregnant. Right after he gave her the pills. He wanted to call an ambulance. He didn't understand what he was doing."

"But you told him not to. And you went there yourself."

"Of course I did. It was my job. What was he going to do, spend the rest of his life with some little uneducated whore? You know how bright he was. I couldn't let him throw his future away. But I had to teach him a lesson. He had to realize he couldn't keep doing this. I made him carry her. I made him tie the rope. It was the only way he could learn self-control."

She believed what she was saying. It sickened me, and I couldn't listen to her anymore. I backed away from the table.

"It doesn't matter. Don't you see?" she said, watching me, her voice uneasy. "David is dead. Julian is dead. Those girls are dead. You can't prove any of this."

"You're right, Melissa. I can't."

A relieved smile spread across her lips. I took another step back.

"But Julian gave me something else—the emails between you and Ted Hale. I can prove you were behind the fire at the Garrison Center. You're still going to jail."

I had the satisfaction of seeing the shock on her face before I turned to walk away.

I made it as far as the pool's concrete deck when I heard the panting of her breath behind me. I saw the heavy metal chair coming down out of the corner of my eye and grabbed it as it swung toward my head, tearing it from Melissa's hands. She lunged forward, unable to stop, and plunged into the deep end of the pool.

I got up slowly. Melissa thrashed at the surface, arms flailing, gagging as she tried to scream.

"Help me!" she choked, but her cry was drowned out by the sounds of her struggle. I watched as she sank lower, her movements becoming more frantic as the weight of the liquid closed over her head. She looked up at me as I stood motionless, and her eyes, magnified by the water, went wide with terror.

Epilogue

***Andromeda* motors out through the** channel in the moist velvet blackness. We share the helm, our hands folded together over the wheel. To our east lies Grand Bahama Island, barely fifteen miles wide in this vast and moving sea. Ten hours and a world away.

Behind us, Melissa Reid huddles in a cell, not far from the place where her husband took his life. Perhaps his ghost haunts her. I hope so. I would like to say the decision to pull her from the water was an easy one. It wasn't. I wanted her to die. But letting her drown would have changed me in ways I could not predict, and it wasn't my choice to make. Melissa's lawyer claims she was a childhood victim of her own father's abuse, driven by decades of suppressed memories to destroy his legacy. It might even be the truth. Something twisted her into the shape she became.

Either way, her future is in the hands of a jury. I have my own future to make.

Ahead of us is uncertainty. The virus is a pandemic now, and in Europe people are dying. The scientists say it is only a matter of time until it laps on all shores. We do not know if we sail toward danger or away from it, or even if we will be able to return home. We are taking a chance.

But no life is without risk. Not the ones who rise at dawn to sow their seeds, not the ones who fight through morning traffic, not the ones who do battle beneath a foreign sky. Certainly not us, floating in a speck of fiberglass on forty-one million square miles of ocean.

Even love is not without risk. We are two souls in a world of billions, and no matter how many years we share, one of us will die, or the two of us will grow apart. It is that knowledge that gives this moment—all moments—meaning. It is the reason we stood before a justice of the peace yesterday, why our hands on the wheel now wear the same ring.

There is a soft glow along the horizon. Josh presses his hand over mine as the moon rises and shines a path across the waves, lighting our way.

Acknowledgments

Thank you to all of those who inspired me to continue Sandi's saga: my parents, who have always told me I could do anything; my husband, who took over my chores and encouraged me to write; my children, Jon, Colin, and Liesl, who embody the best of my characters; my Morattico Creek Ladies, especially Pam, Ronda, and Barney, who gave me direction when I was floundering; the Rappattomac Writers critique group, for their early feedback; Nancy Carter and her waitstaff at the Oaks Restaurant, who poured generous glasses of wine and advertised my books far better than I could; Ann Deaver, who has done everything a friend can do, from attending speaking engagements to bartending at book launch parties; and finally, to all the fans in book clubs who have invited me to their meetings and offered up heartfelt pleas for Sandi's future—here is your happy ending.

A very special thanks to my editor, Cindy Freeman, whose advice is priceless, and to my publisher, Jeanne Johansen of High Tide Publications, for her continued belief in the potential of women writers.

And last but not least, I'd like to acknowledge Jack, our cat, whose literary contributions made while jumping onto my keyboard will live in my memory forever.

About the Author

Ann Eichenmuller is a novelist, marine and travel journalist, and former liveaboard sailor who believes a little tidewater runs through her veins. Winner of the three Boating Writers International awards, her work has been featured in *All at Sea*, *Chesapeake Bay Magazine*, *Chesapeake Style*, *MotorHome*, and *RV Magazine*. She is an avid boater, certified diver, and private pilot whose experiences continue to shape her characters and her stories.

Other books by Ann Eichenmuller

The Sandi Beck Murder Mysteries

Kind Lies

The Lies We Are

The Lies Beneath

Non-fiction

The Writing Rx

The Writing Rx Workbook

Praise for the Sandi Beck Murder Mystery series

"Ann Eichenmuller has delivered engaging characters, a compelling mystery, and a side of romance—all set against Virginia's beautiful tidewater."

Brad Parks, international bestselling author of

Say Nothing **and** *The Last Act***.**

"...a powerful exploration of not just murder and motive, but a determined amateur sleuth's increasingly complex dilemmas of being sandwiched between professional investigators and perps alike. Fans of murder mysteries ...will relish the attention to psychological inspection given in The Lies Beneath...a compelling story."

Midwest Book Review, D. Donovan, Senior Editor

"We were on the edge of our seats from page one...A thrilling, twisting tale of love and deception that riveted us until the very end."

Editor's Pick, Chesapeake Bay Magazine

"Ann Eichenmuller continues to excel in depicting the manner and mores of the modern south as well as infusing her plot with lively characters. She captures the history-haunted nature of the region...."

H. Scott Butler, author, ***Voice from the Shadows*** **and** ***Night Journey***

"A heroine who is a full time liveaboard, set against the backdrop of tidewater....An intriguing mystery."

Boating Writers International Journal 2017

"The story drew me in until I couldn't put it down.... As a longtime fan of mysteries, I found Kind Lies a book I not only enjoyed but can highly recommend."

Carol Bova, author, ***Chesnut Springs*** **and** ***Harboring Secrets***

Made in the USA
Columbia, SC
04 December 2020

26318346R00129